William O. Priestley

The Pathology of Intra-Uterine Death

.

William O. Priestley

The Pathology of Intra-Uterine Death

ISBN/EAN: 9783337403812

Printed in Europe, USA, Canada, Australia, Japan

Cover: Foto ©Andreas Hilbeck / pixelio.de

More available books at **www.hansebooks.com**

OF

INTRA-UTERINE DEATH

BEING

The Lumleian Lectures

DELIVERED AT THE ROYAL COLLEGE OF PHYSICIANS
OF LONDON, MARCH 1887

BY

WILLIAM O. PRIESTLEY

M.D., F.R.C.P., LL.D.

CONSULTING PHYSICIAN TO KING'S COLLEGE HOSPITAL ; AND LATE PROFESSOR OF
OBSTETRIC MEDICINE, KING'S COLLEGE

[*Reprinted for the Author from the* BRITISH MEDICAL JOURNAL.
March 26, April 2, 9, and 16, 1887]

LONDON

J. & A. CHURCHILL

11 NEW BURLINGTON STREET

1887

Dedicated

Charpentier's, Bustamente's, Verdier's, and Whittaker's ; and, besides, we have the well known contributions, illustrating special diseases of the placenta, from the pens of Robin, Virchow, Hyrtl, Hegar, Rokitansky, Ercolani, and others.

It is obvious that a general treatise on Obstetric Medicine can scarcely find room for a full discussion of all that has been done in this branch of pathology ; and, in reference to the special treatises or monographs on placental disease, it may be said that some of them, at least, are out of date. Like all other branches of morbid anatomy, the investigation of diseases in the placenta has made in recent years considerable progress, and opinions and views formerly held in reference to the nature of some of the alterations observed, are now regarded as untenable.

Besides examining many fresh specimens, I have gone carefully over the preparations bearing on the causes of intra-uterine death in all the London museums and some of those on the Continent, and it has been an interesting study, in inspecting these preparations, to compare them with the various pathological views which have been expressed by authorities, both in this country and abroad.

I may state at the outset that the complex and intricate anatomical structure and the alterations associated with the rapid development of the contents of the gravid uterus even in the normal state, render all investigation very difficult. When pregnancy goes its natural course, and development follows its normal progress, the changes which take place are incessant and varying. From the time at which the decidua is first formed in the interior of the uterus to become the outermost of the fœtal membranes, to the formation of the fully grown placenta, there is no pause or cessation in the active changes which characterise the progress of growth. The cells and fibres which build up the tissues day by day undergo progressive change, and the vessels equally undergo modification in size, form, character, and in their relation to surrounding parts. The vegetative process is, indeed, so active that if any derangement occurs, either from accident or disease, the morbid change thus initiated is, or may be, impressed with the same activity, and rapid degeneration takes place, or abnormal growths are produced with surprising quickness.

It can scarcely be a matter of surprise, therefore, that pathological researches into these unstable and ever-changing structures should be beset with difficulties, and that equally conscientious and accurate observers hold different views concerning the nature of some of the pathological results hereafter to be described. The earlier the period of gestation, the greater apparently is the difficulty of pursuing investigations. Then all the tissues are so fragile and delicate that if specimens are procurable their efficient injection is well-nigh impossible, and they are likely to be so contused and broken that their true condition is not easily determined. Notwithstanding all the difficulties, researches have been attempted by very competent observers at every period of pregnancy, and the accumulated results so recorded may to a certain extent be formulated, and some at least of the pathological conditions be thoroughly understood.

Many of the causes which either remotely or directly bring about intra-uterine death are very difficult to trace, and some are so subtle in their influence as to be impossible to detect. Thus the child dies *in utero* with some women in successive pregnancies, and without any clearly assignable cause. The "habit of aborting" has been spoken of, as though it were independent of disease. It is not infrequent to hear of women apparently healthy aborting or losing their children in the later months of gestation ten, twelve, or thirteen successive times. Charpentier mentions the case of a woman who had no living child until the eighteenth pregnancy, and this was born at eight months. Both parents were apparently healthy.

Some women are so prone to miscarriage at any period of gestation, that the slightest imprudence seems to be enough to endanger the existence of pregnancy, and lead to a detachment of the ovum.

This is in marked contrast to other and apparently not healthier women, who will bear an extraordinary amount of violence or injury without disturbance to pregnancy. Mauriceau* relates the case of a woman in the seventh month of pregnancy, who fell from the window of a house, and broke her arm, dislocated her wrist, and, besides, received extensive bruises in various parts of her body, without bringing on labour. Dr. Henry Davies saw a pregnant woman, who, in throwing water out of a window, lost her balance, and fell into the street, breaking both thighs, but she recovered without aborting. Dupuytren has put on record the case of a woman who had severe trau-

* *See* Tyler Smith, "Manual of Obstetrics," 1858.

matic tetanus during pregnancy, and who nevertheless went to her full time.   M. Brillaud Laujardière
relates the case of a peasant who took his wife, while
pregnant, behind him on horseback, and started off
at full gallop, with the object of bringing on abortion.
After shaking her thoroughly in this way, he dropped
her suddenly on the ground without stopping.   This
treatment he repeated twice without success.*   I
have on more than one occasion failed to bring on
abortion when extreme peril to a woman called for
this interference, by passing the sound deep into the
uterine cavity, and stirring up its contents; and one
case is on record in which an intra-uterine pessary
was unwittingly introduced into the womb of a
pregnant woman, and was worn for some time without provoking abortion.

The frequency of embroynic death in the earlier
stages of gestation is approximately shown by the
tables of Whitehead.†   These were taken from the
records of the Manchester Lying-in Hospital, and
give an estimate so far as it relates to women of the
poorer classes.   Whitehead interrogated 2000 pregnant women, whose average age was a fraction below
thirty years, and he found the sum of their pregnancies had been 8681, or 4.34 for each; of which
about one in seven had terminated abortively.   Seven
hundred and forty-seven women had aborted once at
least, some oftener; their average age was 32.08
years; the number of their pregnancies was 4775;
that of their abortions 1222 or 1.63 for each person.

* See T. Gallard, "De l'avortement, &c., au point de but med.-
legal."
† "Abortion and Sterility," 1847.

These figures, however, do not accurately represent the frequency of abortion throughout the whole child-bearing period, and a considerable proportion of the women were pregnant for the first time. In any case, they only afford a calculation of the average number of abortions in the first half of the reproductive period; and inasmuch as abortion is alleged to be more frequent in the latter half of the child-bearing period, it is probably much below the average of the whole. This is rendered the more probable by some further statistics of Dr. Whitehead, which he nevertheless admits are too limited to warrant a general conclusion. Of sixty-four women who were living in wedlock until after the final menstrual crisis, only eight had escaped having an unsuccessful pregnancy, the percentage of those who had aborted being eighty-seven.

Hegar* reckons that there is about one abortion to every eight or ten full-time deliveries.

Quite recently I attempted to draw up some tables on the basis of 1000 cases concerning which I possessed notes of private patients. It seemed to me that as Whitehead's figures were taken exclusively from the poorer classes in a manufacturing town where, according to his account, they were exposed to many privations, and to causes which deteriorate general health, there might be some difference as to the proclivity to abortion in the well-to-do classes. Unfortunately I found that, so far as many of the cases were concerned, the accounts of miscarriage were so untrustworthy or so indistinct as to be value-less. A large number of women had expressed

* " Monat. für Geburt." Band xxi. Sup.

themselves as having had "many" or "several" abortions, and some had persuaded themseves that miscarriage had occurred when there was no satisfactory evidence that pregnancy had occurred at all. I took, therefore, the figures representing 400 patients, in whom the evidence was distinct and unequivocal. All the women had reached at least their 40th year, and hence the history included for most of them the whole of the child-bearing period of life.

The results were as follows : 400 women had been pregnant 2325 times. Of these, pregnancy had resulted in living children 1783 times, and there had been 542 abortions. The proportion of abortions to children was, therefore, 30.40 per cent, or about 1 in 3, while the proportion of abortions to pregnancies was 23.32, or about 1 in 4. The number of women who had borne children but had never suffered abortion was 152 in the 400, or 38 per cent., while the number of women who had borne no living child and only had abortions was 27, or 6.75 per cent. The sum of the pregnancies in 400 women being, therefore, 2325, or 5.81 for each, and the sum of the abortions being 524, it was 1.35 for each.

It will be seen that the proportion of abortions to full-time pregnancies is considerably higher than Hegar's computation. The proportion approximates more closely to Dr. Whitehead's figures ; but there is a larger average of abortions, as the calculation embraces a longer portion of the reproductive period ; and there is another notable difference, which may perhaps be put down to easier circumstances and exemption from bodily toil—namely,

TABLE I.

ANALYSIS OF NUMBER OF WOMEN WHO HAD AND HAD NOT ABORTED.

	Women below 30 years of age (Whitehead).		Women over 40 years of age (Priestley).	
	Number.	Percentage of whole.	Number.	Percentage. of whole.
Women who had not aborted . . .	1253	62.65	152	38.00
Women who had aborted . . .	747	37.35	248	62.00
Total number of women under observation .	2000	100.00	400	100.00
Women who only aborted — that is, who had borne no living child . .	—	—	27	6.75

Table I. illustrates the point that whereas among the younger women the proportion who aborted was about 1 in 3—that is, 1 aborted to 2 who did not—among the older women the proportion was almost exactly reversed, and 2 aborted to 1 who did not.

TABLE II.

ANALYSIS OF PREGNANCIES IN REFERENCE TO ABORTIONS AND TO FECUNDITY.

	2000 Women below 30 years of age (Whitehead).			400 Women over 40 years of age (Priestley).		
	Number.	Percentage of whole.	Number per Woman.	Number.	Percentage of whole.	Number per Woman.
Children . .	7459	85.92	3.73	1783	76.68	4.46
Abortions . .	1222	14.08	0.61	542	23.32	1.35
Tot. pregnancies	8681	100.00	4.34	2325	100.00	5.81

TABLE III.

RATIOS OF ABORTIONS TO PREGNANCIES AND CHILDREN.

	Whitehead.		Priestley.	
	Percentage.	Being about 1 in	Percentage.	Being about 1 in
Ratio of abortions to pregnancies	14.08	7	23.32	$4\frac{1}{3}$
Ratio of abortions to children	16.39	6	30.40	$3\frac{1}{3}$

Table II. shows that the older period is more productive of pregnancies than the younger in the proportion of 5.81 to 4.34 or (4 to 3); but that the percentage of them terminating in abortions is also much greater in the older period than in the younger (23.32 against 14.08). Table III. illustrates the last point in another manner.

that if a comparison is made with Dr. Whitehead's limited data, concerning those women who had passed the menstrual epoch, it will be remarked that while among the poor of the manufacturing town as many as 87 per cent. had incurred abortion, only 62 per cent. of the women in better circumstances had suffered in this way.

Granville, in his work on "Abortion," states that of 400 women 128 of them had miscarried, and among them there had been 305 abortions. Bland [*] computed that, out of 515 mothers, 147 of them had miscarried. Dr. Tyler Smith, writing on this subject in 1858, remarks that, as according to the last census, the married female population in England and Wales between the ages of fifteen and fifty-five amounted to 2,553,894, the loss of fœtal life based on Dr. Whitehead's or any other calculation must be enormous.

As to the particular pregnancies in which abortion most frequently takes place, considerable difference of opinion exists. Dr. Tyler Smith regarded the danger as greater in first pregnancies, particularly among the upper classes, and in those later pregnancies which occur before the cessation of the menses. Whitehead believed that the third and fourth and subsequent pregnancies, and in one or two of the last near the termination of the fruitful period, are most commonly unsuccessful. Schroeder[†] says that there are twenty-three multiparæ who abort to three primiparæ. I am bound to say that I do not think these computations at all satisfactory or conclusive, inasmuch as various elements are not

[*] "Calculations, &c.," 1781.   [†] "Lehrbuch der Geburt."

considered which become important factors in making
the calculation.   Age has a marked influence on the
continuance of pregnancy, be it the first or latest
gestation, and the social circumstances in which the
woman finds her place in life, are not without effect
on her successful child-bearing.   Thus, women of
the better classes incur much more risk of aborting
in their first pregnancies than their poorer sisters,
from the prevailing fashion of taking long journeys
immediately after marriage.   If conception begins
then, it is very likely to break down as the result of
the shaking and fatigue incurred, combined with the
irritation often set up in the reproductive organs,
as the result of the new conditions of life.

The preceding remarks refer more particularly to
abortion in the earlier periods of pregnancy.

Concerning the amount and frequency of fœtal
mortality *in utero* in the later periods of gestation,
no very large amount of information is accessible.
There are abundant statistics by Collins, MacClin-
tock, Sir James Simpson, and others, concerning the
number of still-born children resulting from tedious,
difficult, and complicated delivery, and with these
are included a certain number of children who died
antecedent to the supervention of labour.   But
taking these two together it is obvious that the sum
of both, forms only a small proportion of the absolute mortality which occurs in the later periods of
gestation.   Of 16,654 children born in the Dublin
Lying-in Hospital, and recorded by Collins,* 1121
were still-born.   Of these still-born children, 801
were either premature, or if at the full time, were

"Practical Treatise on Midwifery," 1835.

putrid, and their deaths were therefore not due to injuries during delivery, or what may be called traumatic causes.

The relative period of utero-gestation in which intra-uterine death most frequently takes place, has been variously stated, and for certain reasons cannot be very precisely determined. It is probably very frequent in the form of abortion during the early weeks of pregnancy, and then it may produce so little disturbance in a woman's health as to be scarcely noticed. Among the poor this is certainly the case, and consequently an estimate of its frequency among them is practically impossible. Madame la Chapelle * regarded it as most frequent in the sixth month of utero-gestation. Cazeau † believes abortion to be most frequent in the two or three first months, and Depaul ‡ states its greatest frequency to be between two and a half and three and a half months. Jacquemier,§ on the other hand, declares abortion is not less frequent in the sixth month than in the first half of pregnancy. Whitehead's figures show that of 602 cases of abortion, 275 occurred between two and a half and three and a half months, and 147 between three and a half to four and a half months. (*See* Table IV.)

The stage at which development has arrived, about three to three and a half months, points to a period when, *pro tanto*, abortion may be supposed the more readily to be brought about, and so coincides with Whitehead's statistics, just quoted.

---

* "Pratique des Accouch."   † "Traité des Accouch."
‡ " Leçons de Clinique Obstét."
§ Art. Avortement : " Dict. Encycl."

TABLE IV.

SHOWING THE PERIOD OF PREGNANCY AT WHICH ABORTION OCCURRED IN 602 CASES, THE RELATIVE NUMBER OF STILL-BORN AND LIVING CHILDREN, AND THE NUMBER LIVING AT THE END OF A MONTH AFTER BIRTH (WHITEHEAD).

Period of Pregnancy at which Abortion occurred.	Number of Births at each Period.	Number still-born.	Number living at Birth.	Number living at the end of a month after Birth.
2 months	35	—	—	—
3 ,,	275	—	—	—
4 ,,	147	—	—	—
5 ,,	30	—	—	—
6 ,,	32	24	8	—
7 ,,	55	38	17	3
8 ,,	28	23	5	1
Total	602	85	30	4

Then the villi of the chorion have become more concentrated on the decidua serotina, and the young placenta is in progress of formation. There is great increased vascular activity in all the tissues, and yet a certain instability, for the vascular loops projected from the maternal circulation are beginning to surround the fœtal villi in a delicate sort of network, and the spaces which intervene between the membranes, so obvious in the earliest weeks, are not yet obliterated. Besides, the union between the membranes and the uterine walls is less stable than later on, and so separation more readily occurs. Hence a greater liability to blood extravasations, not only into the layers of the decidua, but also between the several membranes, and more especially between the decidua reflexa and the chorion. From the twelfth to the sixteenth week the phenomenon of " quickening" occurs, and if anything hinders or prevents the ascent of the uterus into the abdomen, abortion is precipitated. Morgagni and Desormeaux * are of opinion that abortion is more frequent with female than with male embryos, but give no statistics; and Cazeau's reasons for thinking this may be true is scarcely a sound one—namely, because at term there are sixteen boys born to every fifteen girls.

Some of the indirect causes which lead to intra-uterine death may be regarded as general rather than specific in their effect. In the case of domestic animals we find abortion, which is not infrequent among them, attributed to a series of indefinite causes, as bad and wet seasons, insufficient and unsuitable food, &c.; and in women, apart from injuries and specific diseases, abortion and death of the fœtus during pregnancy are, by most authors, regarded as brought about by influences which impair the general health and lower vitality, as well as by mental and emotional causes, which are necessarily more potent in the human subject than in the lower animals.

An inquiry into all the circumstances which conduce to, or more directly produce, intra-uterine death, extends therefore over a wide range of subjects, and embraces a variety of pathological considerations. Not only does it involve a minute inquiry into the several morbid constitutional states in the woman which may tend to destroy the offspring, but involves also an inquiry into various deviations of health which may produce a like result on the side of the male parent. It includes various morbid changes which take place in the uterus and its appendages, in the fœtal membranes and placenta,

* *Vide* Charpentier.

and, lastly, in the embryo itself. Various classifications of the causes of intra-uterine death have been made by Spiegelberg, Leopold, Barnes, and others.

I do not propose to follow closely any of these classifications, but shall take first the causes acting through the male parent; then those which act through the intervention of the mother; and, lastly, those which more particularly belong to the fœtus itself, although possibly remotely related to both parents.

1. *Causes of Intra-uterine Death referable to the Father.*—Authorities concur in stating that the death of the embryo, after conception, is due, in some cases at least, to defects in the male parent. The fault is, as it were, *ab initio*. Conception takes place, but it is vitiated from the beginning by some alteration in the fecundating fluid. The male parent may be too young or too old to impart the necessary potency to the spermatic fluid, and so the product of conception breaks down and drops like untimely fruit, because it does not possess the necessary amount of vitality to prolong its development. The same thing is seen in plants as in animals. The pollen-cells are some- imperfectly developed, as the result of an unhealthy state of the plant; or the pollen may be injured or spoilt, before or during the time it is applied to the pistil, and the result is an imperfectly formed seed or fruit, which never reaches maturity. This is particularly noticeable in diœcious plants, and in these experiments can readily be verified. In birds' eggs, again, it is often observed that they cannot be hatched, although no imperfection can be discovered in them. The fault here is probably to be sought in

the imperfect impregnation by the male. It seems probable also that some of the forms of monstrosity are due to faulty conditions in the male parent, and these, in a large proportion of cases, lead to abortion or premature fœtal death. Debauchery, various diseases and injuries from which men suffer, may so deteriorate the constitution as to impair the procreating power, and so cause abortion in the woman.

Devilliers* points out that procreating power is essentially distinct from that of development ; and hence, that a man may possess the power to fertilise, but his whole strength may be expended in this act, and may not extend beyond, so that there is no further development. He further states that the faculty of development is relative. Thus a weak man may impregnate a robust woman, and, by so much as she has strength to impart, the vitality of the germ may be carried on entirely under the influence of the woman. Instances are recorded of women who have aborted in every pregnancy by a first husband, and by a second have gone to the full time. I know of one case where a man, the subject of slight albuminuria, married a young woman apparently in perfect health. They had one child, delicate and fragile, within a year, and the wife aborted successively in three subsequent pregnancies—the husband growing weaker year by year, and eventually dying of uræmia. Since then, I have inquired of several authorities on renal affections, whether they had remarked a special proclivity to abortion in the wives of men who were the subjects of albuminuria, or saccharine diabetes. I have not

* " Dict. Med. et Chir. Pract., &c." : Jaccoud, art. Avort.

been able to procure any precise information on the point, but the general outcome of opinion is that, during the progress of these maladies, the vital powers become so exhausted, that sexual power and desire fall into abeyance ; and that it is only during the slighter forms of disease that they are likely to continue. My friend, Dr. Frank, of Cannes, has related to me the case of a diabetic man married to a healthy young woman. Their first child was born alive, the diabetic tendency being slight. After this the wife had a series of abortions, generally in the fourth or fifth month, the diabetic condition in the husband having become more confirmed. Singularly enough, the wife herself eventually died after her husband of albuminuria.

In the "Arch. Générales de Méd.," 1860, is a curious paper by Constantin Paul, in which he shows that lead-poisoning, or saturnine intoxication as it is called, not only injuriously affects the child *in utero* when the mother is the subject of it, but indirectly also when the father is affected. In this way it may lead to the death of the fœtus *in utero*, and produce abortion or premature expulsion. In many cases, also, where the child is born alive, the poison may so lower its vitality that it does not long survive its birth. Thus, of seven women whose husbands suffered from lead-poisoning, there were thirty-nine pregnancies. Out of these there were eleven abortions and one dead-born child, and of twenty-seven children born alive, eighteen died in early infancy, while only nine survived.

Syphilis.—Perhaps the most potent of all poisons in producing intra-uterine death, at all stages of

c

pregnancy, is the poison of syphilis, and this whether the disease exists in the male or in the female parent. I shall have to speak more fully afterwards of its effects when the woman is the subject of syphilis. Here I propose to say a few words only on its influence on conception in the male. It is readily understood that if a man be affected with syphilis he may communicate the disease directly to a woman *in coitu*, and the usual result will be a local affection, followed by constitutional symptoms, and a general poisoning of all the fountains of life—so much so, indeed, that the fecundated germ as part of the maternal system is blighted from the first. But it is, perhaps, not so readily understood that when a woman has shown no indication of syphilis in her own person she may become impregnated by a spermatic fluid, which carries with it so potent a syphilitic virus that, in its development, it sooner or later kills the product of conception, and this, in its turn, so poisons the maternal blood that the woman eventually becomes tainted with constitutional syphilis. Charpentier, in his "Traité des Accouchements," gives a good illustration of this indirect influence of syphilis in the male on conception, and it is but typical of facts accumulated by other observers.

A student of medicine contracted an indurated chancre, followed by syphilitic roseola. This was carefully and immediately treated, and he had no other sign either then or afterwards. Two years after the primitive affection, this young man married. Although he had shown no indication of syphilis in the meantime, he was so anxious on the subject, that he submitted himself to a fresh anti-syphilitic course for three months before his marriage. His wife's first pregnancy occurred some months after the marriage. She went to her full time, and her child when born had syphilitic pemphigus. It was carefully treated, and apparently recovered, inasmuch as up to four years of age it seemed healthy and vigorous. At this time it took whooping cough, followed by double pneumonia, and a blister was applied to the back of its chest. In forty-eight hours the whole blistered surface was covered with "plaques muqueuses," and it died in forty-eight hours later, in the opinion of those attending it, not of the pneumonia, but of visceral syphilis. Two other consecutive pregnancies of this wife ended in abortion between three and four months. The fourth pregnancy went to the full time, but the child died twenty-four hours after birth of convulsions. The fifth pregnancy again ended in abortion between three and four months. Notwithstanding this history, the mother continued in good health, and showed no signs of syphilis. At her own instance, nevertheless, she submitted to a course of anti-syphilitic treatment, and her husband again adopted the same plan. Nearly seven years elapsed without pregnancy, when a sixth supervened. This followed its regular course, and the woman was in due time delivered of a healthy vigorous child. This, nine months after its birth, when last reported on, had shown no indication of syphilis.

The idea that syphilis could be transmitted directly from the father to the foetus without visibly affecting the mother, was long doubted and combated, but it has been sustained in later days by

Trousseau, Depaul, Vidal, Ricord, and by Diday, whose treatise on Syphilis has been translated for the Sydenham Society. In our own country, Professor Harvey* and Mr. Jonathan Hutchinson also have adduced very cogent evidence in proof that the mother may be infected by syphilis through the medium of the fœtus, and there is every reason to believe that, in many instances where syphilis is, so to speak, latent in the husband, it is not communicated to the wife unless she becomes pregnant by him ; in other words, that coitus without conception does not impart the venereal taint to the woman.

It has occurred to me on more than one occasion to treat cases of pregnancy in which there was a strong presumption that the male parent not only begot a syphilitic child, but that the child in its turn infected the mother. For instance, a young man having suffered from both primary and secondary syphilis two years before, and being apparently cured —as all external signs of venereal disease had disappeared—married a healthy wife about his own age. The wife soon became pregnant, and seemed to go on well until the fourth month of gestation, when, about the time of quickening, she began to have great irritation of the vulva, and mucous tubercles made their appearance all over the vulva and round the anus. The throat became affected about the same time, and syphilitic psoriasis made its appearance on the face and chest. Pregnancy went on to the end of the seventh month, when the woman was delivered of a dead child, putrid, and of a placenta infiltrated with nodules of whitish deposit. The mother dis-

* *Vide* "On the Fœtus in Utero," by Alex. Harvey, M.D., 1886.

tinctly stated that she had no sore in the earlier part of her pregnancy, and there was no indication of her being the subject of syphilis until nearly halfway in her gestation.

As remarked by Lancereaux,[*] the difficulty in this class of cases is to determine when the contamination took place. The father may have had some sore hidden in the urethra and not detected, and the mother may have had some primary lesion which had passed unperceived. In further proof, however, of what has been stated, and of the persistence of syphilis when apparently cured, Vidal[†] refers to three physicians who, believing themselves cured of syphilitic affections, married. The children, the issue of these marriages, presented, a few days after birth, evident traces of syphilitic affection, their mothers never having manifested any suspicious lesion. Lancereaux remarks that this "collection of facts furnished by men well informed and placed in conditions of observation often very different from each other, cannot leave any doubt as to the exclusive action of the father in the inheritance of syphilis."

Baerensprung, the latest authoritative writer on this subject, in his work "Die Hereditaire Syphilis," cites forty cases occurring in his own experience of hereditary transmission by the father, and although infection in all his cases did not lead to the death of the foetus *in utero*, yet they afford evidence of the point under discussion, namely, the infection of the ovum directly by the male parent. Diday quotes several instances where syphilis was thus transmitted

[*] " On Syphilis," trans. for Sydenham Society, 1868.
[†] "Traité des Maladies Vénériennes."

by fathers ; and Baerensprung gives fourteen cases in which the father was exempt from any manifestation of syphilis—it was, so to speak, latent—and yet both the mother and child were infected by him. Baerensprung further concludes, from numerous observations made by him, that syphilis in the father is transmissible during the primary and secondary periods only, not in the tertiary period, or, if so, in a much slighter degree.

2. *On the part of the Mother.*—Before speaking of the specific diseases and local pathological causes which may produce intra-uterine death on the part of the mother, it may be well to glance at the general conditions which conduce to this end. The same general causes which influence sterility, and which have been indicated by Dr. Matthews Duncan,* are concerned in a greater or less degree in the production of abortion and premature death of the fœtus. Thus constitutional conditions, external agencies which depress the general health, unhealthy habits and occupations, extremes of heat and cold, climate, locality, under-feeding and over-feeding, prematurity or old age ; in fact, anything in the mother which tends to deteriorate strength and vigour, must be counted as productive of embryonic death. Some of these influences, as we have seen, are indefinite in their effects, equally in the human subject as in the lower animals. Others are more specific and better defined. Thus, as wild animals in confinement are apt to bring forth abortions, so deviations from normal modes of living, in an insidious way, mar the reproductive faculty in women. Unnatural ways of

* " Lectures on Sterility," 1884.

dressing, particularly tight-lacing and the like, late hours, absence of healthy exercise in the open air, confinement in close rooms, all tell in the long run in producing deterioration of the individual, and just as the unhealthy tree will produce monstrous leaves or flowers, or shrivelled or seedless fruit, so we have the analogues in abortions, dead fœtuses, sickly children, and monstrous products of women. The change from a temperate to a hot, relaxing climate, I have noticed, predisposes women not only to over-profuse and frequent menstruation, but also to abortion. English women going to reside in India are prone to abort. This may in part be due to the luxurious habits of life and the relinquishing of healthy exercise so often superadded to the hot climate. These especially produce sluggishness in the portal circulation and congestion of all the pelvic blood-vessels.

So far as I know, we have no data by way of enabling us to determine the relative effect of over- or under-feeding on intra-uterine life. That both have an effect is undoubted. We have the analogy shown in the vegetable kingdom, where starved trees and plants produce abortive fruit and seeds. On the other hand, over-manuring or over-nourishment of plants leads to a great growth of tissue, but it conduces to sterility or imperfectly developed fruits. In the poorer class of patients, reported upon by Dr. Whitehead, as we have seen, 87 per cent. had suffered abortion, but in the more affluent class from which I have taken my figures, 62 per cent. only had aborted. But these figures do not throw much light on the effects of over- or under-feeding, as happily it by no means follows that the majority of women who can afford it feed to repletion; nor, on the other hand, are women who become hospital patients, as a rule, so imperfectly fed as seriously to interfere with the processes of nutrition and reproduction. I hold a strong conviction, nevertheless, that over-feeding is more pernicious in its effects on the product of conception than under-feeding. The indulgence in larger quantities of food and stimulating drinks certainly tends to produce sterility, and in like manner it imperils the safety of the germ, when once fertilisation has been effected. Besides overloading all the tissues with more material than they can assimilate, and in this way disturbing every function, it more especially disturbs the portal circulation, leads to a congested condition of all the pelvic viscera, and thus favours blood extravasations into the fœtal envelopes, or provokes abnormal uterine conditions. Among authors who have noticed this kind of influence I may mention that Stolz* has observed that fat women are often sterile, and if they conceive they are apt to abort. He believes this depends on nutrition taking an abnormal direction, and the nutritive fluids destined for the nutrition of the embryo are thus insufficient for its development.

I have notes of the effects of anæmia, of high altitudes, of inter-breeding, of plural births, of too frequent or too rapidly succeeding pregnancies, of prematurity and advanced age, and of temperament, as influencing pregnancy adversely; but I must not dwell upon each of these in great detail.

* "Des Accouchements."

Anæmia in the mother is a well-recognised cause of fœtal death, and large and sudden losses of blood from the maternal circulation may also cause death of the child *in utero*. Convulsions are said to have been produced in the child before its death, when the mother has suffered from much depletion, and syncope in the pregnant woman, long continued, will so suspend the utero-placental circulation as to kill the unborn child. Anæmia going beyond the normal limits so impoverishes the blood, that it affords but feeble nutriment to the growing embryo, and so it may perish from sheer inanition. Anæmia does not necessarily prevent pregnancy, and when conception occurs in a woman already anæmic, this condition is apt to increase. As one authority says : " Anæmic women are prone to abort habitually, for in them the genital function is imperfectly performed—menstruation being irregular, scanty, and painful. It may be from a lack of activity and tone, for these women are usually pale, of feeble constitution, and subject to leucorrhœa." Jacquemier* remarks of them, that from the commencement of pregnancy the uterine neck is soft, partly open, very low, and acts in an indirect manner in favouring abortion. The state, he adds, " is allied to a state of congestion or irritability of the uterus."

Anæmia in the mother is recognized as a cause of fœtal death by Leopold,† Spiegelberg,‡ and other writers. In normal pregnancy, Cazeaux§ says there

* " Dict. Encycl." : art. Avortement.
† " Lehrbuch der Geburt."
‡ *Ibid.*
§ " Traité, &c., de l'Art des Accouch."

is a sort of relative chlorosis or anæmia. Long ago the changes in the blood produced by pregnancy were investigated by Andral and Gavarret, and their views have been more recently confirmed by Nasse ("Archiv für Gyn.," 1876). The whole blood mass, according to these authors, is notably increased, and particularly in the latter half of pregnancy. There is increase of water and a diminution of the red corpuscles. The white corpuscles in some cases increase to such an extent as to produce what Regnault calls a "normal leucocytosis." Fibrin diminishes until about the sixth month. In the last three it is increased above the usual standard, and the blood cups when drawn off. All the vessels are more distended, more especially the pelvic ones, and there is everywhere increased arterial tension, with more rapid pulse. This physiological anæmia of pregnancy may be so pushed beyond normal limits that it not only imperils the condition of the child but exhausts the mother.

Gusserow* relates five cases of pregnancy in which nothing but excessive anæmia could be detected, and they all ended fatally.

It is to be noted, however, that pernicious or excessive anæmia in the pregnant woman does not necessarily lead to abortion. It may end fatally to the mother without being preceded by abortion. When present, however, in moderate degree, it clearly has an influence in destroying the product of conception, sometimes by starving it *in utero*, at other times, it may be, by leading to disease in the membranes or placenta.

* "Arch. für Gyn." 1871.

High Altitudes have been stated to be incompatible with successful pregnancy. Lancerotte and Jourdanet* state that in certain mountainous regions, the women habitually descend into the valleys when pregnant to avoid miscarriage. The way in which the elevation so acts is not explained.

Of Inter-breeding.—It may be said that this in plants as well as animals produces weakness and malformation in the progeny, and a tendency to premature death. The abortions of plants so produced is typical of that observed in animals. There is a tendency to the formation of double flowers, of seeds which do not ripen, and, if apparently perfect, they do not germinate.

Plural births also conduce to bring about intra-uterine death. Shorthouse has pointed out that "twinning," as it is called, is apt to favour abortion in horses, and like observations have been made in the human subject. Braun, Chiari, and Spaeth† have produced some evidence to prove that abortions are comparatively more frequent in plural than in single pregnancies. More dead children are born, and monstrosities are also common, with multiple births, while children born alive are more difficult to rear.

Neither *prematurity* nor *advanced age* in the parent is favourable to the continuance of pregnancy. Immature plants do not ripen fruit, and young animals, or girls who become pregnant before maturity is reached, are apt to abort, or, if the full time of gestation is reached for once, the reproductive power may be so exhausted as to lead either to

* *Vide* Charpentier.   † "Clin. der Geburt." 1855.

absolute sterility in the future, or to subsequent abortion. Charpentier states that he has seen girls of thirteen or thirteen-and-a-half and fourteen years go to the full term, but these are exceptional cases.

Again, an old bitch, as Dr. Duncan has told us, often ends her career by producing a dead or premature puppy, and it is a prevalent opinion that the last born of women may either be an abortion or an idiot. It is certainly a fact that the children born of the later pregnancies in women are often not so well developed physically nor mentally, nor so well endowed, as the earlier children ; and this disparity is the more marked if in the meantime the mother's health has deteriorated, from disease or vicious habits, such as drinking, &c. It is a noticeable feature in the cases occurring in my own practice which I have analysed, that abortion frequently ends the reproductive faculty in wives ; but whether this fact means that the function of the generative apparatus is exhausted *per se*, or that the general powers of the constitution have been so expended on previous child-bearing, or from some other cause, as to preclude the growth and nourishment of further offspring, is not clear. Jacquemier asserts that it is not uncommon to see women abort with the greater facility the nearer they approach to the age when aptitude for fecundation ceases. Depaul* does not admit this, but Dr. Duncan's remark on the influence of age on sterility has a direct bearing on this point. Dr. Duncan says : " I know of no cause of sterility or its allies—excessive production, pluriparity, abor-

* " Leçons de Clinique Obstet."

tion, &c.—that can be compared with age in extent and power."

Broadly, then, general causes, contra-distinguished from the specific, resolve themselves into any adverse influences which enfeeble and depress the general health of the individual parents, and so impair the procreative power. There seems to be a rule, to which, however, there may be exceptions, that a certain measure of vitality meted out to the individual may be sufficient to maintain and prolong individual life indefinitely, but there must be a superfluity of this vitality to ensure the successful procreation of healthy offspring. In many cases, where the death of the embryo arises from obscure or apparently inscrutable causes, there is no doubt that some inherent weakness exists in the body of the parents, which, while it permits conception, affords so small an amount of initial vitality to the germ, that it dies down, out of mere feebleness, and the death of the embryo thus only antedates, as it were, the death of the feeble children in infancy who have just survived long enough to be expelled living from the interior of the womb.

Some writers, as Madame Boivin * and Madame La Chapelle,† have spoken of epidemics of abortion ; but these, when inquired into, have been found to be associated with famines, sieges, and the like. Nägele and Hoffman ‡ have made some observations on the subject, and during the siege of Paris in 1870-71, abortion was noticed as particularly fre-

* " De l'Art des Accouchements."
† " Pratique des Accouchements."
‡ *Vide* Charpentier, " Traité Pratique des Accouchements."

quent. "The children born at that time are said to be one and all of a very weak constitution, and are still called '*enfants du siège*.'"[*] Here emotional causes, and constant dread of "the Prussians," were no doubt important factors in bringing about the results mentioned ; but the utter weakness and want of food suffered by large classes of people must also have told in a marked degree. When epidemics of abortion have been studied in domestic animals, they have probably been due to some epidemic disease or plague making havoc among them, of which abortion was the secondary effect; or to the presence of ergot either in the grain or on the grasses upon which they had been fed.

Professor Nocard, of the Veterinary School of Alfort, speaks of an epidemic of abortion among cows which is essentially propagated by infection. He says : "L'avortement épizootique semble bien être une maladie microbienne du fœtus et de ses envelopes, maladie à laquelle la mère reste absolument étrangère."[†]

Principal Veterinary Surgeon Fleming points out that Franck, of Munich, originally demonstrated that epidemics of abortion in cows depended on the presence of microbes, and he shows that there is abundant evidence of this fact published by observers both in France and Germany.[‡]

Some recent authorities seem to doubt whether ergot in grasses is so frequently a cause of abortion in cows as was supposed. Mr. Harker,[§] of the

[*] "Pall Mall Gazette," April 3rd, 1884.
[†] *See* "Times," October 13th, 1886.
[‡] *Vide* Fleming, "Veterinary Obstetrics."
[§] *See* "Times," October, 1886.

Agricultural College, Cirencester, is among these; and the experiments of Dr. Wright, referred to by Christison, seemed to indicate that ergot had no power of inducing abortion in the lower animals. Nevertheless, there is some curious evidence in favour of ergot in grasses producing abortion in cows, in *Land and Water* for 1884; and it is elsewhere stated that abortion among cattle in New Zealand was comparatively rare until the introduction of rye-grass, and its becoming affected with ergot, when it caused great losses to the farmers (Fleming).

I have now to speak of the

Direct and Specific Causes in the Mother.—Some acute diseases of a specific kind in the mother have a very marked and direct influence in destroying foetal life. This is especially observed in reference to forms of illness which are attended with pyrexia and increase of temperature, and the danger to the child *in utero* bears a strict relation to the height of the temperature and the amount of systemic disturbance. It may indeed be asserted that, *cæteris paribus*, in proportion to the gravity of the maternal affection so is the danger to her progeny. It is well known how serious is the complication of some febrile affections with the puerperal state, and it seems almost to be the rule that if a pregnant woman is attacked by any of the exanthemata, or in fact by any disease which is attended by pyrexia, and the attack assumes a severe form, death of the foetus is brought about, and is followed by its ultimate expulsion.

Take, for example, Small-pox. Serres, quoted by Charpentier, states that in twenty-seven cases

which he records, there were twenty-three abortions
with twenty-two maternal deaths. This is a sufficient indication of the serious complication small-
pox is, when combined with pregnancy. Cazeaux*
asserts that there is a great difference in reference
to the effects of small-pox both on the pregnancy
and on the life of the mother, according as the affection is *discrète* or " confluent" in its character. When
" confluent" small-pox attacks a pregnant woman,
it acquires by the fact of pregnancy existing a particular gravity, and abortion is the rule, followed by
the death of the mother. Abortion is stated to be
most frequent at the suppurating stage, but it may
be at any period in the progress of the affection, and
in the later periods of pregnancy the child is sometimes expelled living and sometimes dead. Dr.
Barnes, who published some cases of pregnancy
complicated with small-pox in 1868,† lays down the
proposition that Nature hardly tolerates the con-
current progress of an active disease with pregnancy, and that abortion in these cases may in
some sort be regarded as a conservative process.
In the three cases he records the children were born
alive, and he concludes that the morbid poison of a
zymotic disease, aggravated by further blood-poisoning resulting from arrested or disordered secretory
function, sets up uterine contraction, and so expels
the foetus without interfering with its vitality.
When the child dies, a variety of causes have been
assigned for its death—the state of the maternal
blood, the infection of the child by the mother, and

* " Traité des Accouchements."
† " Obstet. Trans."

the increase of the maternal temperature acting injuriously on her child. The fœtus once dead, it becomes *ipso facto* a foreign body, and must be expelled.

It has been observed that uterine hæmorrhage is frequent at all stages of pregnancy during the progress of small-pox. This hæmorrhage, according to Spiegelberg and Hervieux,[*] is due to hæmorrhagic endometritis, which separates the membranes from the uterus, and in the earlier months leads to abortion, or later to premature labour.

When the child dies in the later months as the result of small-pox, Brouardel [†] regards the death as due to alterations in the maternal blood, which becomes charged with an increased quantity of carbonic acid, and both asphyxiates the child and brings on premature uterine contraction. Spiegelberg and Charpentier regard the death of the child as due to the increase of maternal temperature incident to the disease, and consider that hæmorrhage, when present, although it may favour uterine expulsion, yet plays only a secondary part in producing fœtal death. It seems established that during the suppurating stage of small-pox the temperature is the highest, and then expulsion from the uterus most frequently takes place. Children thus expelled, if born alive, have been observed to die soon after from convulsions. Whether this is due to the disease having been conveyed by the mother to the child can only be surmised. Be this as it may, the mother can no doubt communicate the disease to the infant *in utero*, for children have been

---

[*] " Gaz. des Hôpit." 1864.   [†] *Vide* Charpentier, Tr.

born covered with small-pox pustules, generally less advanced than those of the mother. In some cases, however, the mother and child have taken the disease simultaneously, and the pustules have shown the same stage of development in each.

Scarlatina, measles, erysipelas, diphtheria, typhoid fever, and its congeners, come within the same category as small-pox; each and all are inimical to pregnancy.

Scarlatina.—From the scanty records, it may be inferred either that scarlatina is not frequent during pregnancy, or else that its relation to the puerperal state after delivery has absorbed the attention of authors to the exclusion of the earlier period. The disease is well known to be an especially perilous complication in the puerperal patient, but Cazeau expresses his belief that pregnant women are not apt to contract the disease, and Montgomery thought the poison when absorbed during pregnancy might remain latent until delivery, when its characteristic effects would be produced. Nevertheless, Bourgeois[*] mentions an epidemic observed in Vienna, in 1801, where the disease assumed a very grave form, and all pregnant women miscarried, most of them dying.

Measles, like scarlatina, has a tendency to provoke premature emptying of the gravid uterus and to destroy embryonic life, but its effect is less virulent in this respect than small-pox and scarlatina. Levret notices it in these relations, and regarded it as partaking of the gravity of other eruptive fevers during pregnancy, and nearly always provoking abortion. Bourgeois, in the " Mémoires de l'Académie de

[*] " Mémoires de l'Acad. de Méd." 1861.

Médecine," states that of fifteen cases of measles during pregnancy there were eight abortions or deliveries before term. The signs of abortion generally showed themselves towards the end of the disease, and the disease itself was usually less virulent if attacking the patient in early pregnancy than at a later period. When a woman was near the full term, and was seized with measles, the signs of labour began in the midst of the fever, and grave symptoms were generally developed. The child was usually born dead or died soon after birth.

De Tourcoing, mentioned by Playfair, states that out of fifteen cases the mother aborted in seven, these being all severe attacks. Some cases are recorded in which the child was born with the rubeolous eruption upon it.

Erysipelas also, if attacking a pregnant woman, may, like other affections attended by pyrexia, lead to abortion or premature labour. If the elevation of temperature be great, the life of the fœtus may be compromised. According to the opinion of authorities, it is less grave in its effects than small-pox or scarlatina, and about on a level in this respect with measles.

Typhoid Fever and its congeners have received a considerable amount of attention in their relation to pregnancy. At one time Rokitansky and Niemeyer were quoted as believing that pregnancy gave a sort of immunity from typhoid, but the later opinions of Jenner and Murchison do not bear out this statement. Murchison and others have shown that not only many pregnant women contract the disease, but they may be the subjects of some other varieties of fever, as typhus and relapsing fever. Murchison says, if a woman far advanced in pregnancy is attacked with typhoid or enteric fever, the case is almost certain to be fatal ; death being usually preceded by abortion. He further says that abortion during the progress of typhus is the exception, and if labour is induced by the disease near the full time, the child lives. In relapsing fever, on the contrary, pregnant females, no matter at what stage of pregnancy they are attacked, almost invariably miscarry. Of thirty-six pregnant women who took the fever, under Smith and Jackson, all miscarried but one. If pregnancy is far advanced, the child is always stillborn, or only survives a few hours.

According to some observations published by Weber in 1870 (in the Berlin "Klin. Wochensch."), of sixty-three cases of typhoid in pregnant women, there were twenty-three abortions, forty going to the full time. Of 322 cases collected by Charpentier, abortion and premature delivery occurred 182 times ; in 140 cases pregnancy was not interfered with. When the child was born prematurely, it was often dead or died soon after birth. Charpentier states that typhoid has been observed more frequently in the early than in the later months of pregnancy, and if uterine action is brought on in the earlier stages, it more certainly leads to the death of the embryo. Spiegelberg alleges that the danger is not so much influenced by the form which the fever assumes, as by the period of pregnancy at which the attack begins. The danger is greatest in the earlier months, because it is apt to lead to more serious uterine hæmorrhage than in the later months, when it may only induce premature labour.

Pneumonia.—Of the non-specific forms of disease

attended by fever, I may instance pneumonia, which has always a special gravity when complicated by pregnancy. If severe, it almost invariably leads to emptying of the uterus, and then it depends, to some extent at least, upon the date of the pregnancy and the rapidity of its expulsion as to whether the child is born alive. I have on more than one occasion seen abortion produced in the earlier months as the result of a sharp attack of pneumonia or pleuro-pneumonia, and I particularly recollect one case I attended with my friend Dr. Henri Gueneau de Mussy where, during an attack of pneumonia, a fœtus was expelled at the fourth month, of a deep red colour, and the placenta was retained. The complication thus arising was a very serious one, as with the activity of change going on in the body of the patient the retained placenta showed signs of very rapid decomposition, and consequent contamination of the maternal blood. The placenta was at length removed, but with great difficulty, on account of the rigid contraction of the uterus, and from that moment there was an amelioration of all the symptoms, and the patient eventually recovered.

The causes of the expulsion and death of the fœtus during pneumonia are said by Churchill,* Cazeaux, and others, to be the violence of the cough and other attendant symptoms. Grisolle† considers that the importance of the organs affected, the suddenness of the attack, the intensity of the fever, and the number of sympathetic phenomena, disturb all the bodily functions, and are sufficient to account for the interruption to pregnancy.

* "Midwifery."   † "Traité de Pathol. Intern."

Ricau* and Chatelain† state that the hindrance to respiration accumulates carbonic acid in the blood, which thus becomes inimical to fœtal life, and induces uterine contraction. Ricau, who wrote an interesting thesis on this subject in 1874, collected forty-three cases of pregnancy complicated with pneumonia, and in these the fœtus was expelled prematurely in twenty-one cases, or nearly half, eleven of the children being not viable.

Pleurisy may also, if severe, imperil pregnancy in the same way.

The feverish state which follows surgical operations frequently leads to abortion and premature labour, if the constitutional state of the mother is seriously disturbed, and this apparently apart from the reflex effect of such minor operations as, for instance, tooth-extraction, which has been followed by abortion. I have repeatedly noticed, after surgical operations on pregnant women, that as soon as there were distinct evidences of the patient going wrong from septic poisoning, uterine disturbance has set in, and if the symptoms increase hæmorrhage begins, which is followed by the expulsion of the embryo. In other cases the emptying of the uterus has been almost the last act of vitality before the death of the patient. Thus, in the case of a woman who, being five months pregnant, had submitted to colotomy for obstruction of the bowels, irritative fever set in after the operation, and she eventually died of blood-poisoning. A few hours before death, the uterus was emptied by a sudden

---

* "Thèse," 1884.   † *Vide* Charpentier.

expulsive effort, the child being extruded enveloped
in the membranes and placenta entire. There was
scarcely any flooding, and the uterus contracted firmly
afterwards. It seemed, so to speak, that Nature,
finding life was surely departing from the mother,
made an effort to save her offspring, the last and final
act of her being. Since the child was too premature
to be viable, the effort was unavailing.

The study of the way in which acute diseases,
attended with elevated temperature, bring about
intra-uterine death and expulsion of the embryo is
very interesting.

In 1833, Hohl* found that the temperature of the
mother not only influenced the child, but he found
also that it increased the pulse of the fœtus, and a
diminution of heat made the fœtal pulse slower.
Huter† made similar observations in 1861. In six
cases he noted a marked increase of the fœtal pul-
sations corresponding to increased frequency of the
maternal pulse. Fiedler,‡ in 1862, watched two cases
of typhus with pregnancy, and he found the pulse of
the fœtus was increased in frequency like the mother's
pulse, and it showed similar morning remissions and
evening exacerbations. In the charts he made, he
found the fever-curve of the mother's pulse parallel
with the frequency of the fœtal heart. Kaminsky,§
during an epidemic of typhus and recurring fever in
Russia, in 1866, saw eighty-seven cases with pregnancy ; fifty-five were in the first half of gestation,
thirty-two in the second half. As soon as the

* " Die Geburtshülf Explor." 1883.
† " Monatss. für Geburts." 1861.
‡ " Archiv der Heilkunde," 1862.
§ " Moskauer Med. Zeit." 1866.

temperature of a pregnant woman reached 40° C. (104° F.), he observed the child to become disturbed. (1) There was increased activity of its heart, parallel with the increased temperature of the mother. (2) Increased restless movements of the child, the higher the maternal temperature. These signs were marked until the temperature reached 42.5° C. (108° F.), when the movements ceased, and he inferred the child was dead. Danger began at 40° C., and increased with each advance of temperature. The more intense the feverish state of the mother, the surer was the death of the child. The child so killed was not necessarily thrown off immediately, but might be retained for some time. In only two cases in the latter half of pregnancy was uterine hæmorrhage observed, while it was much more frequent in the first half. Similar observations were made by Winckel,* in 1869, and Löhlein, in a grave case of erysipelas, counted the child's heart-beats at 200 in the minute.

These observations suggested to Runge the idea of making some experiments on the effects of high temperature on the gestation of lower animals, and in the " Archiv für Gynecol." for 1877 his results are published. He placed a series of pregnant rabbits in a well-ventilated box, and raised its temperature in ten minutes to 50° C. (122° F.). The temperature of the animal increased 1° in each five minutes, and the animal died in forty minutes from " heat-stroke " —analogous, I presume, to sun-stroke—if not removed from the box. But the remarkable thing was that the fœtuses *in utero* died when a certain temper-

* "Pathol. der Geburt." 1869.

ature was reached which was not sufficient to kill the mother. Runge took the maternal temperature every ten minutes, and killed the animals, with certain precautions, when it reached an elevation varying from 39° to 42° C. On the uterus being opened, the fœtuses were found sometimes dead, sometimes living, and their temperature was constantly found some tenths of a degree higher than that of the mother. They were dead every time the temperature rose to 41.5° C. (106.7° F.), and were always alive when the maternal temperature was not higher than 40.5° C., or a little over 104° F. At intermediate temperatures they were sometimes dead, sometimes living. The chief lesions were dilatation of the right ventricle of the heart, which was distended with blood, and retraction of the left ventricle, which was hardened by contraction.

From these experiments Runge concludes that:

1. The temperature of the fœtus is habitually higher than that of the mother, and keeps higher when the mother's heat becomes abnormal.

2. That the fœtus dies solely from the heat before it becomes fatal to the mother.

3. That the temperature of the mother if only raised for a short period to 41.5° C. is fatal to the fœtus.

In reference to this last deduction, it has been remarked that the danger probably does not at once cease with the reduction of the mother's temperature to normal, for Claude Bernard has seen animals submitted to experiment die several days after being removed safe from a heated stove.

These experiments of Runge's are extremely interesting, and I thought it might be easy to ascertain whether the inference he draws from them is correct, that the animal heat is proportionately higher in the foetus than in the mother, even when no abnormal condition is present. In order to elucidate this point, Mr. Tyrell Brooks, of the Physiological Laboratory in King's College, kindly undertook to make some experiments under my direction. It seemed at first an investigation of no great difficulty, and yet it was less easy than might be supposed. It was necessary, in order to avoid the infliction of pain, to put the animals under chloroform, and rabbits were found so sensitive to the anæsthetic, that their ordinary temperature was speedily altered, and it sank progressively with the depth of the anæsthesia. Nevertheless, by careful management, and by wrapping the body up in warm flannels, the heat was fairly kept up during the continuance of the experiment. Dr. Sclater, of the Zoological Society, was good enough to lend me the very sensitive thermometer which had been used for taking the temperature of the python during incubation at the Zoological Gardens, and in this instrument the column of mercury would run up the entire length of its fine tube in from three to six seconds. This we used in one experiment, but it was found that good sensitive clinical thermometers answered practically very well, and it was necessary to use three at the same moment, so as to make the temperature in the several localities relative. Thus, one was placed in the vagina, the temperature being taken there ; afterwards an incision was made into the abdomen and uterus—a thermometer was placed in the cavity of the womb, and another in some part of the body of a fœtus, the vaginal thermometer still being retained, and its variations carefully watched. The result showed that in all the experiments where vitality was not so suddenly lowered by the chloroform as seriously to disturb the animal temperature, there was a marked difference between the vaginal, the uterine, and the fœtal temperature. Thus, in a large pregnant white rabbit marked with black, the vaginal temperature was 100° F., the uterine temperature 101.4°. Both temperatures were taken simultaneously. A fœtus being found, a thermometer was introduced into its mouth, and another into the uterine cavity. The uterine temperature was then 100°, the fœtal 100.6°. Ten minutes later a second observation was made on another fœtus, three thermometers being used. The uterine temperature was then 99.1°, the fœtal (taken in the mouth) 99.3°, the vaginal 98°. In another ten minutes the other cornu of the uterus was opened, and a third observation taken. The uterine temperature was then 99°, the fœtal 99.5°, and the vaginal 98.5°. The fœtal temperature in this case was taken in the cavity of the peritoneum, which probably accounts for the higher relative temperature. After another ten minutes' interval a fourth fœtus was exposed, and the temperatures were—uterine 97.9°, fœtal (taken in the mouth) 98.8°, vaginal 97.7°. The natural temperature of the rabbit is about two degrees higher than in the human subject, but it will be observed that the animal heat gradually sank during the experiments, apparently as the result of

the anæsthesia. The relative height of the temperatures nevertheless remained the same, the fœtal
being invariably the highest.

The temperature of the cat is nearly that of the
human subject, and in one of these animals near the
full period of pregnancy, deeply chloroformed, the
vaginal and uterine temperatures being taken simultaneously, the former was found to be 99°, the uterine
100°. Some time was here lost on account of
hæmorrhage occurring from divided uterine veins.
A fœtus at length being secured, the temperature
was taken and found to be : vaginal, 98°; uterine,
99.6°; fœtal, 99.5°. There was probably some error
here, due to the placenta of the fœtus being separated from the uterus several minutes before the
temperature was taken, for in two other observations
on fœtuses in the same uterus the temperature was
as follows :

Vaginal, 98.2°	Vaginal, 96.5°
Uterine, 98.4°	Uterine, 99°
Fœtal, 99°	Fœtal, 99.3°.

These experiments were repeated on other animals,
but these details are a fair sample of the whole. In
all the uterine temperature was relatively higher
than that of other parts of the pregnant animal, and
in all, except in one instance, where a shock was
given to the vitality of the fœtus, the fœtal temperature was higher, sometimes considerably higher than
the general temperature of the body of the mother.
Further, the temperature of the fœtus, although not
sinking so fast as the maternal temperature, was
manifestly influenced by it, declining at a somewhat

less rapid rate, but still keeping a sort of relation to the heat of the mother's body.

All the facts collectively are very instructive. It follows that if the temperature of the mother is raised either as the result of experiment, or from diseased action, the temperature of the fœtus will rise with it, and inasmuch as this is higher from the first, the fœtus will arrive at the heat indicating danger before the mother does. Winckel indeed remarks that it is probable the fœtal warmth rises in quicker proportion in the fœtus, because the liqour amnii, part of whose function it is to conduct heat from the fœtal body, becomes itself over-heated, and so ceases to control the fœtal temperature. I may mention that I have taken the temperature of the fœtus while *in utero* in a case of breech presentation. In this case I put a clinical thermometer into the fœtal anus, and the temperature then was five-tenths of a degree higher than in the maternal vagina. Gusserow has shown that the temperature of the fœtus immediately after birth is constantly from 0.1° to 0.3° above that of the maternal uterus and vagina.

It seems to be well known to physiologists that wherever great activity of function is going on in animal bodies there will be an increase of temperature. Professor Gerald Yeo informs me that there is increase of heat in the liver, beyond what is observed in other parts of the body, and this is most notable after a meal. The observations of M. Valencienne and Dr. Sclater have demonstrated that a considerable increase of heat is generated in the body of the female python during incubation, but the remarkable thing, and one perhaps which has not been sufficiently appreciated, is that regions of the body in mammiferous animals, where rapid nutrition or change are going on, may have a considerably higher temperature than the rest of the body, and it is just possible that some suggestions for treatment by way of controlling local temperature may arise out of this.

The next point of inquiry or conjecture is, how does increase of heat destroy the fœtus *in utero?* In other words, what is the *modus operandi?* Is it from "heat-stroke," somewhat analogous to "sunstroke," which, according to Runge, killed the adult rabbits when long exposed to high temperature? Houlier* has stated his belief that death is owing to degeneration of the myocardium. The heart at first becomes excited, then paralysed, and there is coagulation of the myosin. The same author states that in a child born of an eclamptic mother with a temperature of 40° C. at the moment of birth, he found granular degeneration of the cardiac vessels. I am, however, informed that it would require a temperature of 60° C. to coagulate myosin, so that some other explanation must be sought for. From the highly congested appearance of the fœtus expelled during the continuance of high fever temperature in the mother, it is obvious, that as the result of the heat, all the capillary blood-vessels become overcharged, and a state of hyperæmia is engendered, which is quite incompatible with fœtal life. Not only is the cutaneous surface of a deep livid colour from distension of the capillaries, but every tissue in the interior of the fœtal body is gorged with blood, as in a state of active inflammation. These changes

* *See* Charpentier, "Traité," &c.

of themselves one may imagine would be sufficient to account for the movements of the fœtus first becoming restless, then convulsive, and at last ceasing altogether. On microscopic examination of the congested tissues, I found the capillaries distended with blood, and the globules heaped up in confused masses, with here and there indications of rupture, and more or less of extra-vascular exudation.

It will be observed that, while the heat-theory affords a tolerably clear explanation of the cause of death *in utero* during the progress of diseases in which the maternal temperature is raised largely above the normal standard, it yet furnishes no adequate explanation of those cases in which the fœtus is frequently and rapidly expelled from the uterus, alive or dead, during the progress of some of these affections. It is true that the child may die from increased internal temperature, and be long retained after its death. It is also true that, in a large number of instances, the fœtus is expelled alive ; and if sufficiently developed it may continue to live, although it is prone to succumb after birth, even if near the full time.

The explanation of this tendency to forcible uterine contraction is, I take it, to be found in some observations of Brown-Séquard* in 1851. This distinguished physiologist showed that the circulation of dark venous blood—that is, blood imperfectly aerated, or from any cause rendered impure and charged with carbonic acid—had a remarkable effect in stimulating the nervous centres and contractile tissues. He made the deduction that oxygen gave and

* See " Journal de Physiol."

created contractile force ; carbonic acid brought contraction into play. These elements properly correlated and balanced, are in consonance with the continuance of pregnancy. If blood accumulates in the uterine sinuses, not only does distension act in promoting rhythmical contraction, but the carbonic acid of the blood is still more potent in bringing the uterine muscles into play, and so stagnation is prevented. Anything, therefore, which disturbs the systemic circulation, and more especially anything which prevents or retards the proper aëration of the maternal blood, acts as a direct incentive to uterine action ; and if this passes beyond the normal physio-logical limits, abortion or premature labour is the result.

In pneumonia, in the eruptive fevers, and in other diseases or injuries attended with febrile excitement, we have this pathological state directly induced, and hence the liability to emptying of the uterus. The same explanation would apply to asphyxia in the mother. It is recorded* that, during a razzia in Algeria, conducted by the Duc de Malakoff, hundreds of Arab women were suffocated in the caverns of Dahra, and it was found that many of those pregnant had aborted. The same thing occurred in a similar exploit under the celebrated Chevalier Bayard. In some forms of heart-disease, and in some of the other acute or chronic lesions of the circulation, similar pathological conditions may be produced, and so lead to premature uterine action.

There is still another complication occurring in connection with pregnancy, and said to be attended

* Tyler Smith, "Manual of Obstetrics."

with remarkable increase of heat, which can scarcely be passed over without notice.

In *Eclampsia*, or puerperal convulsions, it is well known that great peril attends the child. If labour and rapid delivery follow the supervention of convulsions towards the end of pregnancy, the child may survive, but convulsions are almost uniformly fatal to it if labour does not come on. The child is then expelled later, marked by such changes as are peculiar to the longer or shorter time it is retained *in utero*. The nearer the attack of convulsions comes on to the completion of pregnancy, the greater the chance of its preservation, and the chance is the greater if convulsion comes on for the first time during labour, and the case admits of speedy delivery. The cause of fœtal death in eclampsia has been attributed to the convulsions interfering with the hæmastosis of the blood—that is, producing asphyxia.

Braun,[*] of Vienna, believes uræmia to be the cause of death. The fœtus is impressed by the first or second access, and almost always dies after a certain number of attacks. If the mother dies, and the child is removed by the Cæsarean section, it is always dead. It is asserted that if the child is perchance born alive, much urea is found coming from the cord ; if dead, much carbonate of ammonia is found in the blood. It is further asserted that uræmia may kill the child without eclampsia having come on, and that the children of eclamptic patients are often albuminuric.

In seeking for the explanation of fœtal death in puerperal convulsions, Winckel[†] claims that he first

* "Lehrbuch der Gesammt Gyn."   † "Berichte und Studien."

E

pointed out a remarkable rise of temperature in the mother during the paroxysms. The French dispute his priority, and Charpentier, in controverting his claim, makes an attack upon him which shows that the anti-German feeling has permeated even the realm of science. He endeavours to show that Kien, a pupil of Hirtz, made the first serious researches with the thermometer in eclampsia, and after him Bourneville,* a pupil of Charcot's, who, in 1871 and 1875, made observations on thirteen patients, to which he adds four of Budin. Bourneville concludes that the temperature increases from the beginning of the attacks to the end; it may run up to 43° C. or 109·4° F. In the intervals, a high temperature is maintained, and this is slightly increased with each paroxysm. If the case terminates fatally to the mother, the temperature goes on increasing until death, but, if better symptoms supervene, the temperature declines.

In view of the researches of Runge, therefore, it may be that fœtal death in eclampsia is due to such elevation of temperature in the mother's body as is incompatible with the safety of the child. When the temperature does not reach so high a standard, the death must be attributed to uterine contraction producing imperfect aëration of the blood, or vitiation of the blood from uræmic poison.

It is stated that there is a very marked contrast in the temperature of the patients suffering from puerperal eclampsia and those stricken with convulsions the result of general uræmia, and it is asserted that the thermometer indicates a positive diagnosis between the two; for while in eclampsia

* "Archives de Tocol." 1875.

the temperature always rises, and may run up, indeed, to 43° C., in uræmic convulsions and coma—and equally in men and women—the temperature invariably falls progressively, and sometimes falls to 30° C. With some exceptions, it falls until death. The authors mentioned, therefore, conclude that eclampsia is not from uræmia, because the temperature is different in the two cases.

Hoffmeier* states "that in thirty-three cases of simple nephritis twenty children died, thirteen only lived. In 104 cases of nephritis with eclampsia sixty-two children died and forty-six lived—that is, on a total of 137 births eighty-two infants died and sixty-one only lived. Rayer, Fordyce Barker, and Hubert, of Louvain, admit the frequency of abortion and premature labour in women who have albuminous urine, and Braun estimated the fœtal mortality in such cases at eighty per cent." †

There are some diseases of women, attended by abnormal increase of temperature, in which the tendency to abortion and premature labour is greater than in healthy women, and yet in which the higher temperature probably plays but an unimportant part in contributing to fœtal death.

In *Phthisis* there is an admitted fertility among women which is almost abnormal, and the tendency to abortion and premature delivery, although not very striking, is yet greater than among healthy women. We are indebted for much precise information on this subject to theses published in France by M. Ortega and M. Gaulard, quoted by Charpentier.

* *Vide* Charpentier.
† "At the recent meeting of German scientists and medical men, at Strasburg, Dr. Fehling, of Stuttgart, read a memoir on habitual death of the embryo in kidney disease. In the first case under his

Mr. J. Scott Battams, in the "Lancet" of 1883, gives some statistics relative to this subject—as well as on the influence of syphilis.   Seventeen mothers bringing phthisical, rickety, or atrophic children for advice had collectively been pregnant ninety times—twenty-four of these pregnancies had terminated in abortion —and there had been thirty-seven infantile deaths. Mr. Battams remarks that these figures illustrate the well-known fertility of phthisical women.   Lebert (Archiv für Gyn. 1877) says that "advanced phthisis prevents pregnancy.   In early stages it does not do so, and pregnancy as a rule will go the full time.   Pregnancy, abortion and delivery determine the development of phthisis in those predisposed to it. Children born of phthisical parents are ordinarily feeble ; often they are first scrofulous and then tuber-

observation, premature expulsion of a dead fœtus occurred six times and there was no evidence of syphilis. At every pregnancy, anasarca, albuminuria, and death of the fœtus, with severe cramp of the abdominal muscles, occurred between the fifth and six months ; the dead fœtus was expelled from three to ten weeks later. In the second case, similar symptoms appeared in a young unipara ; the fœtus died, and thereupon the albuminuria abated. In the third case, the patient had borne two healthy children. During her third pregnancy, albuminuria and characteristic changes in the retina occurred ; and during the fourth she was seized with hemiplegia ; in both a decomposed fœtus was expelled at the fifth month, with subsequent decrease of the albuminuria. In the fourth case, the patient in her first pregnancy aborted at the fifth month ; then she gave birth at term to a recently dead child. In the third pregnancy great œdema and albuminuria supervened, the child was still-born, and the mother died of uræmia. Dr. Fehling believed that in all these cases kidney disease existed before pregnancy, which aggravated the renal symptoms. Winter had described two cases of premature detachment of the placenta, normally situated, where albuminuria existed. Dr. Fehling found atrophy of the villi of the chorion, with wedge-shaped or spherical infarcts in the placenta, in his cases, similar to renal infarcts. The infiltration of the chorionic villi and vessels of the umbilical cord with small cells, as seen in syphilis, was absent, nor did any of the embryos exhibit a trace of congenital syphilis."—*British Medical Journal.*

culous." The well marked anæmia which is so constantly a concomitant of phthisis is no doubt largely concerned not only in leading to intra-uterine death, but in the production of feeble progeny when the children are born alive.

The measure of vitality in children either intra- or extra- uterine, bears a sort of relation to the strength or exhaustion of the mother at the moment of conception, and during pregnancy. In the early stages of phthisis the disease seems to be arrested by the occurrence of pregnancy. An impulse is given to nutrition generally,—but later when the growing foetus makes more demand on the resources of the mother, the disease advances more rapidly. It has been remarked also that when phthisis comes on during gestation or is developed in those predisposed to it as the result of exhaustion by child-bearing—a renewed pregnancy rarely goes to the full term.

Diabetes.—Saccharine diabetes deserves a moment's notice in relation to its influence on fœtal life. The presence of sugar is common as an ingredient of the urine in the course of pregnancy, and no harm may result from it, but when diabetes with its usual attendant symptoms is fully developed, the results to intra-uterine life are very adverse. In a paper published by Dr. M. Duncan on Puerperal Diabetes, in 1882,* it is stated that in seven of nineteen pregnancies in fourteen mothers, the child died during pregnancy, having in all these reached a viable age. In two more the child was feeble, and died a few hours after birth, making an unsuccessful result in nine out of nineteen pregnancies. The dead child was sometimes described as enormous, or its weight

* "Obstet. Trans."

extraordinary. This was probably in part at least from dropsical infiltration. Hydramnios was frequent, and sugar was found in the liquor amnii.

Jaundice, in some of its forms, has a decidedly adverse effect on fœtal life, Cazeaux, Hervieux and Bardinet speak of an "abortive jaundice." Epidemic forms of jaundice indeed have been observed affecting alike pregnant and non-pregnant women, and in those pregnant, the affection always assumed an exceptional severity. In the simpler or more benign forms associated sometimes with the gravid condition, the jaundice may be only due to functional derangement or to physical pressure. These forms are not generally serious unless attended with much pyrexia, when the element of high temperature comes into play. In the more malignant types, the intensity of the blood-poisoning, as observed by Woillez, was so great, that some of the patients died before abortion or delivery could take place, and in those a shade less severe collected from the writings of different observers, there were forty-two abortions or premature deliveries in sixty-eight cases, with thirty maternal deaths. The abortion generally took place from three to five days from the beginning of the jaundice, and it was generally after the abortion that the gravest symptoms set in. The rise of temperature in these instances could not be the cause of abortion or of fœtal death, for the temperature of the body nearly always fell, and Traube has proved that the elements of bile in the blood have not only the effect of lowering the general temperature, but of paralysing the heart's action. It is probable, therefore, that the poison contained in the blood played a similar rôle to

that of carbonic acid—preventing the proper aëration
of the blood in the placenta, and exciting uterine
action. Davidson, in the "Monat. für Geburt." 1867,
and after him Dr. Barnes, speak of acute atrophy
of the liver in the mother during pregnancy as
inimical to the child. In almost all cases observed,
abortion set in, and thus the product of conception
was destroyed.

Heart Disease, according to Dr. Angus McDonald,[*]
has a tendency to shorten gestation, while pregnancy
aggravates heart disease in the mother. The effects do
not usually appear until midway in gestation, and then
the distress may become so extreme as to threaten the
life of both mother and child. It can be readily understood how the congestion of the pelvic circulation, and
the imperfect aëration of the maternal blood, may so
alter the condition of the uterine circulation as to
produce fœtal death even if the mother survives.

Chorea also may endanger pregnancy. Dr. Barnes[†]
has pointed out that it may lead to abortion as well
as be a dangerous complication for the mother.

Malignant Cholera.—I have it on the authority of
medical officers who have observed epidemics of
cholera in India, and more recently in Egypt, that
pregnant women when stricken with the disease
nearly always abort, or if further advanced in
pregnancy are seized with the symptoms of labour as
soon as the symptoms assume a grave form. The
effects of the disease in connection with the gravid
state have been studied more particularly by
Bouchut, Henning, Drasche and others. Bouchut[‡]

---

[*] "Heart Disease during Pregnancy, Parturition, and Childbed."
[†] "Obstetrical Trans.," vol. x.   [‡] "Gazette Medicale," 1849.

has put on record twenty-five abortions in fifty-two pregnant women seized with cholera, and remarks that the number of abortions would probably have been greater had not some of the women died so rapidly from collapse that there was not time for abortion. Henning in one epidemic noted twenty-seven abortions or premature labours in thirty-nine cases of cholera. Of these there were twenty-two fœtal deaths and nine of the mothers died. Besides he collected eighty-five cases from various sources, and of these there were fifty dead infants and thirty-five living. Bouchut attributes the child's death to mechanical conditions, uterine contractions coming on with the cramps or convulsions of the voluntary muscles, and these would either expel the fœtus, or stop its nutrition and the aëration of its blood. Cazeaux looks upon asphyxia as the cause of fœtal death. The coagulation of the blood and its stagnation in the vessels suspends the utero-placental circulation and so leads to death. Slavjansky dwells upon the tendency to uterine hæmorrhage in these cases, and considers it due to a special endometritis of the decidua, characterised by thickening and softening of the membrane. In some cases he examined, small collections of blood were found all through the meshes of the tissue and down even to the muscular coat itself. These effects, however, may have been in a large measure due to the intense congestion produced by the muscular contractions, and to look upon fœtal death in these rapid cases as produced by endometritis would seem to be looking too far away from the obvious and immediate cause pointed out by other authors—viz., the sudden perturbation of the placental circulation, and its eventual suspension.

The morbid conditions I have specified, with their allies, if they stop short of producing expulsive efforts, may yet produce congestion and possible extravasation of blood in the placenta. They may thus so injure the nutritive and depurative functions of that organ as to compromise the life of the fœtus. These congestions and extravasations in moderate degree may interrupt the utero-placental circulation, and destroy the child without leading to its immediate expulsion; but if more intense and rapid so as to produce at once irritation of the uterine walls as well as disturbance in the placenta, they excite the uterus suddenly to contract, and delivery speedily follows.

I have spoken of certain morbid poisons acting upon the product of conception through the paternal organism. There are some specific poisons, both inorganic and organic, which, getting an entrance into the maternal blood, act more directly on the contents of the gravid uterus, and either kill the child or lead to its premature expulsion before it is capable of maintaining a separate existence.

I have no time to go into the proofs, which are now ample enough, that poisons can be transmitted through the maternal organism and destroy the product of conception, sometimes, indeed, without much perceptible effect on the mother, so far as the specific poison is concerned. Thus lead-poisoning acts deleteriously on pregnancy in the female as well as on the male. Other poisons have been named, both organic and inorganic—arsenic, mercury, savin, and the like.

The morbid organic poison, which is probably the most pernicious, and has the most extended adverse influence on fœtal life, is syphilis. I have spoken of the effects when transmitted by the father. Its power in destroying fœtal and infantile life, when the mother is the subject of venereal disease, is now almost universally admitted by authors, both in this country and abroad.

Syphilis was mentioned in this relation as long ago as Astruc. And yet it is curious to note, considering the unanimity of opinion about it at the present time, how comparatively recent is the recognition of its lethal power in this respect. Dr. Whitehead was one of the earliest and best writers on abortion in this country, and on turning to his book published in 1847 I find the following: "The complaint in question was not suspected of being so frequent a cause of abortion as it has since appeared to be, nor did it until very recently engage a particular share of attention. I remember it was the opinion of my lamented and eminent friend, Mr. Fawdington, that abortion in a great proportion of cases was occasioned by a condition induced by the venereal taint." And he goes on to express his entire confidence in the accuracy of his friend's observation. Since then the evidence has so accumulated concerning the influence of syphilis in destroying children *in utero*, both early and late in gestation, as to be overwhelming. For example, in some comparatively limited statistics of Mr. Scott Battams, given in the "Lancet" for 1883, ten syphilitic mothers produced forty children, of whom twelve had died, and they had suffered among them twenty abortions, or half as many as they had borne children. Of fifty-three syphilitic women observed by Fournier,* twenty-eight only went to the full time, and there were twenty-five abortions or premature deliveries. Of 390 pregnancies with syphilis recorded by Lepileur, 249 went to term, and there were 141 abortions or premature births. In the larger tables collected by Charpentier† from the data of Fournier, Lepileur, Weber, and others, it appears that of 657 pregnancies in syphilitic women there were 426 deliveries at term, many of the children, however, being still-born, and there were 231 abortions, or 28·4 per cent. of the whole. Evidence, indeed, might be multiplied almost indefinitely, and, viewed in this respect alone, the ravages of syphilis appear most deplorable.‡

The non-professional public can, of course, know little of the insidious and noxious influence of syphilis so manifested, and of the way in which it affects large numbers of women and children, innocent of any trace of immorality. Did they fully realise the disastrous consequences of permitting a diffusion of this loathsome disease without let or hindrance, they would bestir themselves to adopt preventive measures against its propagation, and until such a time as it could be absolutely prevented, would be glad to aid partial projects for its diminution, even when such projects seem in some degree to clash with the

---

* " Syphilis." † *Loc. cit.*

‡ It is besides abundantly proved that syphilitic disease may not only destroy the embryo at all stages of its development *in utero*, but also that if the child is born at full term it may show evident traces of venereal taint at its birth, or if apparently healthy when born of syphilitic parents, it will develop infantile syphilis before many weeks or months of its life have elapsed, and either die or remain a miserable object afterwards.

generally understood idea of the liberty of the subject, or run counter to cherished notions on what has been termed the "State regulation of vice."

In women who are the subjects of syphilis, abortions often succeed each other in frequent repetition, and with a persistency belonging to no other cause. It has, moreover, been often remarked that when there are no external indications of maternal syphilis, the succession of abortions, or of dead children in more advanced pregnancy, is traceable to a latent form of the disease which manifests itself in this fashion. Fournier especially dwells on this point, and holds that women who are most deeply and viscerally affected are most liable to abortion, although it may happen to those affected in all degrees, even the most lightly. Confirmatory evidence of Fournier's position is educed by the effect of anti-syphilitic treatment, which very frequently succeeds in stopping the tendency to abortion. Some cases of abortion without apparently syphilitic symptoms in the mother, are no doubt due to the transmission of venereal taint from the father.

The effect of syphilis has been now so carefully studied that some general laws have been formulated concerning its effects on human gestation. Thus it has been proved (1) that if a woman has syphilis before conception she is much more predisposed to abortion than a woman taking the disease after conception; (2) if conception and syphilis commence together, abortion or premature labour with a dead child are the rule, but treatment is more potent in preventing them; (3) syphilis acquired after the mid-period of pregnancy has less influence on the child, and it may escape altogether.

Perhaps the worst feature in the relation between syphilis and pregnancy is its persistent and extended influence. It is impossible to say when the effect of the poison will be expended, and long after all outward signs of the disease have vanished in the bodies of both parents, the tendency to abortion may remain, or there may still be the production of dead children, or of feeble emaciated children if born alive, showing external evidences of venereal taint ; or, lastly, in the absence of these, so small an amount of vitality that the children are reared with difficulty.

One of the ways in which syphilis brings about intra-uterine death, as will be seen later, is by producing disease in the foetal appendages. There can be no doubt that the venereal poison is transmitted to the embryo through the maternal blood, and thus it may affect all the tissues in the gravid womb, sometimes manifesting itself in one locality, sometimes in another. Thus it may attack the body of the foetus or its placenta and membranes. We have both the direct evidence of such transmission, and also the collateral evidence derived from the transmission of other agents, through the maternal circulation.

Belonging to this section of the subject as recognised causes, under certain conditions, of intra-uterine death, are

The local affections of the generative organs in women.

Uterine congestion no doubt plays an active part in inducing abortion. Jacquemier enlarges

* *Loc. cit.*

on this cause of intra-uterine death, and Charpentier remarks that he treats the subject in a way quite magisterial. Jacquemier says the congestion may be active or passive, and he believes it the commonest cause of abortion. It excites abnormal contractions, determines frequent extravasations between the uterus and membranes or placenta, and causes apoplexy by rupture of the utero-placental blood-vessels. All women are not equally predisposed, but those chiefly who are liable to uterine congestion before pregnancy begins—who menstruate too profusely, and have other symptoms of uterine or general congestion. To these pregnancy brings new features into play. The whole circulation becomes more active and more easily disturbed, and there is greater local relaxation. As the catamenial periods are normally periods of congestion, so in women predisposed at all times to hyperæmia of the pelvic organs, the monthly times become a source of peril during pregnancy.

The various inflammatory affections of the uterus and its appendages act injuriously on the child *in utero* during the course of pregnancy. Acute inflammations are fortunately rare apart from external injuries. The chronic forms of inflammation affecting the walls and cavity of the uterus, as I shall show subsequently, very commonly lead to abortion by producing disease in the foetal membranes. The chronic forms affecting the cervix, such as induration and ulceration, have a less marked effect, inasmuch as they are external to the womb cavity, and unless they penetrate there do not necessarily interfere with the course of pregnancy. Hyperplasia of the neck as well as of the body may perchance interfere with the

proper expansion of the uterine walls during development, and so lead to a state of irritability which
terminates in expulsion, but just as in malignant disease of the cervix, there may be much induration of
tissue there, and yet pregnancy will go to the full
time. Erosions and ulcerations of the os are common
enough during pregnancy as the result of congestion
incident to that state, and if they remain superficial
and are not over-treated, they do no great harm.
Cazeaux says that even when they penetrate into the
cervical canal and have a tendency to become fungous
or vegetative during the course of pregnancy, they do
not imperil its continuance. He believes, however,
and Richet agrees with him, that these conditions
existing before conception, are more likely to lead to
abortion. Dr. Henry Bennet* distinguishes between
the simple forms of ulceration, which, he says have
little influence on pregnancy, and others of a more
profound character. These he regards as frequently
leading to premature delivery, and when penetrating
into the canal of the cervix and characterized by
destruction of tissue, as rendering abortion almost
certain.

Whitehead endeavoured to show that the presence
of vaginal leucorrhœa, which may or may not be
associated with inflammatory conditions of the uterus,
had a marked influence in predisposing to abortion.
Thus of 2,000 pregnant women, 1,116 had leucorrhœa
when the inquiry was made. 936, or eighty-three
per cent., had purulent or sanious discharge ; of these
544, or fifty-eight per cent., had previously miscarried
—the discharge in the remaining 180 cases being

* "Inflam. of the Uterus."

absent or trivial in amount. There is nothing very conclusive as to cause and effect in these figures, and they may simply mean that delicate women were equally liable to abortion as to vaginal discharges.

The various displacements of the uterus, if extreme in character,—retroflexion or version, ante-flexion, prolapsus, tumours in the uterine walls, in the ovaries or elsewhere in the pelvis,—malignant disease of the uterus,—pelvic hæmatocele or cellulitis, may each and all lead to abortion or premature labour, and on the other hand experience teaches that mechanical displacements or organic diseases may in some cases be present in a very marked degree, without interfering with the course of pregnancy.

There is a drawing of a placenta in Guy's Hospital, which, otherwise healthy, is entirely altered in its shape by the compression of fibroid tumours in the uterine walls. The unevenness of the interior of the uterus has turned up the edge of the placenta in all its circumference and made the fœtal membranes so considerably overlap the uterine surface, that fully one-half of it must have been separated from its connection with the uterus.

Pelvic Adhesions.—Madame Boivin* noticed that in women liable to frequent abortion, the womb was often bound down by pelvic adhesions, probably due to previous pelvic peritonitis. This has been noted by other authors, and there can be no doubt that when such adhesions do exist, if they are at all firm or extensive, they must prevent the proper expansion of the gravid uterus during its development, and eventually lead to abortion.

* "Recherches sur une des Causes de l'Avortement," 1828.

Direct irritation of the uterus and vagina, and in-juries produced designedly or by accident, may of course lead to premature expulsion of the ovum and its consequent death. Under this head may be classed, too frequent or violent coitus ; falls or blows on the pelvis, jolting on horseback or in carriages, and plugging the vagina for any purpose. All these may lead to separation of the membranes, or irritation and dilatation of the os uteri, with consequent hæmorrhage and abortion. I need not say that various gyneco-logical proceedings, such as passing the sound, injudicious insertion of pessaries, and treatment with the speculum, as well as all operations about the uterus during pregnancy ; oxytocic medicines, whether given for criminal purposes or otherwise— all are apt to be followed by voiding of the uterine contents, especially in sensitive women.

Reflex Causes.—The late Dr. Tyler Smith* drew attention to the frequency of reflex or excito-motor causes of abortion, and particularly to the effect of irritation of the mammary nerves. He averred that he had seen abortion produced during lactation from the irritation of constant suckling. He inferred that it was not mere weakness or exhaustion producing the effect, because the mammary secretion may cease on the occurrence of impregnation, but a plentiful supply of milk returns after the occurrence of abor-tion. It is well known that the uterus may be made to contract after delivery by putting the child to the breast ; and Professor Scanzoni, in view of these facts, has proposed irritation of the mammæ as one of the methods of inducing premature labour. The results

* *Loc. cit.*

F

of the method have proved too uncertain for general adoption. But reflex motor actions originating in other organs besides the mammæ are acknowledged to have the effect of inducing abortion in some cases. Thus irritation of the trifacial nerve during the cutting of a wisdom-tooth, or from toothache, are said to have this effect. I have seen abortion brought on by the extraction of a tooth, but I do not think this peculiar to dental operations, as I have seen it follow other minor surgical proceedings, apparently from the nerve-disturbance they produced, as there was no marked increase of temperature.

Quite recently I was confronted, not for the first time, with the question, "Is it desirable to remove the breast by surgical operation during pregnancy. The patient was about thirty years of age, six months pregnant, and she had a tumour, believed to be malignant, in the right breast. It had somewhat rapidly developed, and the axillary glands were enlarged. The whole aspect of the patient was unhealthy, if not cachectic, and it was deemed advisable to remove the breast as speedy as practicable. The eminent surgeons consulted in the case hesitated to operate during the continuance of pregnancy, as one of them at least had recollection of similar cases ending disastrously, abortion coming on after the operation, and the patient dying as the result of the double injury. From my own experience, I was able to say that abortion seemed chiefly to have been provoked under such circumstances when the breast wound was going wrong, and there were evidences of constitutional irritative fever. In fact, that although there is such well-known and intimate sympathy between the nerves of the breast and the uterus, the abortion was less due to reflex action than to elevation of maternal temperature associated with septicæmia. In these days of antiseptic surgery, where healing by the first intention is the rule, removal of the breast and other similar operations may certainly be undertaken with less risk of abortion than formerly. In view, nevertheless, of the fact that abortion sometimes comes on from the reflex effect of all operations, however trivial in character, it is well to abstain from surgical proceedings during pregnancy, unless urgently required. In the case I have referred to, it was at one time proposed to bring on premature labour, and to operate on the breast as soon as the puerperal period was passed. The proposal was eventually abandoned, because some time must elapse before the child would be viable, and the disease in the breast was extending. Consequently the operation was performed at once, and the patient made a good recovery without aborting.*

In undertaking any operation upon a pregnant woman it is important to recollect that the uterus is more irritable at times which correspond to the catamenial periods. It is well, therefore, to avoid these periods.

Intense and persistent gastric irritation has also been known to bring on abortion, and this notwithstanding the fact that a pregnant woman is sometimes brought almost to death's door, by continued

* According to Massot (Schmidt's "Jahrbuch") and Cohnstein (Volkmann, " Saml. Klin. Vorte," 1875) operations on the genito-urinary organs are most likely to be followed by abortion, and Spiegelberg says that no operation on pregnant women should be performed at the time of the menstrual epoch, as abortion is more likely to occur then.

nausea and vomiting, without provoking any sign
of uterine contraction. Vesical, renal, and rectal
irritation may act in like manner. Lastly, ovarian
irritation undoubtedly favours the occurrence of abortion, and consequently there has been observed a
marked tendency to abortion at times corresponding
to the catamenial periods, more especially in women
who have been the subjects of ovarian dysmenorrhœa.

Nearly akin to excito-motor causes are the effects
of mental emotion on pregnant women. There is no
doubt greatly increased nervous tension in all pregnant women. Fright, anxiety, a sudden impression
made upon the mind or body, may not only initiate
uterine contraction at any period of pregnancy, but
there is reason to believe that a sudden mental shock
may at once kill the early embryo or more mature
child, even if it be retained some time afterwards.
Repeatedly it has occurred to me, as to others in
practice, to have patients dating the exact time of
their child's death *in utero* to some alarm or shocking
occurrence which has profoundly affected the whole
nervous system. The immediate effect described
was first violent perturbation and undue active
movement of the child for a brief interval, followed
by cessation of fœtal movement, and absolute
quiescence in the future. In a few rare instances
the woman has been mistaken in supposing her child
to be dead after a shock or fright she has experienced,
but in a large number of cases the relation between
the cause and the effect has been too clear to be
accounted for by mere coincidence, and the child has
sooner or later been expelled dead, possibly both
dead and putrid.

It is no uncommon thing for a woman in early pregnancy, on the receipt of bad news, which much perturbs her, to be seized with uterine hæmorrhage, ending in abortion. Condemned women prior to execution have been known to abort beforehand, and, under the influence of terror and pain, martyred women in former days are said to have aborted at the stake. So potent is mental influence on the stability of pregnancy, that I have had reason to believe the mere dread of miscarriage has in some women been an important factor in bringing it about, and I have known pregnant women who had previously miscarried get into such violent mental agitation as the time approached when they had aborted before, that the event they feared was precipitated, and pregnancy was brought to a premature conclusion.

LECTURE II.

I PROCEED now to speak of the causes of intra-uterine death which are associated with faulty conditions of the fœtal envelopes and fœtal append-ages, and I shall take those first which properly belong to the earlier part of pregnancy.

In the earlier stages of its development, the ovum is in shape like an egg, and consists of the central embryo, with its surrounding envelopes. The outer one, or decidua, which lies next to the uterine wall, is the earliest in its formation, for it appears in the uterine cavity before the descent of the fecundated ovule from the Fallopian tube. It is now well known to be the product of the uterus itself, and to consist of the mucous membrane lining the interior of the womb, thickened and modified in such a way as to fulfil the necessary requirements of a fœtal envelope. A membrane in all respects like this, both in external appearance and minute structure, is sometimes expelled from the unimpregnated uterus at the catamenial periods in cases of dysmenorrhœa. It is then produced by an over-activity of formative elements, which occurs as the result of some reflex irritation, probably in the ovary, and which simulates the commencement of pregnancy. The expul-

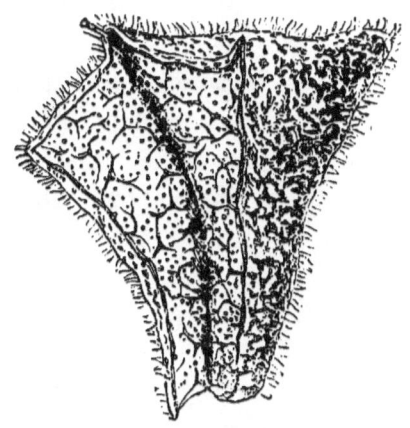

A dysmenorrhæal membrane expelled from the uterus of an unmarried woman, showing the follicular apertures on the internal surface, and the openings corresponding to the Fallopian tubes. (After Coste.)

sion of such membranes, therefore, does not always mean that an abortion has taken place, for they may be formed and extruded without impregnation ; but, in a considerable number of cases in which these membranes are thrown off by married women, they are the result of conception. This is inferred from their frequent recurrence so long as sexual relations are continued, and their cessation when coitus is intermitted. Besides, the catamenial period is often missed once, at least, before expulsion, in women who at other times are perfectly regular. When entire, these membranes generally appear as membranous sacs, of triangular form, corresponding to the shape of the uterine cavity, and the walls of the sac are thick or thin according to the amount of

organised material of which they are composed. The
outer surface is commonly rough, and, if the preparation is placed in water, shreds or flocculi float out in
the fluid. When laid open, it is a common thing to
find the cavity quite empty. The inner surface is
smooth, and marked everywhere with the apertures
of hypertrophic glandular follicles, but there is no
embryo. The ovule has either missed getting into
the decidual cavity, or it has been endowed with so
small an amount of vitality that it has undergone
solution before it could plant itself in the decidual
tissue. The reflex stimulus which has come from
the ovary or tube, in whichever locality fecundation
took place, has been enough to evoke the formation
of the decidua in the womb; but the ovule being
wanting, development is arrested, no decidua reflexa
is formed, and the useless decidua vera is eventually
thrown off as a foreign body. Here the fault in
procreating power, as distinguished from generative
power, may be either with the male or female; and,
if the woman is otherwise healthy, it is quite as
likely to be some defect in the fertilising fluid as
faulty ovulation on the part of the female. These
decidua of early pregnancy are in many cases found
covered with coagulated blood, and the cavity may
be filled with clot, soft or semi-fluid, if recently
deposited there—firm and partially decolorised, if
some time has elapsed since its extravasation. But
these membranes are not always expelled in their
entirety. More frequently they are thrown off in
detached portions or shreds at variable intervals, and
mixed with the fluid or coagulated blood which
escapes at the same time. It is no uncommon

occurrence for a patient, or even the medical man, to infer that the supposition of pregnancy has been erroneous, because no substantial mass has been expelled—the discharges being taken for an over-profuse and perhaps deferred period.   Eigenbrodt and Hegar,* in a memoir " On Apoplectic Destruction of the Decidua," assert that in some cases the presence of the elements of the decidua could only be ascertained by the aid of the microscope.   This accords with my own observation.

Akin to this is another defect of development which has been described by Matthews Duncan† and copied into the various textbooks.   This consists, according to the author named, in a defective development of the decidua round the ovum.   The egg then comes in contact only with a limited surface of the mucous membrane which corresponds to the serotina, and as it is not supported, as usual, by growth of the decidua around it, it becomes, as it were, pediculated, and is easily detached from its limited adhesion.   This is probably one of many faults of development occurring in early gestation. In one specimen I examined which had been expelled as an abortion, the ovule had evidently failed to get inside the decidual cavity, and began its development on its outer rough surface, attaching itself, as it does in extra-uterine pregnancy, to the surrounding structures.   The surrounding structures were partly the outer surface of the decidua, and partly the wall of the uterus, and for three-fourths of the circumference of the ovum the clear trans-

---

* " Monat. für Geburt." Bd. xx. 1863.
† " Researches in Obstetrics."

parent chorion was quite uncovered, its villi there being either atrophied or never developed. The decidua seems in some instances to be detached from the uterine wall, and to lie so loosely in the uterine cavity, more especially if atrophied or imperfectly developed, that one can imagine the ovule as it enters the uterus from the Fallopian tube dropping between the decidua and uterine wall.

We get some sort of idea, now that our knowledge is more precise concerning the formation of the decidua, and of the behaviour of the ovule when it enters the uterine cavity, of the way in which placenta prævia and other variations in the site of the placenta are produced. Ordinarily the thickened decidua fills pretty fully the cavity of the uterus, and the ovule is received into the cushion so formed, to be sustained in the upper part of the uterus. When, however, the decidua is less luxuriant in growth, its cavity will be larger, and the fertilised ovule may then drop down to the lowest part of its cavity, and become implanted there. Dr. Robert Lee* has recorded the appearances of a very early placenta prævia, which bears out this idea, and such an anatomical fault favours the occurrence of abortion, although we know by experience that these cases may go on to the later periods of pregnancy.

The varieties of insertion of the ovum into the decidua, and the several forms of hypertrophy and atrophy, with other anomalies of the same membrane, have been elaborately studied by Kussmaul†, Hegar‡,

---

* "Theory and Practice of Midwifery."
† "Von dem Mangel, &c., der Gebämutter." 1859.
‡ "Monatssch. für Geburts." Bd. xxi. Supplement Heft.

and Dohrn * in special and excellent memoirs, which
are well worth perusal.   It seems obvious that a too
scanty formation of the decidua may lead to the
growth of a placenta too small for the needs of the
embryo.   Charpentier believes that an arrest of
development in the decidua reflexa, or its premature
destruction, are frequent causes of death in the
embryo.   The egg then is covered in a large part of
its extent only by the chorion, and may be suspended by a sort of pedicle from the decidua serotina.
It has thus a very limited attachment to the decidua,
and is easily disturbed.   Probably, indeed, pregnancy cannot go on with so slight an attachment,
and it is a variety of a similar kind which Rokitansky†
has called " Cervical Pregnancy."

When the ovule has been successfully implanted
in the decidua, and the normal development of the
decidua reflexa and other structures are going on in
progressive series, there is great tendency in some
women to go wrong, apparently from mere weakness
of the outer structures which form the ovum.   The
decidua is commonly composed of so lax a tissue, and
is so abundantly supplied with blood-vessels undergoing various modifications of size and distribution,
that during early pregnancy it is prone to suffer from
extravasations of blood into its parenchymatous substance, more especially in delicate women.   It is true
that the uterus is so suspended in the maternal pelvis
as to be affected in the least possible degree by
ordinary locomotion and by accidental concussions ;
yet, in some women, the union between the pregnant
uterus and the decidua is so unstable, that a fall or

* " Monatssch für Geburts." 1863.   † " Lehrbuch der Path. Anat."

stumble, or a shaking of any kind, may be quite sufficient to detach a portion of the latter, rupture the intervening vessels, and cause extravasation of blood. Small and circumscribed clots produced in this way are frequently found between the uterus and decidua ; at other times they are in the meshes of the decidua itself, or both may be conjoined. If limited, these extravasations need not interrupt the continuance of pregnancy. If more extensive, and separating a larger portion of the decidua, they necessarily interfere with the nutrition of the ovum, produce death of the embryo, and precipitate abortion. When the escape of blood from the vessels is confined to a limited space at the upper part of the uterus, it may cause uneasiness, but no external hæmorrhage will be noticed. If it takes place near the cervix, the blood more readily finds exit from the uterus, and is discharged by the vagina, thus becoming a manifest symptom of threatened abortion. Blood-clots in every stage of transition, and every variety of firmness and colour, may be observed in some aborted ova. The latest are deep red or purple, and those older pass through the several tints of chocolate brown to yellow, like apoplectic clots elsewhere.

The same results may ensue from contractions of the uterus, either provoked by local irritation directly applied, or from reflex causes, as, for example, suckling a child after a fresh pregnancy has commenced. It is well known that abortion is frequent if a new pregnancy begins during the time that a mother is suckling her child.

Occasionally, during the very early stages of gestation, blood flows directly into the decidual cavity, and fills it with coagula. The result is, either that all trace of the embryo and its immediate surrounding structures are obliterated, or the embryo is compressed and destroyed by the invading flood, rudimentary portions only of it being discovered. More than once under these conditions I have found the embryo, wrapped in its small and budding chorion, detached from the decidua and floating in the semi-fluid blood contained in the decidual cavity. The decidua reflexa had not yet been sufficiently developed around it to give it a stable attachment. The small aborted ova of this early period are frequently thrown off entire in triangular or ovoid form, the outer layer being the decidua, which encloses, first, firm layers of fibrin, and, as one proceeds to the centre, soft clot.

In the second to the third months, the decidua reflexa or ovuli is fully formed, and the villi of the chorion are everywhere imbedded in its substance. Then another form of hæmorrhage may occur. In this, the blood is not alone extravasated between the decidua vera and the uterine wall, or into the meshes of the decidua itself, but between the decidua reflexa and serotina, and the chorion or outermost of the true fœtal membranes. In the process of development the villi of the chorion are pushed into the decidual tissue, and are soon surrounded by the blood-vessels which are to form the maternal placenta. The decidua is then a highly vascular membrane, especially at the site of the future placenta, and the maternal vessels which everywhere ramify through it undergo a development which in the human body is unique. Appearing first as capillaries, they rapidly enlarge, and eventually become sinuses, which are filled with maternal blood, and in which the fœtal villi are eventually suspended.

It can scarcely excite surprise that these delicate and rapidly dilating maternal vessels should be very liable to rupture. Hæmorrhage taking place in this locality, floods the loose tissue of which the decidua reflexa is composed, and destroys or compresses the chorion villi implanted there. It may be so extensive as entirely to surround the embryo. At the earlier periods, when there is a considerable space between the decidua uteri and reflexa, it may be limited to the circumference of the latter membrane, which, when cut into, is found to contain clot with or without traces of the chorion and embryo. Later, when the decidua reflexa is in apposition with the decidua uteri throughout its whole extent, and the amnion is formed, the cavity, if exposed from within, exhibits eminences or projections from the walls, which may seem like projecting cysts if the blood is imperfectly coagulated ; but they represent hard and firm bosses or nodules, when the blood has been long enough deposited to become solid. The force of the extravasation has in fact pushed forward both the chorion and the amnion, and diminished the size of the cavity. There are all possible gradations in the amount of blood so extravasated, and the morbid appearances vary from slight thickening or consolidation to the extreme forms seen in the drawings and preparations on the table. The nutrition of the embryo is necessarily arrested if the extravasation be extensive enough to interrupt the normal circulation through the imperfectly formed placenta, and the embryo may be found stunted and shrivelled, suspended by its umbilical cord from some part of the amniotic cavity. If the ovum has been long retained after these morbid changes have taken place, the embryo will appear small in proportion to the size of its containing cavity, for there can be no doubt that when the central embyro has perished, the membranous envelopes may go on growing until they are expelled by uterine action. In some specimens again, the embyro deprived of its nourishment breaks down and dissolves, leaving only the remains of a slender or rudimentary umbilical cord, and not uncommonly also a distinct umbilical vesicle, imbedded between the chorion and amnion.

These extravasations of blood between the chorion and the decidua constitute the typical " apoplexy of the ovum" described by many authors. It is found in a multiplicity of forms and modifications, and is, no doubt, produced by a variety of causes. Thus it may be produced by faults in early development, or by any cause which produces detachment of the well-formed decidua from the uterine walls, or from rupture of its blood-vessels. Gendrin said he saw one case where blood tore its way through both chorion and amnion, and overwhelmed the embryo, and Hegar gives another. A drawing in my possession, by Westmacott, shows the cavity of the decidua reflexa entirely occupied by a blood-clot, no trace of embyro or its special envelopes being found.

Wagner, in his " Traité de Physiologie," states that in the majority of cases an extravasation of blood at the time of the formation of the decidua reflexa is the first cause of the death of the fœtus. In some cases, notwithstanding this, the egg may grow, but the embryo is then not properly nourished, and so a disproportion of different parts of the egg occurs.   The extravasation of blood may therefore be the cause of disease in the decidua and of malformation in the fœtus.

Hegar says, and Verdier* agrees with him, that anomalies in the insertion of the placenta, and abnormal insertions of the allantoid and umbilical vessels, predispose to apoplexy, as well as hypertrophy and atrophy of the various parts of the decidua.

In examining ova which have been extruded as the result of abortion during the earlier period, one is often struck with the amount of compound granular cells, as they are called, and of distinct fat or oil-particles, not only mixed up with the parenchyma of the decidua, but contained even in the interior of the decidual cells and fibro-cells, thus constituting a true fatty degeneration.   Sometimes the decidual blood-vessels, namely, those which permeate every-where the decidual tissue, and ramify among the villi at the site of the future placenta, have undergone fatty change, and this is more marked near the seat of the hæmorrhages.   At one time I thought this was due merely to the after-changes in the extravasations of blood produced by traumatic and other causes, but I subsequently found this fatty change in portions of the membranes distant from the clots, and occasionally I have found the whole decidual structures affected by this form of granular degeneration.

I have elsewhere pointed out† that in the parietal decidua which does not take part in the formation

* "Thèse," 1868.   † "Devel. of Gravid Uterus."

of the placenta, a granular or fatty degeneration sets in as soon as its function is superseded by the organisation of the placenta. The drawing there shows the glandular follicles in the third month, filled with fat-granules prior to their final disappearance, and similar fatty molecules are scattered over the parenchyma generally. In the normal condition this fatty degeneration does not extend beyond the border of the placenta, but it can readily be understood that in such close proximity, it may invade the placental decidua also, when impaired nutrition or other cause predisposes it to decay.

On becoming acquainted with the remarkable researches of Ercolani,* I found he believed that the true cause of extravasation and of the formation of clots between the decidua and chorion in early pregnancy, to be this fatty degeneration of the cells of the decidua serotina, which ought to be forming the young placenta. These cells so transformed out of the decidua, when in a state of fatty degeneration, imperfectly support the pressure of blood in the sinuses, and hence, as he says, there is a breakdown and veritable interstitial hæmorrhage. The rupture of the layers of serotina permits the blood to pass from one cotyledon to another, and necessarily produces a slackening of the maternal blood in the imperfectly formed sinuses. Thus a true thrombosis is produced, but preceded by morbid change of structure, not arising out of a normal state as supposed by Bustamente,† whose views I shall notice presently. Sirelius,‡ of Helsingfors, also

* "Delle Malattie della Pl.," Mem. 1871.
† "Thèse Inaug.," 1868.　　　　‡ Vide Ercolani.

G

attributed hæmorrhage in the early formed placenta to the breaking down or rupture of the decidual structures forming the boundaries of the lacunæ, thus producing coalescence and arrest of circulation, with extravasation.

That the presence of a pathological fatty degeneration in the structures of the decidua will, in many cases, account for the occurrence of hæmorrhage both in the parietal decidua and in the serotina, is no doubt true, but there are many cases where no such explanation can apply, otherwise there would be very little chance of checking a threatened abortion when once indications of hæmorrhage have set in. The frequent recovery of patients from the symptoms of abortion with the successful continuance of pregnancy to the full time, is sufficient proof either that hæmorrhage is due to other causes than fatty degeneration, or that, in particular cases, the degeneration was at least so partial that only a very limited area of the structures is affected. Thickening and fatty degeneration to a marked extent in the decidual structures is noticeable in many instances of recurring early abortion ; and, as we shall see presently, this may be associated with an inflammatory process. In other cases, separation of the ovum is clearly traceable to some violence or traumatic cause ; then the structures show no indication of morbid transformation, and the extruded ovum frequently tears away with it from the interior of the uterus shreds of the uterine muscular fibre which are found attached to its outer surface.

Apoplexy of the ovum deserves careful study, because it is a very common cause of embryonic

death, and, if one may judge from the large number
of specimens preserved in the various museums,
compared with others, it is by far the most frequent
of all the pathological changes affecting the early
ovum. In almost every museum in London are
examples of the apoplectic ovum in its various
phases, even where there is an absolute poverty of
other specimens illustrating diseases of the ovum,
and it may be inferred, therefore, that it is probably
the most frequent of the immediate causes producing intra-uterine death in the early months
of gestation. The specimens are often wrongly
described in the museum catalogues as " tubercular
ova," or " cystic ova," and other misnomers are
applied to them.

The largest number of the preparations of this
kind in our museums are of ova so advanced that the
two decidua are united in close apposition. This
corresponds to about the third month of gestation.
The chorion has imbedded its tufts everywhere in
the decidua, and the amniotic cavity is distinctly
formed. On account of the size of the aborted ova,
the morbid changes are so marked that they are
obvious to the most casual inspection, and hence they
come to be preserved.

We have no accurate means of knowing the comparative frequency of apoplexy and resulting abortion
in ova at an earlier stage than this, because in the
first weeks aborted ova have less marked characteristics—they are often passed unobserved, or, if
noticed, they are, from their fragility, likely to be
torn and injured during expulsion. For both these
reasons preserved specimens of this kind are much

rarer in the several museums than otherwise they might be.

One of the morbid conditions of the decidua, the presence of which is inferred rather than demonstrated, is congestion.* The inference is drawn from the fact that in some ova expelled during abortion the decidual vessels are found gorged with blood, not only on the outer or uterine surface, but in the deeper layers, and no evidence of other pathological change is observable. The women chiefly predisposed to it are the plethoric, those suffering repeatedly or habitually from disorders of the portal circulation, from heart-disease, and also those who, from any other cause, are the subjects of pelvic congestion generally. Hegar noticed the uterus proportionately larger in those prone to congestion and apoplexy of the ovum.

It is believed that congestion of the decidua is a sufficient and adequate cause, irrespective of any other, to produce rupture of its blood-vessels and extravasation into its substance. It depends, of course, upon the amount and extent of the congestion and its consequent results, as to whether abortion is provoked and pregnancy comes to an end. If blood is extravasated as the result of congestion, it goes through the same changes and phases as when extravasated from other causes. But there is reason to suppose, also, that hyperæmia, arising from whatever cause it may, apart from extravasation, can have the effect, by the distension and irritation it produces, of bringing on uterine action and thus precipitating abortion. This is the more probable

* See Devilliers, "Review Med.," 1842.

as the whole uterus must partake of the congestion, and be proportionately irritable.

Inflammation of the decidua, taking various forms, has been described by Virchow, Hegar, Schroeder, and Spiegelberg. Slavjansky has described an acute form associated with cholera in pregnant women, and leading to hæmorrhage with the death of the fœtus.* These inflammations are, however, generally chronic, and are continuations or extensions of previously existing inflammation in the unimpregnated mucous membrane of the uterus. Three forms have been described as producing different alterations in the decidua.

I. The first, "chronic diffuse endometritis" of authors, produces a thickening or hyperplasia of the uterine mucous membrane, which, when conception occurs, renders it unfit for the reception and growth of the fecundated germ. According to Spiegelberg, the hypertrophy consists in a development of conjunctive tissue, which not only thickens, but indurates the membrane, and extends down to the muscular fibres themselves. The arrangement of the hypertrophied tissues is such as often to give rise to the appearance of cysts, which, however, are probably only the "cups" of Montgomery enlarged. Schroeder regards it as a chronic and diffuse proliferation of the mucous cells, both parietal and reflected. The thickened membrane presents, he says, the large cells of the decidua united *en masse*. By their proliferation, particularly in the deeper layers, they may produce a cavernous structure, and even form cysts. This alteration, he says, produces

* " Archiv für Gynäkol.," 1882.

death of the embryo and abortion, by the irritation which the inflammation produces on the uterine nerves.

Other cases have been described in which inflammation was still more chronic, and where the nutrition of the germ was not interfered with. Madame Kaschewarowa,* a Russian woman doctor, whose researches are sufficiently accredited to find a place in Virchow's " Archives," alleges that she has found the membranes thickened of a fœtus at term, not only by proliferation of conjunctival tissue and decidual cells, but even by smooth muscular fibres of new formation. Hofe† has described other alterations of form, and Schroeder‡ and Spiegelberg§ both state that there may be proliferation of decidual cells, which is secondary to the death of the fœtus, although, if it begins before, it is apt to deprive it of vitality.

In examining early deciduæ thrown off as the result of early abortion I have repeatedly observed a morbid condition, which differs in its histology from the description just given by Spiegelberg, Schroeder, and others, and which does not seem to have been sufficiently noticed. In this the membrane is distinctly thickened and hypertrophied, and its structure is firmer than normal, while its outer surface exhibits none of those floating filaments seen in comparatively healthy deciduæ, but is more or less nodular, and shows indications of being slowly separated from the uterine walls. Microscopic examination shows that there may be an attempt to increase the cell element peculiar to the decidual structure, and that the cells

---

* Virchow's "Archiv," 1868. † "Archiv für Gynäkol.," 1869.
‡ "Lehrb. der Geb." § *Ibid.*

themselves are more frequently split up than usual, and otherwise deformed; but in addition to the cell element, there is besides a copious exudation, which is at first simply amorphous or granular, but soon degenerates into fat. The granular deposit is in much larger proportion than the increase of the cell element or of connective tissue, and it may be free from fat in some portions of the membrane, but is elsewhere pervaded with compound granular cells and oil globules. A condition somewhat similar to this has been briefly noticed by Hegar. It is, I believe, the result of a low form of inflammation, and as it degenerates, which it readily does if at all abundant, it involves the decidual cells, fibro-cells, and blood-vessels in the same morbid change. The inflammatory action is probably due to an unhealthy condition of the uterine mucous membrane prior to conception, or to impaired nutrition afterwards, from faults in the maternal blood. Had the exudation been less abundant or endowed with greater vitality, it would probably have been converted into connective tissue as described by the authors named.

The engraving of a hypertrophied decidua given by Duncan at p. 292 of his "Researches in Obstetrics," is probably an example of one of the forms of hyperplasia produced by endometritis, syphilitic or otherwise. The membrane is described as much increased in thickness, its walls thrown into prominent folds or rugæ, and the cavity was very large in comparison with the small size of the embryo attached to the fundal portion. The embryo had evidently ceased to grow soon after conception, while the decidua had gone on vegetating.

Dr. Duncan remarks that fatty degeneration was present in this as in other specimens of hypertrophied decidua which he examined, and I may observe that fatty change is noticeable in all preparations of this kind which have been retained after the death of the embryo. It is often difficult to say whether the fatty degeneration was a primary change arising from faulty conditions of the maternal blood, and which caused the death of the embryo; or whether it was secondary to fœtal death from some other cause. In either case the fatty change, by the friability it produces, loosens the attachments of the decidua to the uterus, and so precipitates abortion.

A variety of this chronic diffuse endometritis constitutes the "adhesive endometritis" of Braun.* It takes place in the later months, and it then attacks the utero-placental mucous membrane, setting up such irritation that it imperils the life of the fœtus and precipitates premature labour. Strictly speaking, the affection may be regarded as a disease affecting the placenta. One of its results is to produce adhesions between the placenta and uterus, and so complicate delivery. Its presence is characterised by the fœtal movements giving pain, and often besides this, acute pain and tenderness are experienced in the walls of the womb which some have described as "uterine rheumatism." It may be produced by chills, overwork, &c.; and according to Kaschewarowa, it is one of the results of syphilis, or of a pre-existing endometritis.

II. A second form of inflammation affecting the

---

* "Gesammt Gyn.," 1881.

decidua has been described by Virchow* under the name of "polypoid endometritis." It would seem to

FIG. 2.

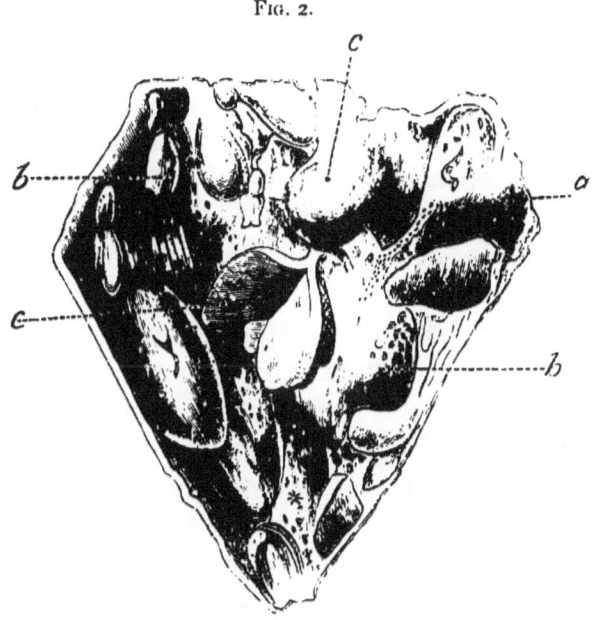

Polypoid Endometritis (Virchow). *a*, fine apertures of the glands ; *b*, larger apertures of glands ; *c*, protuberances, or polypi.

be only a more advanced degree of the inflammatory condition just described, but the mucous membrane is thickened to twice or thrice its ordinary depth, and prominences and projections like polypi protrude from the free internal surface. Where the eminences exist, the uterine gland apertures are obliterated, while they are apparent on other parts of the surface. According to Virchow, the microscopic element, which grows here in excess, is the interstitial mucous tissue, which increases and proliferates in such wise as to cause the hypertrophy. Spiegelberg, Schroeder,

* Virchow's " Archiv," 1861 and 1865.

Dohrn, and Gusserow*, have all verified Virchow's observations with some modifications as to detail in structure. Virchow's case was attributed to syphilis, but there was no proof of this in others. This change is only seen in very young ova, and it always produces an alteration in the chorial villi, which may be in contact with it, disturbing and altering their form; and in some cases, as pointed out by Dohrn and Müller,† causing them to show commencing myxoma. The embryo in nearly all the recorded cases had disappeared.

III. A form of inflammation affecting the decidua has been named "catarrhal endometritis." It is characterised by a persistent discharge from the gravid uterus, which constitutes the "hydrorrhœa" of pregnant women. A woman generally about the sixth month of pregnancy loses suddenly and at intervals a quantity of transparent colourless fluid, analogous to ascitic fluid. This is succeeded by a dribbling more or less prolonged and without pain. The pregnancy may go on to term; and the membranes, as a rule, are found intact. The affection has given rise to much discussion, and there is an extended literature on the subject. Naegele has seen it persist for sixteen weeks without interrupting pregnancy.

According to Spiegelberg, Schroeder, Braun, and Hegar‡, the fluid comes from the cavity of the decidua, which is a secreting membrane even during pregnancy, and hydrorrhœa is only a hyper-secretion

---

* "Mon. für Geburt.," 1866.
† "Bau der Molen," 1867.
‡ Hegar, "Monat. für Geburt.," 1863.

of this membrane depending on chronic inflammation of the decidual glands. A great diversity of opinion has, however, been expressed as to the source of this fluid. Tarnier and Budin, besides the decidual form, speak of an amniotic hydrorrhœa, which occurs as the result of perforations of the amniotic sac far up in the uterine cavity, and, on account of the position of the aperture, do not necessarily precipitate labour. A drawing of a portion of the amnion, with such perforation, is given in their conjoint work on *Mid-wifery*.

Fig. 3.

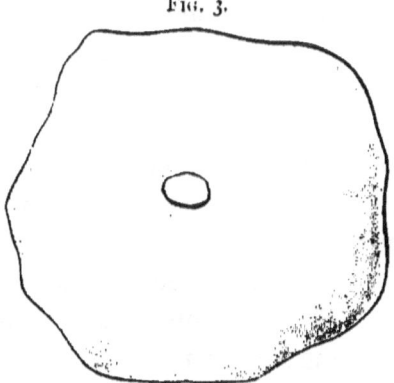

Aperture in the bag of membranes found in the upper part of the sac, distant from the usual seat of rupture. (Tarnier and Budin.)

Hydrorrhœa is a somewhat rare condition, only seventy cases having been collected in the most recent essay on the subject. It is only under exceptional circumstances that simple hydrorrhœa compromises the course of pregnancy; most women affected by it go to the full period. I need not, therefore, dwell further on the subject. Those interested may be referred to the Thesis of M. Stapper,* and to the

* *Vide* Charpentier, "Tr. des. Acc."

"Traité des Accouchements," by Tarnier and Budin, which contains the last and most able exposition on this topic.

A form of catarrhal endometritis I have sometimes met with in early pregnancy, and attended with sero-sanguineous or dark grumous discharges, is more formidable so far as pregnancy is concerned. Its persistence generally indicates chronic disease going on in the fœtal envelopes—of the decidua more especially—and it commonly ends in abortion. There is usually, in such cases, some antecedent history either of injury or of endometritis existing before the advent of pregnancy.

Some of the so-called "moles" consist of the decidua altered and distorted by one of the morbid processes I have just described. A "carneous mole" is so termed because it looks like a fleshy mass expelled from the uterus, and it usually consists of the morbidly thickened decidua which forms the outer covering, and the contents are either laminæ of blood-clot arranged like the layers of an aneurysm, or such remains of the disorganised embryo and its special membranes as have escaped entire destruction. Most frequently, in the case of carneous moles, no trace of the embryo can be discovered.

Morbid Changes in the Chorion.—The pathological change affecting the outermost true fœtal envelope or chorion, which has received most attention, is what is commonly called "cystic or vesicular or hydatid degeneration." In this affection small or large quantities of cyst-like bodies are expelled at intervals from the uterus of the pregnant woman, their expulsion being attended with hæmorrhage, and commonly with the discharge of a large quantity of serous fluid of pinkish colour, which has been compared to red-currant juice. Madame Boivin* stated that she found this disease occurring only twice in 20,375 pregnancies, but I suspect this account does not represent the true frequency of the affection, for most accoucheurs in large practice have met with it, and specimens of cystic chorion, in its various stages, are to be found in almost all our museums. In its earlier phases it is not uncommon, but then may be readily overlooked. When fully developed the appearance of the growth is very remarkable, and must at once arrest the attention of the medical attendant. Although commonly thrown off at first in detached portions, a time comes when uterine action fully sets in, and then a large quantity of cysts may be expelled in one mass, which, in some instances, is sufficient to fill a large basin. The vesicles or cysts of which the mass is composed vary from the size of a millet-seed to that of a grape, and these are intimately united together at various points by thin stems or pedicles. They have been compared to bunches of grapes, but the cysts do not necessarily terminate the stem on which they are suspended, like grapes, but are united in a plexiform arrangement one with another in a sort of network.

In Paré's "Surgery" it is recounted "that the Countess Margaret, daughter of Florent IV., Earl of Holland, and spouse to Count Herman of Heneberg, on Good Friday, in the year of our Lord 1276, and of her age forty-two, brought forth at one birth 365 infants, whereof 182 are said to have been males, as

* "Mem. de l'Art des Accouch."

many females, and the odd one an hermaphrodite, who were all baptized, those by the name of John,

FIG. 4.

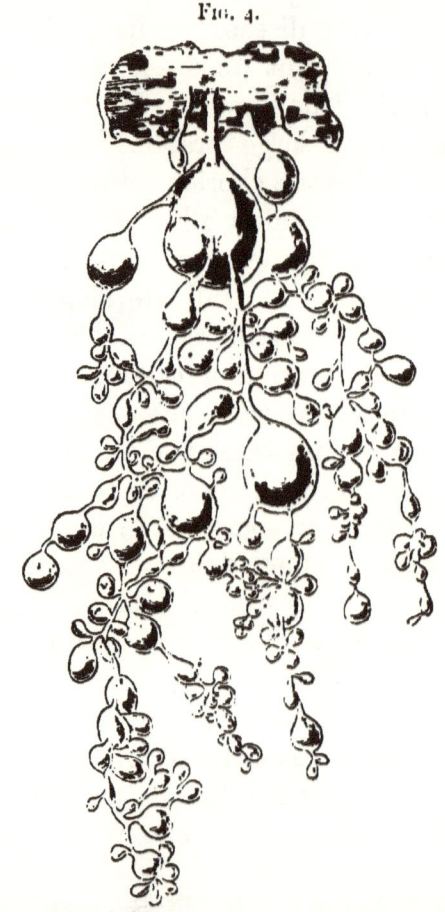

A portion of cystic chorion as seen with the naked eye. The arrangement of the vesicles is seen and also their attachments to the chorion membrane. (Ercolani.)

these by the name of Elizabeth, in two brazen dishes, by Don William, Suffragan Bishop of Treves." It is added: " The basins are still to be seen in the village of Losdun, where all strangers go (on purpose) from the

Hague, being reckoned among the great curiosities of Holland." This account is not regarded by modern authorities as a pure invention. Ambrose Paré was eminently honest, and these 365 children are now regarded as having been merely vesicles of a cystic chorion, magnified into infants by some one whose interest it was to promulgate the illusion.

The published literature on this single disease of the chorion is more extensive than of any affection of the fœtal membranes, and both detached observations and separate monographs exist in several different languages. Cloquet,* Percy,† and Boivin regarded the vesicles of the chorion as true acephalocysts ; but it has been abundantly proved that they are not so, being furnished neither with hooklets nor other minute structures characteristic of true hydatids. Bidlos and Soemmering believed cystic chorion to be a disease of the lymphatic vessels ; and Bartolin, Müller, and Cruveilhier‡ a disease of the blood-vessels. Ruysch§ attributed the formation of the cysts to accumulation of fluid in the cellular tissue which unites the vascular tunics of the fœtal membranes.

Nearly all modern authorities agree in regarding them as the results of pathological changes of one kind or other in the villi of the chorion. The single exception, I think, is Ancelet, who in 1868 published a paper in the " Gazette des Hôpitaux," and he there reverts to an old idea that the hydatid mole is a disease of the decidua.

* " No. 1 de la Faune des Med."
† " Ancien Journ. de Med.," 1793.
‡ Vide Charpentier, " Maladies du Placenta."
§ " Obser. Anat. Clin.," 1691.

Velpeau* seems to have been the first to indicate
that the cysts were not true or independent vesicles.
He regarded them as swollen chorionic villi, the
terminal extremities being enlarged by the accumulation of fluid, as a sponge is distended by water.
H. Mickel† and Gierse‡ said there was hypertrophy
of the natural structures, with œdema of the villi,
which they considered secondary. An excellent
description of the different stages of this transformation and its mode of growth, after Mettenheimer, is to
be found in Sir James Paget's " Surgical Pathology ;"
and Dr. Barnes,§ Dr. Graily Hewitt,‖ and Dr. Braxton
Hicks,¶ in this country, have further illustrated the
various stages of its development in separate papers.
In France, C. Robin's observations have attracted
much attention, and his views are adopted by M.
Cayla, who wrote a well-known thesis on the subject.
Probably the most lucid and notable contribution to
the pathology of this subject is from the pen of the
celebrated Virchow.** He points out that the many
discrepancies in the ideas promulgated concerning the
true nature of cystic chorion are due to incomplete
knowledge of the villous structure in normal conditions.
According to him, the villi consist of a prolongation
of the same mucous tissue which forms the gelatin
of Wharton in the cord. The villi have two essential portions—an epithelial covering (exochorion) and

---

* " De l'Art des Accouchements."
† " Handbuch des Mensch. Anat.," 1820.
‡ " Verhandl. der Gesells. für Geburt.," 1847.
§ " British and Foreign Medical Review," 1855.
‖ " Obstet. Trans.," vol. i.
¶ " Guy's Hospital Reports," 1864.
** " Die Krank. d. Geschw.," t. i.

a substratum or body of mucous tissue (endochorion) which, non-vascular when the villi first appear as buds on the outer surface of the chorion, later contain blood-vessels. The proliferation of the epithelium which Heinrich Müller[*] regarded as the *point de départ* for the production of cysts, Virchow regards as the expression of regular and normal development. The buds or cysts are formed in the same way as in normal growth, and it is the interior of the villus— not in its epithelium—that the particular and morbid transformation takes place. In effect, Virchow regards the cystic chorion as a typical form of myxoma, and he avers that he has found the same productions in other parts of the envelopes. Both Ruysch and Virchow have found these cyst-like bodies in the umbilical cord. Virchow noticed certain buds of the external epithelial covering of the villi which contained transparent cavities; these he called "physalides." Single large dilated cells containing a hyaline liquid he called "physalifores." Wedl had previously described them in his "Histological Pathology;" and Virchow, while confirming Wedl's observation, regarded them as accidental products. Ercolani interpreted their presence after another fashion, and as affording evidence of a different theory of cyst development.

Virchow further states that the mucous metamorphosis of cells seen in the villi of the chorion may disappear in fatty transformation, or the cells may be changed into fibrous elements, thus constituting a "myxoma fibrosum." This change I shall describe later.

* "Der Bau der Molen," 1847.

As long ago as 1858,* before I knew anything of the researches of Virchow, I had pointed out that the cysts of the chorion were not mere dropsical dilatations of the terminal villi, but that the fluid distending them, in the earlier stages at least, was formed or secreted in the interior of beautiful thin-

FIG. 5.

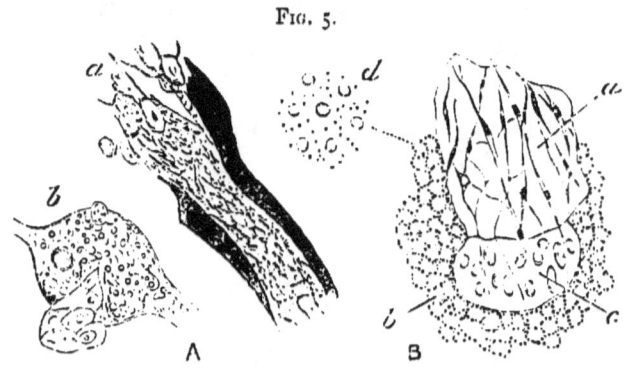

A a, Extremity of a villus in early stage of cystic degeneration; a. shows the first stage of enlargement in the cells of the villus trunk; b, a somewhat more advanced stage, showing hyaline cells escaping from the ruptured capsule of a young cyst. (Priestley.)

B Terminal villus of cystic chorion; a, stellate connective tissue; b, c, inner and outer layers of wall; d, early stage of b. (Braxton Hicks.)

walled cells, which had their origin in the centre of the villus. The microscopic examination I described in my lectures on the gravid uterus as follows:—
"Placing a terminal branch under the microscope, which seemed to the naked eye nearest to the normal condition, it was seen to be enveloped by a granular covering, probably derived from the altered decidua; the club-shaped extremities were observed to be distended with large nucleated cells, and bearing little resemblance to the small and more uniform cellules

* "Lectures on Development of Gravid Uterus."

composing a terminal villus in a healthy state. By
compression the envelope bounding the villus could
be ruptured, and gave egress to the cells. The
fully developed cysts had two coats, like a normal
villus, the external epithelial, the internal delicately
fibrous, but firm and dense. An incision being made
through these (if the preparation was fresh) what
appeared to be a viscous or gelatinous fluid escaped
from the aperture, and this was found to be contained in large transparent cells, with walls of extreme
tenuity, assuming the polyhedral form from the pressure to which they had been subject. The entire contents had much the appearance of the vitreous humour
of the eye, which has transparent partitions running
across, separating the fluid into compartments; the
presence of a nucleus, however, in each compartment
clearly proved it to consist of largely developed thin-
walled cells. In the largest cysts, the pellucid
cells were not readily discernible, having probably
undergone solution. Scattered over the vesicles and
their connecting peduncles were little nodular projections, consisting of cellular buds for new branches,
such as exist in healthy villi. The narrow stems
uniting the cysts were fibrous, with a cellular covering, and sometimes enclosed a small vessel full of
blood. Fat granules were copiously deposited in the
texture of both stems and vesicles."

There is no discrepancy between this account from
actual observation and the view taken by Virchow,
that the morbid change is a true myxoma. The
only difference is that Virchow seems to look upon
the distension of the villi as due to the accumulation
of mucus in the inter-cellular tissue, while I found

the distension produced during early development
at least in the rapid production of thin-walled,
nucleated cells. Possibly both may be right. It
seems highly probable that, in the smaller cysts, large
cells with fluid contents constitute the first stage of
the disease, and, later, these cells form themselves
into spaces traversed by trabeculæ of connective
tissue, and containing the fluid. This is identical
with the process by which the gelatin of Wharton is
produced in the cord. The exuded fluid in both cases
has all the chemical reactions of mucine. It is by no
means uncommon to find in the extremity of a comparatively healthy villus one or more large transparent
hyaline cells. These represent the beginnings of the
cystic change, or the first transformation from the
more uniform cell-structures which compose the
parenchyma in a normal state.

Ercolani* (who wrote in 1876) differs *in toto* from
Virchow and other authors in his view of the production of cystic chorion, and, disbelieving in its
myxomatous origin, he regards Virchow's appellation
for it as misleading. He, like Virchow and Robin,
describes a villus as composed of two parts : one
internal or parenchymatous (tissue chorial of Robin,
mucous tissue of Virchow) which is in direct communication, and in fact continuous, with the chorion.
Besides, this is an external portion, which constitutes
an outer envelope or casing to the villus (the exochorion of Robin). Before the villus penetrates the
decidua, this outer envelope is constituted of an
epithelium which belongs to the fœtal structures, but
directly the villus is embedded in the decidua to

* *Loc. cit.*

form the placenta this epithelial envelope disappears, and its place is taken by a layer of cells derived from the decidua, which he calls the "glandular organ," because in this glandular organ, he conceives, is carried on the process of elaboration by which materials are provided from the mother's blood for the nutrition of the fœtus. Now it is from this outer envelope—the epithelial covering in the primitive chorial

Fig. 6.

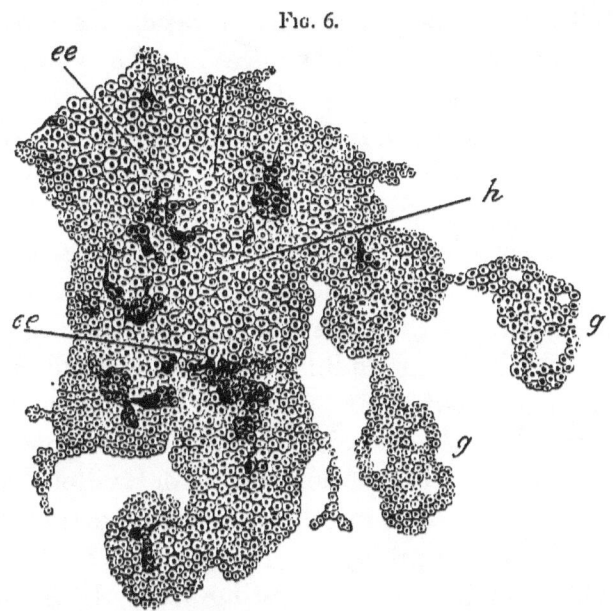

Extremity of a chorion villus, hypertrophied, and beginning cystic degeneration. The cellular structure, seen at *h*, is the epithelial covering of the villus. Neoplasms are springing from the surface of the villus (*ee*), and large dilated cells (physaliforcs) are seen at *g*. (From Ercolani.)

villus, or, if the disease begins later, from the glandular organ in the villi of the placenta—that, according to Ercolani, the proliferations take place which form the cystic disease of the chorion, and not from the mucous tissue or parenchyma, as stated by

Virchow. Heinrich Müller had in 1843 declared that these morbid changes commence with an enlargement of the external envelope of the villi, and that later these buds or enlargements give place to internal cavities which become vesicles. Virchow so far agreed with Müller that the epithelium is the point of departure for the formation of cysts, but he contends that, in the production of vesicles, the parenchymatous or basic substance of the villi must penetrate the new epithelial product, thus carrying with it the mucous cells continuous with the chorionic structure, and which are necessary to the production of the true myxoma. From this view Ercolani emphatically dissents, and he gives various details of investigation to sustain his position. Thus, besides his asseveration, that the buds take their origin in the epithelial or glandular layer surrounding the villi, he points out what had before been indicated by Ancelet, that the vesicles in their development do not necessarily spring from the parent villus trunk, but take their origin in other vesicles, and that some vesicles not only proliferate from large vesicles, but also that the largest often spring from those which are much smaller. This he holds is quite incompatible with the idea of the mucous tissue from the chorion penetrating or sending prolongations into all the vesicles.

In limine Ercolani holds that there may be a formation of cyst-like bodies beginning in the epithelial envelope of a villus, when disease attacks the chorionic villi at a very early period. But when the chorion has united with the serotina to form the young placenta, the typical form of cystic degeneration begins in morbid proliferations of the decidual or glandular organ, and so the disease apparently belongs more to the mother than her offspring. It is worth while to appreciate this point, if it be true, as it may afford some clue to subsequent treatment, which must necessarily be on the maternal side. Ercolani's researches and speculations on this subject are marked by great painstaking and ingenuity, but I confess I am not convinced of the truth of his view as opposed to Virchow's. Ercolani has certainly contributed to produce some confusion in the pathology of the condition by describing myxoma of the chorion and myxoma of the placenta as different affections, and giving to each a separate chapter, while there can be no doubt that both are essentially the same disease with but slight modifications.

The general relation of the cystic chorion to the decidua is sometimes very distinctly seen in the incipient stages of the morbid change. Many years ago the late Dr. McClintock showed me in Dublin a preparation which is mentioned by Dr. Montgomery in his "Signs of Pregnancy," in which a mass of cysts is enclosed between two layers of decidua—the decidua vera and the decidua reflexa. Dr. Graily Hewitt,[*] has also figured a specimen in which both deciduæ are well shown, and the relation of the cyst-like structures to the serotina is delineated. When cystic disease is further advanced, the relations of the various membranes become so confused that the vesicles are inextricably mixed up with the hypertrophied decidual structures, and separation of the two is impossible.

[*] " Obstet. Trans."

There are all possible varieties in the degree and stage of the disease to be met with, and the different appearance of the mass which is expelled from the uterus has given rise to a classification of these "moles," as they are called. Thus we have the "vesicular mole," in which the chief part of the substance passed consists of the pellucid cysts just described, varying in size from a pin's head to the size of a grape. With the cysts, however, is always mixed up a certain amount of a denser envelope—the altered decidua—which either adheres to the cysts or is loosened from them and expelled separately. If the thickness of the outer envelope of the mass greatly preponderates over the cystic structures within, we have another modification of the so-called "carneous mole," which may with propriety be named "carneo-cystic," to distinguish it from the other carneous mole I have described as a mere thickened decidua. In this the mass is made up of a more or less fleshy substance, granular in appearance, and blood-stained, with a small proportion of vesicles. Some time ago I carefully examined a specimen of this kind, which had been expelled from the uterus with all the symptoms of miscarriage. The mass was half the size of a cocoa-nut, and, when cut into, was seen to be composed of a granular, dark red substance, interspersed here and there, at distant intervals, with vesicular bodies. In this case the chorionic villi had degenerated, as in the more marked form of vesicular mole; but the decidua had become proportionately much more morbidly developed than the chorionic villi, and hence the different appearance of the mass. In this and in other instances I have repeatedly examined the microscopic structure of the granular matrix in which the cysts were sparingly or more amply imbedded, and I have rarely failed to find distinct evidences of a definite arrangement of glandular structure, such as exists in the normal decidua. All the elements were, however, enormously hypertrophied; while the glandular particles were infiltrated with fat-granules and the *débris* of blood-corpuscles and crystals. The blood-vessels themselves were surrounded with fat-granules and molecules, and crumbling in degeneration. This fatty degeneration must cause a tendency to separation from the walls of the uterus. The mass then becomes a foreign body, which at length excites uterine contraction, and ends in its expulsion.

When cystic disease of the chorion is far advanced, the embryo either entirely disappears, or, if found, it is commonly shrivelled and wrapped in its amnion in the centre of the mass. In some rare cases, even when the embryo is found, no trace of the amnion is present. It has either not been developed, or, once formed, it has disappeared, and the shrivelled and distorted embryo remains attached directly to the inner surface of the chorion.

Chorionic villi which have undergone cystic degeneration have a remarkable way of forcing themselves not only through the decidua, but into the very substance of the uterine walls. This is strikingly illustrated in a preparation in St. Thomas's Hospital, which is recorded in the "Obstetrical Transactions" by Dr. Cory. The woman from whom it was taken was forty years of age and had had eight children. When more than four months pregnant, she passed a large hydatid mole. Bleeding, with serous discharge, continuing, the uterus was eventually injected with perchloride of iron. The patient died very suddenly after, and it was found that the iron had penetrated to the peritoneal cavity. The uterus shows a portion of cystic chorion still attached to the interior of its cavity, and the cystic villi have forced themselves along the uterine sinuses so far down into the deep structures of the womb that they are close to the peritoneal surface. There was consequently very little tissue left between the cavity of the uterus and the peritoneal cavity. Somewhat similar cases have been recorded by Waldeyer[*] and Jarotzky, Spiegelberg,[†] and Volkmann.[‡]

Cystic degeneration of the chorion is essentially a disease of the membranes in early pregnancy. It has been supposed to begin before the allantois reaches the chorion, and, therefore, before the villi are supplied with vascular loops. That this cannot be always the case is proved by the fact that fœtal blood-vessels are sometimes seen in the stems of the diseased villi and in the vesicles, and also by

FIG. 7.

Cystic chorion forcing its way through the muscular walls of the uterus towards the peritoneum. (After Spiegelberg.)

---

[*] Virchow's "Arch.," Bd. xliv.
[†] "Lehrb. der Geburt."
[‡] Virchow's "Arch.," Bd. xli.

the cases of partial myxoma which have been re-corded.

In early gestation, the whole outer surface of the chorion is furnished pretty equally with villi. Those which are to form the placenta, and which are imbedded in the decidua serotina, soon become more developed, and the rest, under ordinary circumstances, remain for a while stationary or retrograde. If cystic disease begins, it is generally at the crisis of develop-ment, when the placenta is about to take a definite shape, and the villi are concentrating themselves on the placental spot. Then the villi over the whole sphere of the ovum have about an equal growth, although they may be somewhat more luxuriant at the placental spot; and all may be like affected by the myxomatous change. Not only do the villi destined to form the placenta dilate, but the chorial villi, which should become atrophied, increase in volume and hypertrophy. This accounts for the general appearance of the cystic mass when it is expelled from the uterus, the vesicles being pretty equally distributed everywhere through it. There are some few exceptions in which the placenta is attacked by cystic change after the placenta is already local-ised; but the disease then rarely shows itself in an advanced form, the dilatations of the villi being com-paratively small. Instances, however, have occasion-ally been recorded in which living fœtuses have been born with the placenta in a state of partial cystic degeneration, and some of these seem sufficiently authenticated by modern observers to be admitted.

Partial myxomas have been described in which one or more branches of villi alone have been affected, the rest remaining healthy and the child well developed. These cases are, however, rare. When the disease does occur, as before stated, it generally attacks all the villi alike. Still rarer are instances which have been recorded where a twin embryo has perished in early pregnancy, and has eventually been expelled with cystic degeneration of its membranes, at the same time as a living child with its placenta healthy. Siebold gives an example of this, and Dr. Hall Davis has recorded another in the "Obstetrical Transactions" for 1862.

The crucial question, and one which has been much discussed, is, whether the disease of the chorion precedes the death of the embryo, and so causes its death, or whether the embryo dies first, and the cystic degeneration takes place subsequently, and is in some sense the consequence. Most modern authors regard the disease of the chorion as first in the order of events; but Mikschik,[*] Gierse, and Dr. Graily Hewitt have endeavoured to show that the disease is consequent on the death of the embryo. The reasons advanced for this view are, that, in many cases, the embryo has either been arrested in growth or has disappeared altogether; and, further, that in some twin conceptions one chorion has degenerated, the other remaining healthy until term. This view is vitiated, in the first place, by the recorded instances of living fœtuses where the placenta was cystic, notably by Martin of Berlin,[†] Villers,[‡] and Krieger;[§]

---

[*] "Zeit. der Wien. Aerzte," 1845.   [†] "Monat. f. Geburt." Bd. xxix.
[‡] Schmidt's "Jahrb." Bd. xxxix.
[§] *Ibid.* 1864. Dr. Allan Sym, in the "Edin. Med. Jour." for Aug. 1887, has recorded another instance of this kind.

and, further, by the fact that we may have partial myxoma of the chorion with continued growth of the embryo. Graily Hewitt gives, as one of his reasons for regarding the death of the embryo as first in the order of events, its small size in all cases where the chorion has become cystic; the largest he had been able to find was Dr. Granville's example, in which the embryo was only one inch and three quarters in length.

In St. Thomas's Hospital, however, is a fœtus of from three to four months' growth, with cystic chorion fully developed. The fœtus is not shrivelled, as commonly happens in such cases, but seems as though, up to a certain time. it must have been fairly nourished, notwithstanding a very marked twisting of the umbilical cord. The largest portion of the placental mass had in this specimen undergone advanced cystic degeneration, but enough of the villi had, up to a certain time, remained capable of supplying nourishment to the fœtus. A time came at length when the distension of the uterus, from the rapidly growing chorion, brought on uterine contraction and eventual expulsion of the contents. The placenta in this preparation is seen to be as large as that organ commonly is at the full time.

I take it, therefore, that both the direct and indirect evidence is clearly in favour of cystic disease of the chorion preceding the death, and in most cases being the cause of death in the fœtus. There may be exceptional instances where cystic degeneration takes place after the death of the embryo. This may be the case where one placenta of twins only is affected by disease; but this does not invalidate the main position; it only indicates that cystic change in the villi may take place both before and after the death of the embryo.

As to the cause of the disease, Virchow believes that the original fault is in the decidua, which, becoming inflamed and thickened before impregnation, is incapable of receiving and supporting the chorionic villi which try to take root in it. It is converted, so to speak, into a soil incapable of affording nourishment for normal growth, and the result is the production of a monstrosity, which acquires all the characters of a parasite, and kills the embryo by appropriating all the nutrient materials to its own vegetation. It may not be regarded as fanciful to remark that the various forms of mole seem not only to bear analogy, as previously remarked, to monstrous flowers and fruits, but also that the structural parts of these monstrosities find their counterparts in these abortive masses from the human subject. Thus, the carneous mole, with its overgrown decidua, may represent the deformed calyx, and the vesicular mole the distorted and over-developed corolla, being developed at the expense of the central embryonic portion.

Virchow's theory—that the cause of cystic disease in the chorion is to be found in a faulty condition of the uterine mucous membrane—is supported by the fact that the same woman will often produce several vesicular moles in succession, and Virchow asserts that in these women the decidua bears traces of inflammatory thickening, sometimes with polypoid excrescences on its free surface. Depaul* mentions a woman who had the affection three times. There

* "Leçons de Clin. Obstet.," 1872.

is, nevertheless, abundant evidence to show that a
woman may have living children at some later period,
after being the subject of cystic disease of the chorion.
The only objection to Virchow's view which strikes
me, is the fact, previously mentioned, that twin ova
have been expelled in abortion, one of which had
cystic chorion and the other not.   It is difficult to
understand, if disease of the decidua was the cause of
cystic degeneration, how one embryo should be
affected and the other escape.*

The last point in connection with this subject is
the question : Can cystic or vesicular chorion ever
occur in women without conception ?   This question
came before a Court of Inquiry in India some years
ago, and involved both the character of an unmarried
woman and the reputation of a medical man whose
opinion had impugned her chastity.   The medical
man collected the opinions of all the leading
obstetricians in this country, and, although the
balance of opinion greatly preponderated in favour of
vesicular chorion being always the result of impregnation, there was at least one notable dissentient,
who believed that the vesicles might be formed in
the virgin uterus.   We now know so accurately the
way in which these vegetations are produced that
doubt should no longer exist on the matter.   With
our present knowledge it would be just as reasonable
to suppose that a child might be expelled from an
unimpregnated uterus as a true vesicular chorion.

A portion of cystic chorion may be long retained *in*

* Underhill asserts that cystic chorion, in the majority of cases, is
associated with a cancerous or syphilitic dyscrasia.—(" Obstet. Gaz.,"
1879.)

utero without giving rise to active symptoms, and thus unfounded suspicion may arise concerning the chastity of women when this is expelled. The late Dr. McClintock* specially called attention to this, and said, "Hydatids may be retained *in utero* for many months or years, or a portion only may be expelled, and the residue may throw out a fresh crop of vesicles, to be discharged on a future occasion."

There can be no doubt also of the fact, which is well illustrated in Dr. Cory's preparation, previously described, that after a cystic mole has been expelled, a portion of the cyst growth may remain behind and proliferate in the uterine walls, thus keeping up exhausting discharges, and imperilling the safety of the patient. In these cases, therefore, the prognosis should be a guarded one. I need not say that cystic chorion must not be mistaken for true hydatids or acephalocysts, which on very rare occasions have been expelled from the unimpregnated uterus.

Morbid Changes in the Amnion.—The amnion, or innermost fœtal envelope, bears a very close resemblance to a serous membrane. In its earliest development it may be seen raised like a blister over the whole dorsal surface of the embryo, and as it gradually grows away from the fœtus and forms a more distinct cavity to surround it, it increases in firmness and density, and at length coalesces with the inner surface of the chorion to form the future bag of membranes.

In the early stages of pregnancy the amnion does not always escape the effects of extravasation beginning in the decidual structures. The force of the blood extravasation may be such as to

* "Clin. Mem.," 1863.

break down the resistance both of the chorion and amnion, and if the cavity of the amnion is invaded, the invariable result is the destruction of the embryo, with abortion sooner or later. The earlier in pregnancy this extravasation takes place, the greater the likelihood of the inner envelope giving way, for it is then most fragile and most easily ruptured. There is great variation in the amount of resistance offered by the amnion in different cases. This is notable even to the end of pregnancy, for we sometimes find the bag of membranes of which the amnion forms an integral part so thin that the first uterine contractions produce escape of the waters, while in other cases the membranes are so tough as to impede the progress of labour and require puncture for its acceleration. Dubois* says the feeble resistance of membranes may be due to natural structure, I suppose, as some women may have thinner skins than others, or it may be due to alterations consequent on inflammation. However produced, it may, by facilitating rupture and escape of the liquor amnii in early pregnancy, and before the child is viable, lead to intra-uterine death, for it is well known that pregnancy cannot continue long after the entire evacuation of the amniotic fluid.

The question as to whether there is a true inflammation of the amnion has been discussed, and various supposed pathological results have been pointed out. Jacquemier details three cases which he regards as clearly indicating the occurrence of inflammation on its free surface. One of the patients had peritonitis, and aborted five days later; another had been kicked in the abdomen at the third month, and although she

* "Dict." in 30 vols., Art. Hydrometrite.

I

went to the full time, there was a rapid development in size of the abdomen as the result of the injury, and a large quantity of liquor amnii was formed in the uterus. In all the cases the membranes were thickened and traversed by abundant vessels, and in one the containing fluid was cloudy and whitish in colour, with flakes like curd of milk floating in it, which were portions of false membrane detached from the free surface of the amnion.

The adhesions sometimes noticed between the amnion and the umbilical cord, or between the amnion and the fœtus, are almost invariably associated with some malformation or monstrosity of the child, and have been attributed to inflammatory action. The difficulty in accepting this theory is the general absence of other inflammatory signs in such cases, besides the mere adhesion and its associated monstrosity.* The natural history of such malformations further points to some entanglements of embryonic structures in the process of development—these resulting in distortion and displacement of normal parts.

The condition which has received most attention in connection with the pathology of the amnion is what has been termed "Hydramnios," or superabundance of liquor amnii. The presence of a certain amount of fluid in the cavity of the amnion is necessary to the development of the fœtus, but in some cases it is so abnormally large as to endanger the life of the child, and if it does not necessarily bring peril to the

---

* Courtsey says when the phenomena are produced early, it is by the liquor amnii being absorbed, and the membranes then acquire adhesions to the integument of the fœtus. In others, inflammation is the cause, and there are false membranes formed from the amnion.

mother, it may place her in very grave discomfort. Dr. Kidd, who wrote on the subject in the "Proceedings of the Dublin Obstetrical Society" for 1878, limits the term "hydramnios" to those cases in which more than two quarts of amniotic fluid are present. The quantity of fluid is sometimes very large. Baudelocque gives one case where thirty pints escaped from the uterus; other authors give thirty or forty pints. Coming on suddenly in some instances, more slowly in others, the fluid so distends the uterus that it acquires a volume entirely disproportioned to the stage of pregnancy. The result to the mother is that she may suffer greatly from the distension. Respiration is impeded, and the patient may not be able to lie down night or day. The digestion is deranged from physical pressure, and the heart's action is disordered, while other secondary symptoms, such as œdema of the lower limbs and blueness of the countenance, may be superadded.

The effect on the child is to impede its development, and, if born alive, it is commonly too feeble to survive its birth. Frequently the child is affected with dropsy, hydrocephalus, or other complication. Of thirty-three cases mentioned by McClintock, nineteen children only were born alive ; ten of these died a few hours after birth, and nine survived. Often the fœtus dies *in utero*, and may then be retained a considerable time after its death, thus prolonging the discomfort of the mother. The condition has a tendency to repeat itself in the same woman. I saw a patient some years ago in her tenth pregnancy, who was sent to me by Dr. Matthews Duncan, and who had suffered from hydramnios in nine out of the ten gestations, losing most of her children, the first pregnancy being the only healthy one.

There is an extensive literature on the subject, but little is known as to the cause or causes. Mercier noted traces of inflammation in the amnion, but Dubois and Desormeaux cite cases where there was no appreciable lesion of the membranes, and there are no constant appearances in the placenta associated with the condition. Churchill attributed it to excessive secretory activity in the amnion, and various other explanations have been given, but they do not add much to the precision of our knowledge of its causation.

In the case I have alluded to as occurring in my own experience, there was nothing to account for the phenomena beyond a short residence in India, which had impaired the general health, and I found no albumen in the urine.

It has been said to be rare before the fifth month, but in going through the museums, I find many examples of it in the earlier periods of pregnancy; and both from this and my own experience, I infer that it is far from infrequent in the first half of gestation. In St. Mary's Hospital there is a specimen in which the amniotic cavity is from three to four inches long, and the embryo is not larger than a horse-bean. In St. Bartholomew's again there is a large amniotic cavity with no embryo at all.

Merriman,* Robert Lee,† and others, attribute hydramnios to a morbid state of the mother, and particularly to the effects of syphilis. That the

---

* "Synopsis," &c., 1838.
† "Theory and Practice of Midwifery."

liquor amnii may be affected by the state of the mother is evident from many facts. Dr. Duncan,[*] in a paper on Puerperal Diabetes, states that hydramnios is frequent in association with this condition, and sugar has been found in the liquor amnii. Two or three facts have been distinctly made out in relation to its pathology.

1. Scarpa[†] noticed a coincidence between this form of dropsy and the presence of twins. This has been fully confirmed by the observations of Winckel,[‡] McClintock,[§] and others.

2. In pregnancies complicated with hydramnios the child often presents some vice of conformation. Monsters are, in fact, common with this affection.

3. The children born with a superabundance of liquor amnii often present evidences of syphilis, and this whether they are born dead or alive.

4. Hydramnios is comparatively rare in first pregnancies as compared with others.

5. It is more frequent with female children than males. Of thirty-three cases collected by McClintock, only eight were males.

The impression derived from a careful study of all the circumstances is, that hydramnios is not a product of inflammation of the amnion, as some have supposed, but that it arises sometimes from constitutional conditions affecting the mother, sometimes from local causes. The idea of local origin, in some cases at least, is strengthened by the fact that it may occur with twins, one only being affected; and Charpentier mentions a case where the abdomen increased

---

* " Obstet. Trans.," 1882. † " Opuscula di Chir.," 1825-32.
‡ " Path. der Geburt." § " Diseases of Women."

rapidly after local injury from a fall at the fifth
month, and the woman was delivered of a dead child
at seven months, with seven to eight litres of liquor
amnii. In this instance, the placenta was found to
be diseased to a third of its extent. It would thus
seem to be due to some fault in development, as
cystic chorion is a fault of this kind.

LECTURE III.

ONE of the chief difficulties in studying the literature of these diseases as they have been described by various observers arises from the tendency on the part of authors to regard the particular morbid change which they have had the opportunity of investigating as the chief or only disease with which the organ is affected. All other morbid appearances are for them but consequences or complications of a specific and cardinal lesion upon which the rest depend. To give an example, Charpentier avers that the placenta is attacked by only one morbid change. He accepts the investigations of Robin as illustrating the whole range of placental pathology, and believes that when disease has invaded the placenta, it commences always in fibro-fatty change, and consequent on this, blood extravasations, and successive transformations of effused blood, account for all the various pathological appearances associated with the death or enfeebling of the fœtus.

Verdier and Bustamente take entirely another view of these changes. It seems to me that one cannot long investigate the diseases of the placenta without discovering that they are most complex in their nature, and that they proceed from a variety of causes inextricably intermixed—sometimes one pathological condition having the precedence, sometimes another. The placenta is, in truth, as liable to be affected by a variety of diseases as the liver or the lung, and some of its diseases bear not only a striking resemblance to diseases occurring in those organs, but have affinities with them, and may depend on the same causes. Again, confusion has arisen from investigators describing the same morbid condition under a different name, probably because it was observed only in one stage of progress or with some variations, and some have fallen into the error of ranging affections which are intrinsically different under the same appellations.

After the third month of utero-gestation, the various membranes surrounding the embryo have come into apposition; there is no distinct interspace between them, and the fœtus lies suspended in its liquor amnii in the centre of the ovum. By this time the placenta has assumed a definite form, and the embryo is now chiefly dependent upon it for the supply of those materials which are necessary for its growth. It is as yet, however, in a rudimentary form, and instead of having those sinuses, or cavities, everywhere permeating its substance which are peculiar to its structure at a later period, it consists of villi of the chorion, round which loops of maternal vessels have been thrown, in such fashion as to form a complex, but very distinct, network throughout the placental mass. I have repeatedly seen these maternal loops naturally injected in young placenta, diseased, as well as normal, for in some forms of indurated young placenta they are almost as distinctly seen as when the organ is healthy, and microscopic sections are more easily made. Their prototypes are seen in the placenta of some mammalia, which have been described more especially by Professor Turner, and I have thrown out the suggestion that by dilatation and further development, these maternal vessels, appearing at first in the young placenta as capillary loops, become eventually the sinuses of the maternal portion of the placenta, into which the fœtal villi are suspended, as the gills of a fish are suspended in water. There they are bathed by the maternal blood current, and both absorb materials for the growth of the embryo, and also effect the aëration of the fœtal blood, which is so necessary for its well-being. It is obvious, therefore, that a healthy state of the placenta is necessary for the safety of the fœtus, both in the earlier and later months. Until the placenta is fully organised, the nutrition of the embryo is carried on by the chorion villi more or less over the whole sphere of the ovum. But when the placenta is formed, the whole nutritive and respiratory function is concentrated upon it, and the chorion villi degenerate and atrophy over the rest of the chorion membrane.

Extravasations of blood into the young placenta are very common, and they occur as the result of rupture of some of those vascular maternal loops which I have just described. If the extravasations be limited in extent, the life of the embryo may not be compromised; but a more extended apoplexy at once stops its nutrition, and the root-like processes of the young villi become so compressed, that the circulation can no longer be carried on through the minute fœtal blood-vessels which they contain. It is common enough to see clots in varying stages of change in accordance with the date of their formation in young placenta which have been expelled as the result of abortion, and if the ovum has been long retained, and extravasation has been of such extent as to kill the embryo, the whole placenta is generally found to have become indurated and in a measure contracted. The clots have been consolidated, decolorised, and contracted, while the villi in other parts of the organ, not in the immediate vicinity of the altered blood-clots, have become atrophied, and so firmly fused together, that it is almost impossible to separate them for microscopic purposes.

Apoplexy takes place into the substance and on the uterine surface of the full-grown placenta also very frequently. There is, however, this marked difference from the earlier period, that now the placenta is larger and thicker, and isolated clots may be deeply imbedded in its substance, only to be exposed by incision. Others may have been formed between the uterine walls and the maternal surface of the placenta, making a deep depression into the centre of a placental cotyledon, and compressing the placental structures. It is further to be remarked, as a difference in the results of blood extravasations in the young and more mature placenta, that in the latter several successive effusions of blood may take place, forming apoplexies of varying sizes and dates, without so seriously jeopardising the life of the fœtus as it would do at an earlier period of gestation. The larger size of the placenta and its more extended surface afford a better chance of so much of the potential part of it retaining its healthy relations, and so carrying on the placento-fœtal circulation that embryonic life is sustained. This may be, notwithstanding that the whole amount of intended pabulum is not furnished, for the simple reason that a considerable portion of what may be called absorbing radicles have been destroyed, or their function impaired by the local lesion.

Apoplexy, and the various morbid changes associated with it, is, perhaps, of all others, the most frequent pathological condition easily reeognisable with the naked eye in the placenta. This being so, it can scarcely be a matter of surprise that some authors have regarded it as the chief of placental diseases, being the prime factor, indeed, in all placental disease, and the forerunner of all other pathological appearances. To it has been attributed the occurrence of the so-called tubercle, and also the formation of scirrhus in the placenta.

Sir James Simpson,* in his " Memoir on Congestion and Inflammation of the Placenta," which is remarkable for its literary research, describes placental congestion as the forerunner of apoplexy. The congestion, according to him, consists of an extraordinary accumulation of blood in the spongy tissue of the placenta. This only requires to be pushed a degree further to lead to rupture of the vascular coats, and escape of blood into the parenchyma or on the maternal surface of the organ. He then goes on to describe the changes which take place in the

* *Vide* " Obstct. Works," p. 397.

extravasated blood, and the effect on the placental structure.

In 1839, M. Jacquemier wrote a communication on Extravasations of Blood in the Placenta which is still regarded as classical in France, and he gives an excellent description of the pathological appearances observed. He points out that the effects of extravasation vary with the stage at which gestation has arrived. According to him, at an early period the villi of the chorion are so loosely imbedded in the decidua serotina, that there may be said to be space between the two membranes. If, therefore, a rupture takes place in a utero-placental blood-vessel, the extravasation is the more general, and wide spread, because of the laxity of tissue, and thus pregnancy is the more likely to be interrupted. In the later period, the placenta is more developed and compact —the chorion and decidua have become fused together, and if extravasation occurs into the substance of the placenta it is more limited in extent—generally, indeed, confined to the lobe in which the apoplexy has occurred, although more than one lobe may be affected. Jacquemier describes three varieties of placental apoplexy in the later months which I need not give in detail here.

Verdier, who wrote a thesis in 1868, entitled " Researches on Apoplexies and Hæmatoses of the Placenta," goes so far as to say that fibrous changes— scirrhus hardness, fibro-fatty, and those which appear due to inflammation—are due only to extravasated blood and the changes taking place in it.

In 1848, Bustamente published a memoir on Placental Disease, which attracted much attention in

France and elsewhere. Admitting the accuracy of previous observers as to the frequent presence of so-called apoplexies in the placental tissue, and their influence in producing death of the fœtus, he contends that the masses of blood so found are not due to vascular rupture and extravasation, but are produced by thrombosis in the maternal sinuses of the placenta. He points out that deposits are very frequent in the deeper structures of the placenta, and even near its fœtal surface. The mechanism of their production he believes to be somewhat as follows : The whole of the villi constituting the fœtal portion of the placenta, and found equally distributed throughout its entire mass, are bathed with the maternal blood in the lacunæ in which they are immersed. The maternal circulation through these lacunæ is necessarily slow, because it is poured into the placenta by maternal arteries, and, before passing back into the maternal veins, it must pass through the dilatations which con-stitute the placental sinuses or lacunæ. Anything, therefore, which disturbs the utero-placental circula-tion, favours stasis in the placental lacunæ, and more especially in those portions of the placenta which are most distant from the maternal supply. The increase of fibrin observed in the blood of pregnant women, various general pathological conditions which render the blood more readily coagulable, syncope by slowing or arresting the circulation, even for a limited period, —all favour stasis of the utero-placental circulation and resulting thrombosis. The villi, once imbedded in the blood of a thrombosis, although at the moment healthy, speedily degenerate. The loops of fœtal capillaries become granular, and eventually disappear.

The epithelial covering of the villus and the proper fibroid structure of the stem become fatty and disorganized, and the whole tissue eventually shrivels. But this is not the only change which takes place, according to Bustamente, when placental thrombosis has occurred. The blood-clot itself becomes organized. He quotes O. Weber, in Billroth's "Surgery," as an authority on the organisation of extravasated blood, and avers that he has himself seen leucocytes in the centre of placental clots, not near living tissue. These leucocytes develop, and form a connective tissue, with nuclei readily seen by the addition of acetic acid, and firmly unite the villi to each other, thus producing a dense and resisting tissue, the component elements of which it is difficult to separate.

Other and later authors have expressed the opinion that no apoplexy takes place into the substance of the placenta, either in the early or later periods of gestation, without some previous degeneration of structure. Charpentier quotes from a contribution of M. Bailly, who endeavours to prove that some morbid change invariably takes place prior to blood extravasation, and in this way the morbid condition bears analogy to apoplexies in the brain and elsewhere. Charpentier himself, in his elaborate essay on "Diseases of the Placenta," says it is a law that clots are only found in cotyledons of the placenta previously altered by disease. There is a very general consensus of opinion that when effusion of blood takes place into the placenta, it is always, or almost always, from the maternal system; and there are some curious coincidences occasionally noticeable between blood extravasations in the placenta and apoplexies in other parts of the body of the same patient, indicating a feeble resistance in the blood-vessels in more than one organ at the same time.   Latour (" Rev. Med." 1843) has put on record the case of a woman who died of cerebral apoplexy after spontaneous abortion at twenty-eight years.   A painful case occurred in my own practice some years ago illustrating the point.   A lady, most anxious to have children, lost three successively in the latter half of gestation.   In each pregnancy uterine hæmorrhage came on, apparently without cause, and ended in the expulsion of the child before it was viable.   No disease of the child or placenta could be detected, beyond the fact that the twisting or spiral arteries in the centre of each maternal lobule were found to be in a state of partial fatty degeneration.   In the fourth pregnancy, as the result of great care and absolute rest, gestation was carried on to the eighth month, when uterine hæmorrhage set in as before.   The labour being speedy the child was born alive, but within an hour of what seemed a comparatively happy delivery, a sort of convulsive seizure supervened, followed by deep coma, and in two hours later the patient died with all the signs of apoplexy of the base of the brain.

Charles Robin* is one of the chief and explicit exponents of the doctrine that morbid change goes on in the placental tissue preliminary to blood extravasation.   He differs *in toto* from Jacquemier, Verdier, Bustamente, and others, as to the order of pathological events in the placenta.   He insists that no blood extravasations take place in the placenta with-

Société de Biologie.   See " Gazette Médicale," 1854.

out previous disease in the tissue, and the morbid
change which is the most common forerunner of
apoplexy is not mere vascular change, but an alteration of the whole structure of the villus.

As Robin's researches on this subject are regarded
in France as the most important contribution of late
years, I venture to speak of them in some detail.
M. Robin points out that in the early formation of
the chorion a certain proportion of the villi do not
contain vascular loops, but the centre becomes fibro-
cellular, and the nuclei are seen, by the addition of
acetic acid, to be of an elongated form. This centre
is easily distinguished from the elastic sheath, which
retracts and corrugates when lacerated. In some of
these non-vascular villi are fine granules and distinct
drops of oil or fat, highly refracting the light, and
attacked by potash, but not by acetic acid. The
fibro-fatty degeneration of villi is, therefore, according
to Robin, a normal process, by which useless and
non-vascular villi undergo atrophy, but this fibro-
fatty change may become a morbid process, and, by
extending to other and active villi, may first compress
and then obliterate the contained fœtal blood-vessels,
thus producing a solid villus which is composed of
dense fibro-cellular structures admixed with fat, and
whose function is entirely abrogated by the change.
This morbid transformation may occur in the mature
placenta as well as in the earlier stages of its formation, and the ultimate effect is to produce a firmness
and density of tissue, in which it is most difficult to
separate the component elements. The amount of
fatty deposit and its proportion to fibroid change
varies in different cases, and the larger the amount

of fatty granules and molecules, the less distinct are the nuclei of the fibroid structures.

According to Robin, extravasations of blood are always consecutive to placental disease of this or a kindred form, and he contends that this prior change is fibrous obliteration of the villi with fatty degeneration of tissue.

I have mentioned the views of M. Robin here because they have a direct bearing on the production of placental apoplexy, and are associated by him, and those who think with him, as cause and effect—the fibro-fatty degeneration being the invariable precursor of hæmorrhage into the placental substance.

Supposing it to be admitted that some pathological change not unfrequently precedes blood-extravasation into the deeper structures of the placenta, there can be no doubt that effusion of blood takes place with comparative frequency on the maternal or decidual surface of the placenta from other causes. The most common of these causes is an accident of some kind ; or uterine contraction, which tears the utero-placental vessels across, and causes the formation of apoplectic clots between the placenta and uterine walls. Such hæmorrhage may go on to separate the membranes from the uterus down to the os uteri, and then it appears as flooding from the genital passages. If, on the other hand, the results remain at the point of extravasation, the amount of clot may be so considerable that it bulges forward the uterine wall, and can be felt as a projection by abdominal examination, constituting the so-called "concealed hæmorrhage." When the clot is small, it remains in the locality of its formation, and, if pregnancy is not further dis-

K

turbed, it undergoes all the changes peculiar to retained clot elsewhere. Large or small, the clots before disappearing go through various phases. According to Ercolani, the fibrin assumes a lardaceous, yellowish aspect, the appearance of fibrillæ gives place to two kinds of granulations, the one of proteic nature, soluble in alkalies and acetic acid; the other of a fatty nature, resisting these reactive agents. If a clot is to become organised through the process originally described by O. Weber, and afterwards confirmed by Virchow, it may eventually form a distinct neoplasm in the placenta. These neoplasms are rare, but cases have been put on record by Virchow and also by Danyau.

The interference with the life of the child or with the course of gestation depends upon the amount of extravasation, and the excitability or quiescence of the uterine walls under the provocation to contraction.

Inflammation of the Placenta, or *Placentitis*, has been described by Brachet, Dance,* Simpson, Cruveilhier,† and other authors. Simpson described it as consisting of three stages, the first being one of congestion, in which the tissue is engorged by an unusual accumulation of blood in the vessels; the second characterised by the exudations of coagulable lymph, producing a greater density of tissue and eventual induration; the third stage being that in which purulent matter is formed.

Brachet, in the "Revue Médicale" for 1828, gave a very full and precise description of four cases in which the placenta bore a resemblance to the red

* "Report Gén. d'Anat.," tom. iii.   † "Anat. Pathol."

hepatisation of the lungs—was friable, engorged with blood, and dense in tissue. In some sections the structure was yellowish, and strewn with fatty degeneration analogous to fatty liver. He further states that he has seen circumscribed abscesses in the placenta, such as occur in inflammation of other parenchymatous organs. Dance and Brachet both aver that they have seen a deposit of pus covering the entire surface of the placenta, while Jacquemier and Cruveilhier each report the presence of purulent matter as the result of inflammation in the placenta and adjacent uterine veins. Jacquemier teaches, that especially when a portion of the placenta has been separated, inflammation may be set up and pus formed.

In later days a good deal of scepticism has been expressed about the existence of placentitis; at least, so far as its parenchyma or fœtal portion is concerned. Bustamente disbelieves in its existence altogether, and says the evidence rests on the supposed presence of pus, which has been shown to be fallacious; the supposed purulent matter, according to Robin and other observers, being merely pseudo-pus, produced by broken-down fibrin.

It has been further argued that, according to modern theories, inflammation of the placenta is impossible, since there are no capillaries in the maternal portion, and there are no nerves to regulate the contractility of vascular walls in the entire structure. This seems to me not conclusive reasoning. There are fœtal capillary loops in all the active villi, and there are also minute capillaries of maternal origin in processes or dissepiments of the decidua which circumscribe the fœtal villi.

It is true, nevertheless, that the presence of purulent matter in the placenta in most of the reported cases is supported by imperfect evidence. There are only some ten cases of abscess in the placenta recorded, and as no account is given of the microscopic examination of the supposed pus, the evidence is plainly unsatisfactory. Purulent matter has, however, been found and duly authenticated on the surface of the placenta, and in the uterine sinuses at or near the placental site.

That some morbid change analogous to inflammation does take place in the placenta or its neighbourhood, is apparently indicated by the firm adhesions which are occasionally formed between the placenta and the uterine walls,* and from the traces of an exudation which agglutinates and compresses the villi of the placenta. The progress of such inflammatory action is, moreover, often marked by the presence of tenderness over the gravid uterus, with general indications of pyrexia. Braun, Schroeder, and Spiegelberg regard this placental inflammation as not a form of true placentitis, but of chronic endometritis affecting the mucous membrane of the uterus primarily, and only extending to the fœtal structures incidentally. Hegar and Mäier† describe it as a form of interstitial endometritis, in which the villi are agglutinated and compressed by the hyper-

---

* Desormeaux and Dubois say that inflammation not only makes the placenta adhere to the uterus, but also to the fœtus, and so produces monstrosities. On the other hand, Robin holds that adhesions between the placenta and uterus are not due to inflammation, but result from the persistence of the firm condition of the uterine mucous membrane found in the unimpregnated uterus, instead of softening as usual in pregnancy.

† Virchow's "Archiv," 1871.

trophied elements of the serotina, and the development of a new connective tissue.

According to Spiegelberg, it is only through the work of Hegar and Mäier that we have got precise knowledge concerning the so-called inflammation of the placenta. Their memoir is certainly an example of careful work, and is well worth perusal. I regret that I must pass it with so brief a notice. This inflammation begins, according to them, in the formation of soft granular exudation, and ends in the production of induration and disorganisation. The decidual tissue normally consists of elongated cells imbedded in a small quantity of amorphous intercellular substance. When inflammation begins there is an enormous development of fusiform cells with an

Fig. 8.

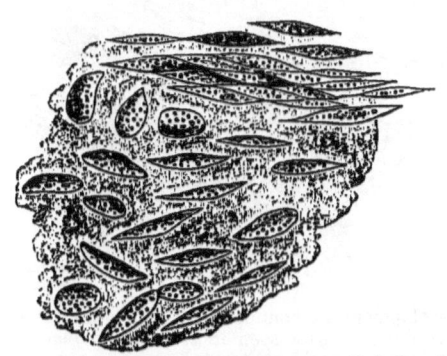

Placental tissue showing granular or slightly striated matrix, with elongated decidual cells, constituting the first stage of interstitial placentitis. (Hegar and Mäier.)

increase of intercellular granular material. Then the cells become deformed, distended with fine fat granules, and eventually the whole structure is converted into fibroid tissue. It is apt to repeat itself in the same individual, and the chronic morbid condition of the mucous membrane, upon which it depends, may lead to earlier abortion in other pregnancies. The recognition of the true cause of this placentitis, as Spiegelberg points out, affords a clue for treatment, and also a hope that its recurrence may be prevented on future occasions.

FIG. 9.

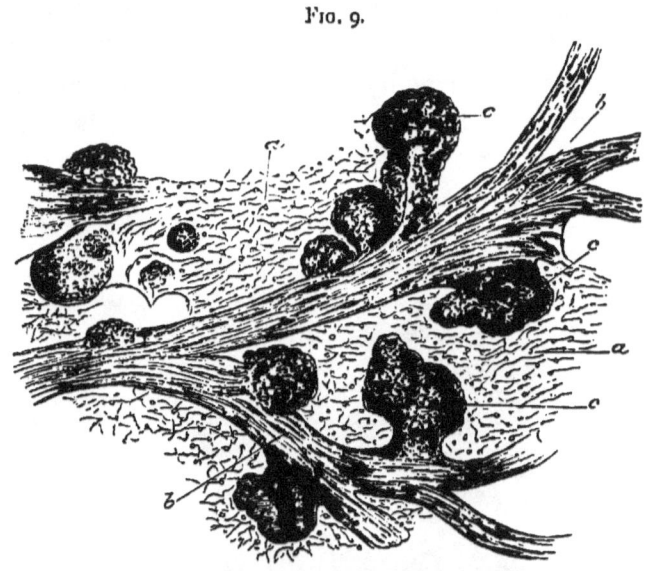

a. Strong development of connective tissue taking the place of the earlier cellular formation seen in the normal placental structure. *b*. Indication of vessels obliterated by the growth of connective tissue. *c*. Extremities of villi atrophied and in fatty degeneration. (Hegar and Mäier.)

Under the influence of this morbid change, the utero-placental vessels and the villi undergo varied modifications, of which the constant result is atrophy and degeneration by compression, in such sort that, passing through various intermediate stages, they become hard, whitish nodules or cords, like old cicatrices, imbedded in the spongy substance of the placenta. This chronic and progressive production of connective tissue, on the surface and in the substance of the placenta, constitutes a work of induration, the net result of which is the obliteration of the double system of fœtal and maternal vessels, and secondary disturbances in the circulation, which are evidenced in thrombosis or in apoplexy more or less extended. The whole morbid process, say these authors, bears the closest resemblance to cirrhosis of the liver.

Neumann * has described a condition which he also regards as produced by inflammation, and which he terms " sclerosis " of the placenta. In this form of disease the villi develop in such luxuriance as to encroach upon the maternal sinuses, and eventually to obliterate them. It may therefore be regarded essentially as an affection of the fœtal part of the placenta. Neumann recognises the fact that this sclerosis of the placenta, in some cases at least, may be the result of an inflammatory process in the decidua, and result in a hyperplasia of its connective tissue.

Meyer,† of Freyburg, while he says that he has never found the condition which Neumann calls " sclerosis of the placenta," describes a morbid process which he has carefully investigated, and which consists of hypertrophic proliferation of the connective tissue in the placenta, with consecutive induration. The more this connective tissue grows, the more the proper parenchyma of the placenta dwindles by pressure and wasting of the vessels ; the whole organ

* " Königsb. Med. Jahrb."
† " Monat. für Geburt.," 1868.

shrivels, and the diminution in the size of the organ results as much from the loss of normal, as the contraction of newly formed tissue. In the normal placenta there is, he says, only a small amount of connective tissue, but there is a large amount in these abnormal cases. This author does not agree with Simpson, Rokitansky, Scanzoni, and others, who suppose inflammation followed by exudation to be the cause of the formation of connective tissue.

There is a sort of general resemblance between the descriptions given by Hegar and Mäier of placentitis originating in the decidual part of the placenta and Meyer's "hypertrophic proliferation of the connective tissue in the placenta." The differences are as to the nature of the process and in the details of microscopic change. Henning has further made an important contribution on the subject of placentitis, and explained how it produces adhesions between the uterus and placenta and membranes.

Placental Phthisis.—At different times, extending over years, I have seen specimens of a disease of the placenta which does not correspond accurately with any of these descriptions. In some of its stages, it bears a close resemblance to morbid changes which have already been described by the authorities I have quoted, and I have endeavoured to trace its connection with these morbid processes. It may, indeed, combine more than one of them in the progress of its development. It differs, nevertheless, in some important particulars of its pathological history, which I shall endeavour to indicate. It has so many analogies to phthisis in the lung, that it may with propriety be named "phthisis of the placenta." Sir James Simpson has previously used the term "placental phthisis;" but he comprehended under this appellation various forms of disease in the placenta which interfere with intra-uterine respiration and nutrition.

In its earlier stages, repeated investigations have convinced me that it is not, primarily at least, a mere increase of the cell structure, nor of the fibroid element in the placenta, as described by Hegar and Mäier, or by Meyer ; but that, in its first stage, it consists of an exudation or deposit, thrown out among the villi, and that it is probably due to some modification of a low inflammatory process.

The disease is not really tubercular in its character, and so far as I can make out it is not associated with any form of bacteria as phthisis is. It seems to me rather the result of an inflammatory process which throws out an exudation or deposit into the parenchyma of the placenta. This deposit may be in masses, or in a more diffused form, and if it be of low organisation, it is prone to crumble in the centre of the masses, thus producing blood extravasation and resulting apoplexies. If the deposit be more sparing in quantity, and endowed with a higher organising power, it becomes gradually converted into fibroid connective tissue, which binds the placental villi firmly together. In either case it seriously cripples the functions of the placenta. The initial deposit separates and compresses the placental villi and prevents their being bathed by the maternal blood. If the deposit breaks down, and apoplectic clots are formed, a considerable portion of the placental structure may be destroyed ; and, lastly, if the fibroid transformation takes place, this so binds and contracts the villi, that all circulation through them is impossible, the cavernous structure is obliterated, and the placenta, in its entirety, or in part, is converted into a dense and inert mass. It depends, of course, on the amount of placenta involved in these morbid changes, as to whether the child lives or dies, and there is an intermediate stage in which the child is born alive, but shows evidence of imperfect nutrition. I have seen a number of instances of this form of placental disease, no two perhaps being exactly alike, and some seeming so dissimilar that they might be taken for different affections. In some placentæ, however, all the various stages may be observed in progress together, thus indicating that they are only different phases of the same pathological condition.

I may state that, as a rule, it is not possible efficiently to inject placentæ of this description, so far at least as the morbid parts are concerned. The finest size injected with considerable pressure will penetrate the vessels of any villi which are comparatively healthy, but none of the injection appears in those which are firmly matted together, proving that the capillaries are occluded or obliterated.

In making microscopic researches, therefore, one has to be content with making thin sections and staining them.

The best example I have met with as illustrating the earlier phases of the disease, is in a placenta preserved in the Middlesex Hospital Museum.

The child was born at the eighth month of gestation, and it was alive, notwithstanding evidence of extensive disease in the placenta, but it seemed to have been imperfectly nourished. The placenta was about the usual size. Several lobules on the uterine surface had lost the usual healthy appearance, and were paler and more prominent than under normal conditions, while to the touch they were firm and resisting. Throughout the whole placenta one could feel indurated portions imbedded in the healthy structure, and some of these extended to the fœtal surface and could be seen as white patches through the membranes there.

On section, the tissue of these firmer portions was found to have lost its normal character, and to have become, so to speak, "hepatized" (*see* Plate I.). These hepatizations were generally situated in the centre of a lobule, with comparatively healthy tissue around, but there were exceptions to this rule, as some masses were irregularly placed. They were in various stages of morbid progress, some of them consisting of mere thickening or induration of tissue from solid infiltration, with no trace of blood globules or blood crystals anywhere; other masses were undergoing a process of crumbling or disintegration in their centre, after the fashion of tubercular masses in the lungs; and in a third form, the disintegration of the centre had attacked both the villi and the blood-vessels; blood was extravasated, and apoplectic clots, limited by layers of fibrin, were undergoing all the usual changes in accordance with the date of their extravasation. In the parts where the changes were more recent, and more or less round the outer borders of all the masses, the villi were found either simply glued together, or they were imbedded in an amorphous or finely granular material somewhat striated, which

was not fat, but consisted of proteic elements not
soluble in the chemical agents which dissolve fat.
Unlike fat granules, the corpuscles of the deposit
were thoroughly coloured by the material used for
staining the microscopic sections.   Here the villi
were as yet but little altered in form, their walls
being only slightly granular or darker in colour, and
blood-vessels were still seen in their interior.   In
portions further advanced, the villi were firmly
adherent to each other, and were becoming disorganized.   Their external membrane was wrinkled
or broken, and their vessels either absent or their
course marked by clusters of minute granules, appearing like exudation from their coats (fig. 10).   Still
further diseased portions, especially where the tissue
was crumbling, showed the villi very much as Dr.
Barnes described and figured them when affected by
fatty degeneration.   The villi were broken up, contained no indications of blood-vessels, and the cellular
structure seemed to have disappeared ; its place now
being taken by amorphous granules, and by spherules
of oil or fat, soluble in ether.

In places, again, where exudation had been poured
out in moderate degree,—and was not undergoing
this retrograde metamorphosis,—the primary round
corpuscles were assuming, or had assumed, an elongated form, as seen in commencing fibroid structure,
and the deposit was being converted into a new connective tissue, firmly binding the villi into one solid
mass, and as it became more organized, completely
interrupting their functions, and rendering those
portions of the placenta dense and inert structures.

Mr. Thurston, lately curator of the museum in

King's College, and now director of the Natural
History Museum in Madras, kindly made sections
and drawings for me (*see* Plate II. fig. I.).

It will be seen that the amount of deposit in some
microscopic sections, taken from parts of the placenta
where the exudation seemed most recent, is so considerable, that it pushes aside altogether the normal
villi. Here and there it crowds them into groups
closely packed together. In one section the field of
the microscope is occupied to a large extent by the
adventitious deposit, instead of sections of villi at
regular intervals. Sometimes the exudation assumes
a somewhat capsular form. The deposit itself is
irregularly striated, and studded with round interspersed corpuscles. There is yet no trace of fatty
change. This is observable only in a later stage,
when disorganisation begins.

Other sections show the effect of softening in producing degeneration of the villi. In the earlier phases
of this degeneration the villi have not yet lost their

FIG. 10.

FIG. 11.

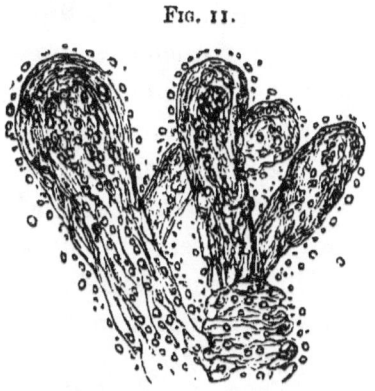

Showing fat granules and
molecules following course
of tortuous capillaries in
villi.

Villi in which all trace of capillary
loop has disappeared, in progress
of disintegration.

cellular structure, but fat granules are seen scattered over their surface, more especially following the course of the tortuous capillaries ramifying in their extremities (figs. 10 and 11). A further stage of this degeneration is indicated in the appearance of villi which have lost all trace of capillary loops,—their outer sheath often broken and retracted, and the cellular structure well-nigh gone, its place being taken by fat granules and oil globules, both on the surface and in their interior.

A notable feature in all the sections where disorganization is not too far advanced, is the great hypertrophy of the contractile coat of the foetal bloodvessels. This is observable in the larger branches, but is most marked in those of intermediate size, before they divide into capillaries. The sections are seen in most microscopic specimens (*see* Plate III. fig. II.), imbedded in the placental substance, and the contractile coat of the artery is observed to be at least twice its ordinary thickness, and marked by the usual minute nuclei arranged in a circular manner round the calibre of the vessel. A similar hypertrophy of the vascular tunics was observed by Frankel in a placenta which he has described as syphilitic, and also by Lawson Tait in his description of a form of placental disease published in the "Transactions of the Obstetrical Society." Lawson Tait regards it as the result of a compensating effort on the part of the arteries to overcome the obstruction found at the extremities of the villi, which eventually ends in their contraction and closure, and looks upon it as analogous to the hypertrophy of the vessels observed in renal disease, and described by Dr.

George Johnson. Hegar and Mäier had previously spoken of this compensating action as likely to lead to extravasation and apoplexy in sounder portions of the placenta.

There is a marked difference between this affection and primary fatty degeneration of the placenta, which is comparable for example with fatty degeneration of muscle. Here there is an adhesive exudation or infiltration distinctly seen to be thrown in among the villi as the first step in the morbid process. In some examples of recent deposit it bears a resemblance to the exudation found in the tissue of the lung in pneumonia as figured for example in Woodhead's "Practical Pathology." The deposit, whatever its exact nature, stops the circulation both foetal and maternal, and the effort to overcome this obstruction probably accounts for the vascular hypertrophy. If the deposit degenerates because of its foreign origin—which it may do as one of the results of the pathological process—it produces also degeneration of the villi, which gradually break up and soften. Thus cavities are formed which become full of blood. In places again where no softening takes place, the exudation becomes organized, and produces a density of tissue, quite unlike that found in the normal placenta.

Some time ago a placenta was kindly sent to me by Dr. Hunt, of Dalston. The patient, after giving birth to two healthy children, had a series of miscarriages at six and a half months, without any known cause. The child usually died about a fortnight before its birth. There was no syphilitic history.

In this case the placenta was smaller than at the

full time ; denser throughout than in the normal state, and was of a paler colour than usual, having a waxy or fatty appearance. Some portions were much firmer than others, and between these firmer portions were parts of comparatively spongy tissue. Here and there were small apoplectic cavities, but none of large size, and they were for the most part old, the blood being changed in colour, and having the appearance of cysts with thickened walls. Some of these cavities were contracted to very small dimensions, and interspersed here and there were cicatrices or patches of indurated tissue, which, from their surroundings, give the impression of blood cysts which had become obliterated by contraction.

The microscopic sections showed pretty uniformly throughout the placenta, except where disease had produced further disorganisation, an exudation thrown in among the villi—in one place separating them widely from each other—in other places crowding them together, so that over the field of the microscope they were most irregularly distributed. The exudation or deposit was in some sections finely granular or molecular, with indications of striæ ; in other sections it had a more distinct fibrous appearance, being constituted of very fine wavy fibrillæ, dotted at intervals with small rounded corpuscles. In portions of the placenta where the exudation was obviously older and the structure more consolidated, the villi were seen to be fused together, by a firm fibroid tissue, having all the characters of connective tissue elsewhere. Here the villi themselves had lost all trace of their ordinary cellular structure, and contained no vessels in their interior. They were shrunken and atrophied, the stems fibroid in structure, with interspersed fat granules. The extremities were misshapen and shrivelled, and had dark masses of amorphous granules occupying their interior. The villi were, in fact, disorganized and imbedded in a fibroid matrix. (See fig. 12.)

FIG. 12.

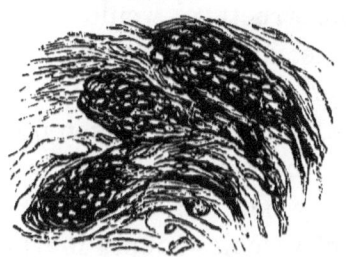

Distorted and atrophied villi imbedded in
fibrous stroma.

In this specimen, as in the preceding one, the coats of the blood vessels were much hypertrophied. This hypertrophy is well shown in the drawing by Mr. Thurston in Plate III. fig. II.

There is a specimen preserved in the Hunterian Museum, which I was permitted to examine. The catalogue shows that "the fœtus was at the eighth month of utero-gestation, and was born dead, with a small diseased placenta. The whole organ had a yellowish, bloodless aspect, and in various parts were flattened circular nodules of amber yellow colour, and thicker than the rest of the placenta. They were not unlike syphilitic gummata. Under the microscope they appeared to have been due to an inflammatory process, altered or followed by fatty degeneration."

" The woman had borne four children previous to

L

her last pregnancy, and two were of weak intellect. No distinct history of syphilis could be obtained."

The above is the account of the preparation taken from the museum catalogue.

The placenta was small and contracted in its entire dimensions. It was of a whitish grey colour, and its tissue was firm and condensed throughout. The component structures would not separate, being hard and brittle, and indissolubly united together. It was well-nigh impossible to tease out a portion for the microscope, but a small broken fragment or a thin section showed the remains of the villi stunted and shrunken. They had lost all cellular structure, and all indication of vascular supply in their extremities, but a section of their trunks still showed the apertures indicating the position of the now contracted arteries and veins in their interior. The villi were now represented by fibroid structures with or without fat granules, and the uniting medium which bound them so firmly together was fibrous connective tissue, either in the form of long fusiform cells, or fully grown fibrous tissue with interspersed nuclei. Plate III. fig. II. is from a drawing by Mr. Thurston of a microscopic section of this placenta.

I might give details of other cases, but I have selected these as illustrating what I am disposed to regard as variations of the same pathological process, originating in a low form of placentitis. The later stages correspond very closely in the results produced, with certain pathological conditions which have been described by eminent authorities I have mentioned under different names, and not necessarily associated with an inflammatory process.

None of the authors seem to have noticed the crumbling in masses of feeble organization in the midst of the placental structure, and the formation of apoplexies in this way. Hegar and Mäier indeed compare the induration of the placenta constituting the later stage of placentitis as they have observed it, to cirrhosis of the liver, and the limited hæmorrhages connected with it to collateral fluxions of blood. The irregular distribution throws increased pressure upon parts of the placenta already weakened by softening, but where the circulation has not yet been obliterated, —and so apoplexy occurs.

It seems to me not difficult to trace the links which unite these various pathological changes occurring in the placenta. They are probably all the result of an inflammatory process assuming different forms. It may be a refinement in pathological precision to insist with Hegar and Mäier that the origin of the inflammation is always in the maternal portion of the placenta, which corresponds to the uterine mucous membrane; and more especially when exudation or deposit is poured out equally into the various structures which form the parenchyma of the placenta, but it would be of some importance if the origin of the pathological processes could be so localized, because, as remarked by Spiegelberg, we should thus have a cue to treatment on the side of the mother, in her subsequent pregnancies. Spiegelberg says inflammation of the placenta is apt to repeat itself in the same individual, and the chronic morbid condition of the mucous membrane upon which it depends may lead to earlier abortion in other pregnancies.

It should be further remarked that not only may

inflammatory changes in the placenta, such as those described, destroy the child or impair its nutrition, but they may favour placental retention at the time of delivery. This may be either by producing adhesions to the uterine walls, or as maintained by Hegar and Mäier in the monograph previously mentioned, by lessening the cohesion of parts of the placenta,—in such wise that even with the ordinary uterine contractions, or as the result of even moderate traction on the umbilical cord to promote the expulsion of the placenta, some solution of continuity may take place, and thus portions of the placenta may be left adherent in the uterine cavity.

So far as I have observed this affection of the placenta, it is most frequently chronic in its course and gradually impairs the function of the organ, until it eventually destroys the child. In some exceptional cases, nevertheless, it seems to run a more rapid course. I have occasionally seen dead children born plump and well nourished, with a placenta so largely affected with the first stage of infiltration that intra-uterine respiration could no longer be maintained, and the history in these cases has been that the fœtal movements after being unduly restless for a short period, ceased altogether a few days before labour came on. The well-nourished condition of the child seemed to indicate that the disease was of recent origin, and killed the child more speedily than by slowly starving it, as in the more chronic form usually observed.

As to the cause or causes of these morbid changes in the placenta, they may be approximately stated to be those which produce impairment of the general health and deterioration in the maternal blood. The patient in the first case I have narrated was not at the time the subject of phthisis, but her family were strumous, and she had lost other children from disease of the placenta. I have seen other cases associated with anæmia, and also with syphilis. In anæmia, it is well known there is a deficiency of red globules in the blood, with a larger proportion of fibrin. This, as well as syphilis and other conditions, may predispose to a low form of inflammation in the placenta, as in other organs of the body, and to such pathological changes as those described.

To recapitulate, therefore, in the order of successive changes observable in this form of placental disease, we have first hepatization or solidification of tissue from exudation. Then softening may take place in the centre of masses of exudation, if the exudation is sufficiently abundant and of low organization,—and as the result of this softening, cavities are formed as in phthisis of the lung, which become full of blood, and constitute one of the forms of so-called apoplexy of the placenta. When the exudation or deposit, which produces hepatization, is endowed with higher vitality— and this may be when it is more sparing in quantity and thus remains in closer proximity to active structures—it does not break down or crumble, as in the preceding case, but becomes organized into fibroid tissue, going through the processes which have been described by other authors. The placenta is thus rendered firm and dense, and its function, as an organ for intra-uterine respiration and nutrition, is completely abrogated. This stage bears an analogy to the change in the lung which is termed " fibroid phthisis," or as Hegar and Mäier have put it, to cirrhosis of the liver.

Fatty Degeneration of the placenta, as first described by Dr. Barnes * in this country, is, according to the author named, analogous to fatty change attacking other organs, as the heart and arteries, for example. In its simplest form it is seen in cases where the death of the child has arisen from some other cause than disesase in the placenta. In the case of a child which died near the full time from intra-uterine small-pox, and was retained some time after, all the villi, as well as the maternal portion of the placenta which I examined, were crowded with oil-globules and compound granular fat particles. The villi were swollen and œdematous, and their external covering was readily separated. The entire placenta was paler and softer than usual, and contained an abundance of serous fluid in all its meshes. Dr. Barnes is careful to draw a distinction between this sort of passive fatty change following the death of the fœtus, which he calls "fatty transformation," as distinguished from "fatty degeneration," which, according to him, commences previously in the placenta, and, if extensive enough, kills the child. This he calls "true fatty degeneration," and compares it to the fatty degeneration of the brain, liver, and muscles occurring in the adult. It is characterised by the morbid changes being partial, invading one or more cotyledons, and the diseased masses are often imbedded in the midst of healthy tissue. The child may be living if only limited portions of the placenta are diseased. If the disease in extensive,

* "Medico-Chir. Trans.," 1851, &c.

it kills the child, and there is an intermediate stage in which the child lives, but its nutrition is interfered with, and it becomes puny and starved. Dr. Barnes figures both the decidual cells forming the maternal part of the placenta, and also the fœtal villi studded everywhere with fat globules. The villi are brittle and firmer than natural. Under the microscope they are seen to be thickly covered with oil-globules ; the proper structures are disorganized ; and the blood-vessels, which are empty, have their courses marked out by the clusters of oil-molecules which follow their tortuous course.

FIG. 13.

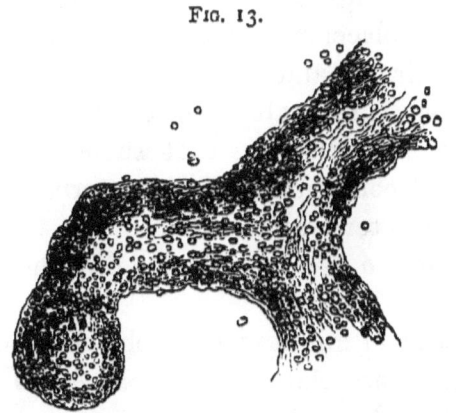

Fatty degeneration of placental villus. (Barnes.)

Kilian * had, prior to Barnes, written on "A New Disease of the Placenta," which partly anticipated Dr. Barnes's observations on "fatty placenta ;" and, soon after Barnes, C. Robin published his monograph, to which I have previously alluded. Robin, as we have seen, does not believe in a purely fatty degeneration, and regards the fibrous transformation of the

* "Neue Zeitschr. für Geburt.," 1850.

villi in so-called fatty placenta as the chief lesion, the fatty deposit being associated with it only as a complication in the obliteration of the villi.

The description of Barnes is certainly accurate so far as some phases of placental change are concerned. The question is whether fatty degeneration of the placenta during the life of the child really occurs as a primary pathological change, or is invariably preceded by some exudation or other morbid process which initiates the fatty metamorphosis. Adventitious deposits are more liable to fatty degeneration than normal tissues; and it is to be noted that, in the majority of examples where fatty degeneration has attacked the placenta, the portions affected are not softer, but firmer and denser, than usual, the villi being almost inseparably united together. It is conceivable, nevertheless, that some depraved and impoverished conditions of the maternal blood may lead to such deterioration of vitality in the placenta, that it begins to degenerate and die, and thus kills the fœtus.

The deposit of minute fatty molecules and of larger oil-globules is associated with most forms of morbid change in the placenta—in some stages, at least. In consonance with the general law that effete and useless parts of the organism undergo degeneration into fat, and so are more amenable to absorption, the placental structures, when altered by disease so far as to be unfit for the exercise of their normal function, begin to undergo fatty change, and this results in atrophy of the part affected.

Fatty degeneration, whether it occurs as a primary change or is the secondary effect of some other pathological condition which precedes it, may produce softening and disorganization of the placental tissue, and so favour extravasation of blood or apoplexy. In other placentæ it leads to atrophy. All the structures shrivel and condense, so that the organ seems like a mass of dense fibroid tissue; it undergoes, in fact, the fibrous transformation which I have previously described. The tendency of modern investigators is evidently to regard fatty degeneration not as a primitive change, but a phase or stage of some other morbid condition which precedes it or is associated with it.

Dr. Druitt[*] regarded fatty degeneration of the placenta as a normal condition towards the end of pregnancy, and as preparatory to detachment at the time of delivery. For him, therefore, fatty degeneration was only the extension to a morbid degree of a condition which exists normally to a certain extent towards the end of pregnancy in all placentæ. There is, it is true, some amount of fatty change towards the end of pregnancy in certain portions of the after-birth which have now no active purpose to serve. This is notable round the margins and in the membranes. The nuclei in the epithelial cells of the amnion are surrounded with a ring of fat particles in nearly all placentæ at the full term; but normally there is no fatty degeneration in the potential villi as pregnancy advances, and it is obvious that the nutritive and respiratory functions have to be carried on for the well-being of the child just as actively up to the termination of pregnancy as at any previous period.

[*] " Lancet," 1853.

Hiffelsein and Laboulbène,* Charpentier, Simpson,† Goodell,‡ Whitaker,§ Cowan,‖ and others, have all made contributions to the subject, and all regard it, however it may arise, as intimately associated with the processes which produce destruction of fœtal life.

Ercolani has describd as synonymous with fatty degeneration of the placenta what he calls " cellular hyperplasia and hypertrophy of the parenchyma of the placental villi." He agrees with the general accuracy of Robin's observations in regarding the presence of fat-granules with fibroid degeneration of the villi as an accidental and not essential complication. The firm and dense placentæ, which have been written upon by Bustamente and Neumann as " sclerosis of the placenta," he considers as essentially due to a hyperplasia not of the connective tissue, but to a cellular hypertrophy of the parenchyma of the villi, either simple or complicated with obliteration of the contained vessels, and also in some cases with lesion of the glandular organ or decidual covering.

It is obvious from the description that the disease described by Ercolani is different from fatty degeneration as described by Barnes, and I have not seen any specimen having the exact characters as those described by Ercolani.

Myxoma Fibrosum.—Virchow has described a very curious morbid transformation of the villi of the placenta, which he terms "myxoma fibrosum." It is quite different from the cellular or fibrous degenera-

---

* " Soc. de Biolog.," 1865.   † " Obstet. Works."
‡ " American Journal of Obstet.," vol. ii.
§ *Ibid.* 1870.   ‖ " Ediu. Med. Journ.," 1854.

tion of the villi described by Ercolani and Robin. It
consists of such enlargement of the stems and villi by
fibroid hypertrophy that they form in some cases

Fig. 14.

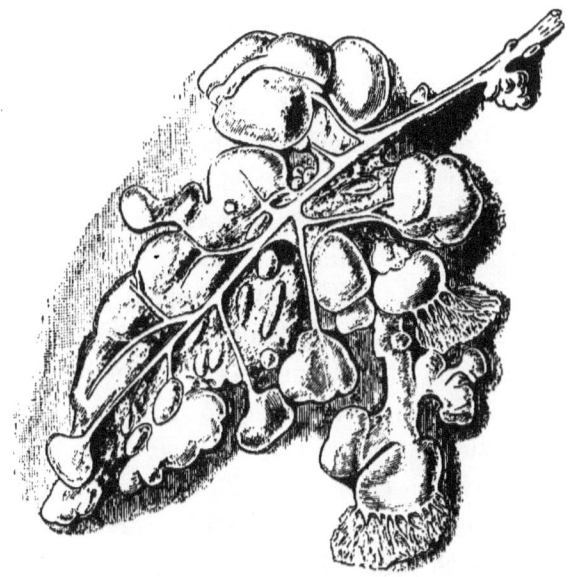

Myxoma fibrosum of the placenta. Virchow (after Storch.)

distinct tumours in the placental structure. The
cases are somewhat rare, but I saw two excellent

Fig. 15.

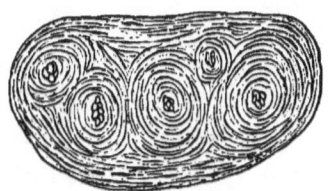

Section of a tumour showing fibroid structure.

examples in Copenhagen which have been described
in Virchow's "Archiv" in 1878, by Storch.

In one, the tumours were as large as hazel-nuts, attached by pedicles to the deeper seated trunks of the placental villi, and, when an incision was made into the substance of the placenta, they projected through the opening like so many adherent hard nodules, or perhaps I may say digitated radishes. Microscopic examination showed that they were composed entirely of fibroid elements formed by a cellular hyperplasia of the central part of the villi, and that they were enlargements or excrescences on the villus trunks, with an external arrangement somewhat analogous in appearance to cystic chorion. Virchow regards the disease as a transformation of the mucous element pertaining to the villus structure into fibroid tissue, instead of the soft myxoma which is seen in cystic chorion. The fibroid change is, however, unlike the cystic chorion, more frequently connected with the later period of pregnancy, although indications of it are sometimes seen in the earlier months, and, therefore, it is described as a disease of the fully developed placenta. Hildebrandt has also described a good example in the "Mon. für Geburt." Bd. xxxi. ; and Dr. Sinclair, of Boston, United States,* another. It is probable that the case of sarcoma in the placenta given by Hyrtl is one of the same kind. In Storch's first case the child was born alive, but feeble, and died an hour after birth. If the placenta is only partially affected, the child, though emaciated, may live ; if the disease is more universal, the child dies.

Œdema, or Dropsy of the Placenta, is characterized by serous infiltration of the villi, by increased soft-

* "Journal of the Obstetrical Society of Boston," 1871.

ness and succulence of texture, by paler colour, and by marked friability. There is not necessarily fatty degeneration, but the outer covering of the villi is more easily broken and detached than usual. Generally the placenta looks larger and heavier in all its dimensions, and its weight before it is drained is greater. The child with such a placenta is often still-born prematurely, and it may be even dead. When born alive it has been found poorly nourished, and sometimes dropsical. The effect on the fœtus of course varies with the extent of the mischief, but if very extensive the serous effusion is supposed to compress the fœtal blood-vessels, and obstruct the double circulation of the placenta. Some authors have regarded it as a post-mortem change, but this is not so in all cases, for children have been born alive with marked œdema of the placenta. Lange[*] found it associated with hydramnios, and generally with chlorois in the mother.

Barnes has observed it in association with hydræmia of the mother, with anasarca and dropsy connected with kidney or other visceral disease, and also with dropsy and peritonitis in the fœtus. On this last point it may be remarked that Charpentier in three cases was unable to find any morbid lesion in the fœtus. Joulin[†] suggests that it is due to some obstruction in the circulation of the umbilical cord, or in the circulatory organs of the fœtus, distending the villi and producing hypertrophy with serous effusion. Simpson found œdema of the placenta associated with obstruction in the cord, but this is evidently only one of the causes or complica-

[*] "Geburtshülfe."   [†] See Whittaker.

tions. Scanzoni* regards it as analogous to cystic dilatation of the chorion villi, but arising in later pregnancy, and the dropsy exists more especially between the villi, instead of in their interior. Klob† avers that œdema predisposes to apoplexy. In this affection the child may not only lose its life from interruption in its circulation, but it may be from its premature birth, as the œdematous placenta, besides being large in itself, is commonly associated with superabundance of liquor amnii, and these together may so distend the uterus beyond what it will bear, that premature uterine action may come on.

Melanosis of the placenta has been described by Ercolani, Henning,‡ and other authors. It does not seem to be in itself a specific disease, but rather an incident and effect of other morbid conditions, and it deserves a passing notice as occasionally associated with disease and death of the fœtus. The tissue of the placenta is stained black or deep purple in detached portions or larger masses; and the colour has commonly been attributed to blood extravasation. Latterly, however, it has been shown to be due to the deposit of granules of hæmatoidin from the colouring matter of the blood. It is situated in the villi or their pedicles, and is free—not contained in cells. Henning believes it due to heart disease or changes in the blood of the fœtus, and Wedl§ noticed it in connection with œdema of the cellular tissue in a child. Heschl thought that deposits of

* " Lehrbuch der Gerburt."
† " Path. Anat. d Weibl. Sexualorgan."
‡ " Studien über den Bau der Mensch. Pl.," 1872.
§ " Allgem. Pathol.," Uhle and Wagner.

pigment only took place when the hæmatin abandons the globules of the blood and becomes attached to the vascular walls, and Ercolani, in quoting Heschl, in connection with his own observations on the subject, considers it especially interesting as indicating the way in which materials pass from the mother to the fœtus through the placenta. He believes he has proved that the hæmatoidin contained in solution is absorbed by the serotinal cells, where it leaves traces, and is then transmitted or secreted into the substance of the villi, where it chiefly accumulates. The pigment granules are formed about the utero-placental or maternal vessels, or infiltrated into the cells which limit the lacunæ, and they reappear in equal if not larger number in the interior of the fœtal villi.

Calcareous or osseous concretions in the placenta have received a considerable amount of attention, as it was supposed they were indications of a degeneration which might influence the life of the child, and besides had some relation to diathesis or conditions of health in the mother which it might be desirable to counteract for successful pregnancy. Practically it has been found that calcareous depositions in certain portions of the placenta, and even in comparative abundance, may be present without compromising the existence of pregnancy or the child's life. The commonest form is shown on the uterine surface, where stellated or irregular patches, hard and gritty, are often seen studded over the decidual membrane. They are not distinctly crystalline, but amorphous, and under the microscope resemble fragments of chalk aggregated together as they might appear to the naked eye if larger. Acetic acid does not affect them, but they are dissolved by nitric acid with effervescence. Robin states that they are formed in the cells of the decidua and are composed of carbonates and phosphates of lime and magnesia. It is sometimes easy to dissect off the decidual layer of the placenta, and with this carry off the chief part of the chalky spicules, which may be well seen in the dried preparation. They follow the decidua, however, into the inter-cotyledonary spaces when the decidua dips inwards to form boundaries to the maternal lacunæ.

Besides being in the decidua, they have been found to exist in the extremities of the villi and in their pedicles. Lobstein, Meckel, and Cruveilhier considered them as ossifications of the capillary walls of the vessels, and Späth, according to Whittaker,[*] regarded them as superfluous lime salts in the blood of the fœtus, which are deposited in the extreme capillaries. Decker and Millet[†] found a placenta with more than 200 calculi adherent to the vascular ramifications, the largest of the size of a nut. They are frequently associated with adherent placenta, and Garin mentions an instance where the deposit was three lines in thickness. Another case is mentioned by Carestria, where fully half the placenta was involved, and where the chalky substance formed plates on the fœtal surface. They seem particularly prone to develop themselves in any adventitious deposit, and as placental adhesions are no doubt due in some cases at least to inflammatory action in the decidua during pregnancy, this probably accounts for

* " American Journ. of Obstet.," vol. iii.
† *See* Ercolani.

their frequent presence in cases of adherent placenta. They are found at all periods of pregnancy, but more especially at the full period of gestation, and hence Heschl* thought that they were but indications of the ripeness or maturity of the after-birth— all placentæ at full term showing some signs both of fatty and calcareous change. In an observation in a case of calcareous placenta made by Ercolani, all the villi were affected by fibrous transformation; and this author believes that the calcareous productions are but a metamorphosis of adipose substance in degenerating decidual cells. Lobstein thought they were indicative of protracted gestation, but, according to Späth, of nineteen cases in which calcareous concretions were present, there was only one in which there was a probability of over-maturity of the fœtus. Of the nineteen cases, however, there was one of congenital rachitis, one of spina bifida with hydrocephalus, and one of slight hydrocephalus. (Whittaker.) The presence of·calcareous deposits in the placenta, therefore, seems associated with some pathological conditions un-favourable to the welfare of the child, although the adverse influence does not proceed far enough in most cases to extinguish life. Madame Boivin remarked that it was reproduced several times in the same woman, and Carus affirms that it occurs oftener in some countries than in others. Dr. Barnes alleges that calcareous deposits are frequently associated with scrofula, tuberculosis, and poor living, and he draws a parallel between such deposits occasionally found in the brain in tubercular subjects, but more

* *See* Whittaker.

especially between such deposits found in the tubercular lung—the lung in the air-breathing subject being the homologue of the placenta *in utero*. It must be admitted, nevertheless, that calcareous concretions of the placenta are very frequent in seemingly healthy mothers, who produce well-developed children. I have found them in placentæ of women unusually robust, and have imagined they were sometimes at least the product of a gouty diathesis, more especially as this diathesis was distinctly traceable in the family history.

As may be inferred from these observations, calcareous deposition in the placenta takes place as the result of various causes. It may occur as one of the pathological results of degeneration of tissue, and it may occur from constitutional conditions present in the mother or child influencing the composition of the blood.

Cysts of the Placenta have been described by several authors. These are not to be confounded with cystic chorion, being situated commonly on the fœtal surface between the chorion and amnion, or in the substance of the fully developed placenta. They occur singly or there may be several. Those which lie between the chorion and amnion sometimes attain a considerable size, and project towards the amniotic cavity. They are commonly like vesicles more or less translucent, with slightly turbid contents, the turbidity being due to fat granules with disintegrating fibrin and perhaps the débris of blood corpuscles. They have been supposed by Millet* to be filled with fluid identical with the gelatin of Wharton in the cord,

---

* *Vide* Ercolani.

and to be offshoots indeed from this; and it is possible such an explanation may account for some of the varieties, but for others a different origin must be sought.

Bustamente believed some of the cysts at least to be the result of previous blood extravasation or hæmatocele, and this explanation is probably the true one, for many of those which are imbedded in the substance of the placenta. As Ercolani suggests, the term cyst in these cases is obviously incorrect. In some apparent cyst-like cavities projecting forward beneath the membranes on the fœtal surface, the cavity is filled with coagulated fibrin, and the remains of disintegrated blood, while the walls are formed of laminæ of fibrin and degenerated and compressed placental villi. In one of Ercolani's cases a large number of small calcareous concretions were found mixed up with the fibrous laminæ forming the so-called cyst wall.

A good specimen of a serous cyst developed on the fœtal surface of the placenta, and having two coverings, showing it to be both beneath the chorion and the amnion, is to be found in St. Thomas's Museum.

Tumours of various kinds have been described as occurring in the placenta. Klob mentions a case which occurred in the Rokitansky Institute, where a fibroid tumour of nearly the size of a child's head was found loosely adherent between the amnion and the inner surface of the placenta near the cord. Tumours of less size have been put on record by Danyau*—one of them eleven centimètres in length and eight in breadth. It was on the fœtal surface

* " Memoir sur deux cas de Tumeurs volum, &c."

of the placenta, covered by the membranes, and near the circumference. It was slightly lobulated and enclosed in a sort of capsule. It was dense like scirrhus, and was hard and resistant on section, like a fibroid. Blood-vessels were found on its surface and penetrating to its interior. Whittaker mentions a remarkable specimen in the Hyrtl collection, which like the last was attached to the fœtal surface. It had a vascular connection with the placental mass, and was like a placentula or supplementary placenta. In structure, however, it was found to be sarcomatous.

Other so-called tumours are no doubt the result of blood extravasations, the bulk of the mass being made up of clot and disintegrating villi in various grades of transformation. Barnes mentions one of this character in St. George's Hospital, and others are to be found in the museums. When of this kind they are of all sizes, and may appear like tubercles or projections on the fœtal surface of the placenta, covered by the amnion, or they may be so large as to project as a mass towards the amniotic cavity. If it be true that blood clots may become organized, as taught by Weber, Virchow, and others, some of the apparent neoplasms may originally have been blood clots ; but it is certain that others are simply hyperplasias or hypertrophies in previously existing structures.

Syphilitic Placentæ.—It is important, if possible, to answer the question, Is there a syphilitic placenta? —that is, a form of disease in the placenta associated with syphilis which may be recognized by examination. Much diversity of opinion has been expressed concerning this matter, and various descriptions have been given of the syphilitic placenta which do not agree.

That syphilis is a potent cause of placental disease and abortion has been recognized by some of the oldest authors. Astruc mentioned it as far back as 1796, but Murat (according to Deschamp*) was the first to describe certain appearances as belonging to the syphilitic placenta. To illustrate the diversity of opinions in recent times, I may mention that Verdier regards a thickening of the arterial walls produced by a form of arteritis in the fœtal part of the placenta as characteristic of syphilis. After thickening, the vascular walls degenerate, and the vessels become obstructed. Rokitansky[†] associated some of the fibrinous deposits found in the placenta with the syphilitic taint. These had a syphilitic aspect on section, whatever that may mean. Lebert,[‡] before him, had observed yellow granulations which had the same structure as tubercles, but he did not regard them as of special importance.

Gusserow and Klebs[§] observed a morbid hyperplasia of the decidual cells in a case where the father was syphilitic, but Straussman[||] and Madame Kaschewarowa have since shown the same changes in the placenta where there was no suspicion of syphilis. Virchow,[¶] who always brings a certain originality into his work, has made some observations on syphilitic placentæ. Virchow points out that in

---

* " Thése," 1880.
† " Lehrbuch der Path. Anat."
‡ " Comptes rendus," 1852.
§ Virchow, " Archiv," Bd. xxvii. s.
|| " Verhandl. d. Berlin Geburts.," 1863.
¶ " Path. der Geschw.," Bd. ii.

studying this subject we must remember the envelopes consist of two portions, the fœtal and the maternal. He then proceeds to point out that syphilis may produce two forms of endometritis during pregnancy, the one attacking that part of the decidua which enters into the formation of the placenta, the other the parietal decidua, or vera, which is away from the placental spot. The first form produces thickening and fibrous induration which may cause atrophy of the villi. In the second form the most marked effects were shown upon the decidua vera. It was thickened and covered on its uterine side with growths almost polypoid, composed of very vascular proliferating mucous tissue, with no trace of fatty degeneration. Virchow considers this change is analogous to mucous papulæ, or flat condylomata, observed elsewhere on mucous membranes in connection with syphilis.

Straussman has thrown some doubt on the supposed specific character of this lesion by finding it in the case of a mother who had not the least symptom of venereal disease. Henning regards these proliferations as simple angiomas. Virchow's observations on this subject seem to me to refer rather to the effects of syphilis on the ovular membranes in early pregnancy than to the full-grown placenta. Fränkel[*] is the author whose researches in later days have received most attention in Germany and France, and they bear the impress of great care. Fränkel's conclusions, which he says are founded on the examination of over one hundred placentæ, point distinctly in favour of there being a syphilitic placenta, which may be recognized by certain definite characteristics. The placentæ

[*] " Arch. für Gynäkol.," 1873.

mostly belonged to syphilitic, mature, or immature children, and he took the indications pointed out by Wagner, of Berlin,* as peculiar to syphilitic fœtuses, to be unfailing evidence that syphilis was present. Wagner has pointed out that in all syphilitic children there is a peculiar band of tissue between the shaft of the bone and the cartilage of the epiphysis, which is in a state of inflammatory irritation. The microscope, as well as the naked eye, shows that the changes thus produced are unlike any other changes, and consequently are specific. Taking this test as a basis, Fränkel states that the evidences of placental syphilis vary according as to whether the syphilitic virus is derived from the mother or the father. If from the male parent, the villi constituting the fœtal part of the placenta are chiefly or primarily affected, but the disease may extend thence to the maternal part. The villi undergo a peculiar cellular hypertrophy, with thickening and proliferation of their epithelial covering, which alters and distorts their form in a remarkable manner. There is a particularly marked hypertrophy in the coats of the vessels, with consecutive obliteration of their canals. This morbid change Fränkel calls by the awkward name of "disfiguring granulation-cell disease." The placentæ in their entirety were in the early stage of the disease unusually large, notwithstanding that in most cases the fœtuses were atrophied and shrivelled. After the hypertrophy, came one of atrophy, in which the vessels were completely obstructed, the epithelial covering of the villi disintegrated, and fatty degeneration in full progress. Fränkel insists strongly on one

* Virch. "Arch.," Bd. i. p. 305.

point, namely, that although fatty degeneration of the villi, blood extravasations, &c., may be present in

FIG. 16.

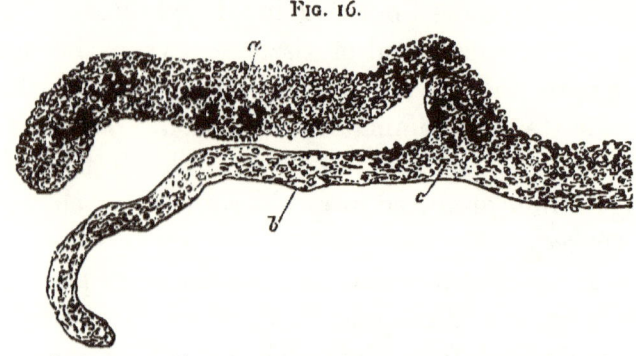

Villus of placenta, affected with "disfiguring granulation-cell disease." (Fränkel.) *a.* Portion of villus covered with granulation cells; *b.* normal villus deprived of its epithelial covering by maceration; *c.* junction between sound and diseased structure.

placental syphilis, they are secondary, the primary disturbance being increase in the normal cells of the villi, a revolutionary growth brought about by diseased blood.

When the mother was the subject of syphilis the pathological lesion was more complex, and the changes were especially marked in the decidual or maternal part of the placenta, but also might extend by contiguity to the villi or fœtal portion. The changes in the decidua took the form of disease described by Virchow as placental endometritis, or by Slavjansky* and Kleinwächter† as "placentaris gummosa." These consisted of increased growth of the connective tissue, and enormous hypertrophy of the large decidual cells, these so crowding and compressing the villi that their circulation was interrupted, and the result was interference with the nutrition and

* "Prager Vierteljahrs.," 1871. † *Ibid.,* Bd. cxiv.

placental respiration of the fœtus. I believe Henning was the first to call attention to the intimate

Fig. 17.

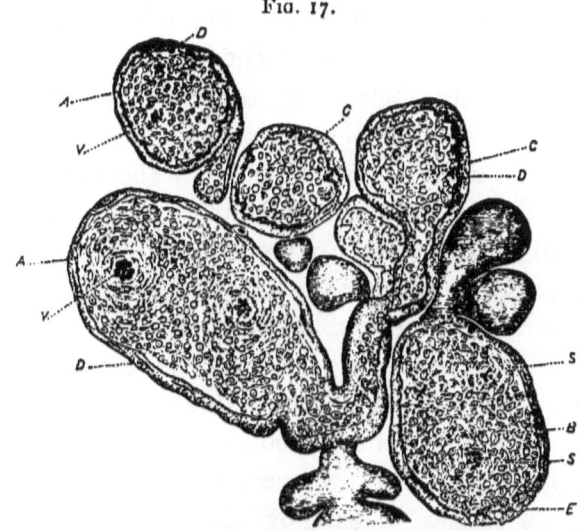

Section of villi affected with "disfiguring granulation cell disease." *A.A.* Luxuriant cell development in the interior; *V.V.* lumen of blood-vessels with hypertrophied walls; *B.* villus in which only a trace of blood-vessels can be seen at *S.S*; *C.* villus without trace of vascular canal; *D.* epithelial covering. (Fränkel.)

relation of the cell-growth to the vessels in syphilitic placenta, and his observations are confirmed by Fränkel. If both father and mother were syphilitic, the lesion was of course a mixed one, and in all there were variations, consisting of changes of colour, dark hyperæmic patches, alternating with paler structure, and frequently smaller or larger blood extravasations.

The late Dr. Angus Macdonald,* of Edinburgh, wrote a paper confirming these observations of Fränkel, and asserted that although the syphilitic placenta may be mistaken for a fatty placenta, and,

* "Obstetrical Journal," 1875-6.

in fact, had been so mistaken by Kilian and Robin, this is easily rectified by miscroscopic examination. In these cases the death of the fœtus is the result of progressively increasing defective blood-supply, owing to the changes described.

I have on different occasions had the opportunity of examining placentæ in the early months of gestation with certain peculiarities of morbid change which I considered were undoubtedly due to syphilis, and which bore some resemblance to Fränkel's descriptions. For example, I examined the placentæ in two separate pregnancies of the same individual. She had contracted syphilis immediately after her marriage, and at the same time became pregnant. During the early part of her pregnancy the vulva became the seat of specific sores, mucous tubercles, and warts. Later her body was covered with patches of syphilitic psoriasis. She miscarried in both the first and second pregnancies in the fifth month. Both the placentæ exhibited changes very closely resembling each other. On the uterine side of the placenta the decidua was much thickened, and there was great increase of all the cellular and fibroid structures which normally constitute that membrane. Prolongations of this dense tissue were sent down into the substance of the placenta, and seemed to terminate about half-way through its thickness. The effect of this dense layer was apparently to compress and contract the sinuses or lacunæ, to do away with the spongy character of the organ, and so to prevent the growth of the villi into the sinuses. The villi next to this layer were stunted and atrophied. Those near the fœtal surface were hypertrophied, and were beginning to undergo fibroid or fatty degeneration or both. In all the microscopic sections, hypertrophy of the arterial coats in the fœtal blood-vessels was noted, and those nearest the maternal surface were absolutely obliterated. Here was a case in which syphilis in the mother was clear and distinct, and where the changes in the maternal portion of the placenta were most marked, supporting the doctrine that it is this portion which is most affected when the mother is syphilitic in early pregnancy.

So far as my observation goes, I do not think we are yet able to say with precision that any one specific lesion of the placenta belongs alone to syphilis, although some morbid appearances are more constant than others in connection with syphilis, as, for example, the changes described by Fränkel. In addition to the hypertrophy of the villi delineated by Fränkel, and the morbid changes in the decidua just described, I have seen fibroid deposits, such as those observed by Rokitansky, some unchanged, others undergoing fatty transformation. Again, I have seen the yellowish granulations of varying sizes looking like tubercles as observed by Lebert, but I have also seen most, if not all, of these pathological appearances where no syphilitic history could be traced. The nearest approach to precision in this respect is to say that, as a general rule, when the decidual or maternal portion of the placenta has become so far changed by hyperplasia as to arrest the utero-placental circulation and the full development of the placental villi, that this is probably due to maternal syphilis. It finds its analogy in the changes which take place in the mucous membrane in the uterus and elsewhere when the blood is undoubtedly poisoned by syphilis, and also in the thickening of the decidua during the early pregnancy of syphilitic women, which has been described by Virchow and Dohrn as "endometritis papulosa et tuberosa." When fibrinous and pseudo-tubercular deposits are found in the placenta in connection with syphilis, they are probably only the expression of a depraved or impoverished condition of the blood, which may be equally associated with anæmia or with some form of dyscrasia. When there is marked hypertrophy and degeneration of the villi, the maternal portion of the placenta being less affected, the syphilitic taint more probably comes from the male parent, and the mother may show no signs of the disease. Both Depaul and Tarnier, among modern observers, dispute the existence of absolutely specific lesions in the placenta as the result of syphilis.

De Sinéty, one of the latest writers quoted by Charpentier, did not find placental lesions in all women affected with syphilis, but where lesions were present he was able to demonstrate three important points : (1) Hypertrophy of the placental villi ; (2) fibrous degeneration of them ; (3) islands of granulation belonging to the caseous form of degeneration. This coincidence of the fibrous and caseous forms of degeneration is found in syphilitic gumma, notably in gummata of the liver. De Sinéty had not found this combined degeneration except in syphilis. He does not know if any other disease may produce the combined changes, and does not decide the question as to a specific placental lesion in connection with syphilis.

In reference to all diseases which affect the placenta, it is to be noted that the effect on the life of the child bears a direct relation to the amount of damage done to its tissues, and impairing its double function as an organ for respiration and absorption. In cases of separation of the placenta a portion still adherent to the uterine walls may be enough to sustain the life of the child, for a time at least, and, in like manner, when the placenta has become diseased, if some portions of it only remain sound, vitality may still be maintained in the body of the fœtus. If the morbid process be slow and chronic, there will probably be progressive emaciation, and if the child be born alive it will have all the appearances of being starved during its development. If the placental disease is more acute and rapid, and affecting a large area of tissue, the child's movements become at first more restless than usual, and then become less marked and distinct as they subside into absolute quiescence. With the aid of the stethoscope the beats of the fœtal heart have repeatedly been noted in cases of suspected placental disease to become slower and slower, and thus to furnish important indications for the induction of premature labour.

Among the further causes of fœtal death *in utero* which I cannot here overtake are the pathological conditions of the umbilical cord, ante-partum hæmorrhage, extra-uterine gestation, and allied conditions, the malformations and diseases of the unborn child— the most fertile cause of the latter probably being syphilis.

Did time permit I might say something besides, concerning the changes taking place in the body of

the fœtus when it is long contained in the uterus
after its death ; of the inferences to be drawn as to
the cause of its death from the appearances it presents after long or shorter periods of retention, and
other kindred topics.

I must, however, hasten to say a few words on the
subject of preventive treatment.

Treatment.—And now, it may be asked, what are
the remedies suggested for these many and varying
causes of intra-uterine death ? The answer must,
I fear, in regard to a large number of them, be considered as eminently unsatisfactory. Notwithstanding all that has been done, we are yet only on the
threshold of those investigations which must reveal
to us eventually the best methods of obviating death
in unborn children. In the meantime, so far as the
prevention of some of the forms of intra-uterine death
is concerned, we are absolutely in the dark, and the
therapeutics of the subject are still as a closed book.

Fortunately this need not be said of all. A careful
study of the several pathological conditions in the
parents, combined with the local expression of the
results of those conditions, enables us in some cases to
formulate methods of treatment and lay down rules
for guidance which in practice have been attended
with happy results.

Whenever, therefore, a woman has once or more
frequently lost the product of conception at an early
or later period, careful inquiry should be made into
the health of both parents, and any previous history
of illness should be accurately scrutinised. If the constitution of either parent be found at fault, measures
must be taken to amend this. The question of

syphilis is so important, and the venereal poison is so persistent and all-pervading, that no pains must be spared to ascertain whether this is the root of the misadventures. If a patient has once had syphilis it is impossible to say when the effects on the constitution have entirely passed away, and many men who have believed themselves to be cured and free from every taint of the disease, find the evidence still remaining in their wives' frequent abortions, or in the indications of syphilis in their living children. When, therefore, either patient has suffered from syphilis in the near or distant past, and the wife has recurring abortion, or has her children die *in utero* at a later period of gestation, the presumption is that syphilis is the cause. Both parents ought at once to be put under anti-syphilitic treatment before a fresh conception is permitted, and this ought to be sufficiently prolonged to give it a fair chance of producing satisfactory results. Diday recommends that the physician should not be contented with submitting both parents to anti-syphilitic treatment prior to the occurrence of pregnancy, but that with each successive pregnancy, as it occurs, the mother should at once recommence a mercurial course, even if she has no visible indications of the disease. I can testify that I have repeatedly seen good effects from small doses of bichloride of mercury, with bark, given during the first three months of gestation, when there has been no opportunity of commencing the treatment before conception began ; and under this method, with a careful diet and régime, women who had repeatedly miscarried before went to the full time.

Similar favourable results have been observed to follow the administration of iodide of potassium. M. Goshkevich, quoted in the " Brit. Med. Journal " (July 1, 1885), advises its use in habitual abortion, even when no syphilitic symptoms have been recognized, and testifies to its utility in saving fœtal life. It must be left for the medical man in charge of a case to determine whether in any given case some of the approved forms of mercurial treatment are most appropriate, or a course of iodide of potassium. Possibly both may be judiciously combined, or one course succeed the other. Depaul has such confidence in mercurial treatment that he urges it should be adopted in all cases of recurring abortion, even when no syphilitic history is traceable in either parent. Charpentier, by way of enforcing this precept, records a case in which a woman had four consecutive abortions without known cause, and in which both parents not only denied any knowledge of syphilis, but no traces of the disease could be found upon them. The two parents were then subjected to an anti-syphilitic course, and two children were born subsequently quite healthy, and with no trace of disease upon them.

I may mention, for what it is worth, the case of a patient who had aborted in five successive pregnancies. In the sixth she was salivated by accident in the third month. On this occasion she went her full time, and was delivered of a living child.

In attempting to form a just estimate of the effects of mercurial treatment in syphilitic cases, it is but fair to say that the venereal poison has a natural tendency to attenuate itself and wear out, in such way, that, apart from treatment, pregnancy may at length be continued to the normal term in women who have repeatedly miscarried from this cause before. In these cases each successive pregnancy may have longer duration, until eventually a living child is born. The value of mercurial treatment is nevertheless almost universally acknowledged. So far as my reading goes, there is only one notable dissentient to its utility. Desprès, a French author, looks upon mercury as the cause of all the evils which it is expected to remedy, and to be itself a cause of abortion. It is probable that some of the forms of mercury (the bichloride, for example) in very small doses over a continued period, and so regulated as not to produce ptyalism, have a beneficial effect in other than syphilitic cases, for more than one reason. The treatment certainly has a good effect on some constitutions. It restores the secretions, regulates the bowels, and, if combined with bark, improves the appetite and aids nutrition. I have frequently seen patients fatten while taking the bichloride. Further, it is an acknowledged remedy for certain forms of uterine hypertrophy, and more especially acts on the mucous membrane. In those instances, therefore, where the uterine walls are thickened, and their elasticity impaired—in those cases where chronic endometritis so hinders the formative power of the uterine mucous membrane that a faulty or diseased decidua is produced—an alterative mercurial course may best fulfil the indication of treatment demanded, and indirectly hinder the repetition of abortion. If inquiry shows that the health of either parent is disordered or deranged from some other cause than syphilis, care must be taken to trace out the nature of the deviation in health, and so to define it that treatment fulfils its purpose. It cannot be too much insisted upon that not the mother only, but the father also, must be put under supervision. If there is any constitutional peculiarity or diathesis, it must be met by appropriate means—the strumous diathesis by tonics and cod-liver oil, with such improved climatic conditions as may be feasible ; the gouty rheumatic by limitations of diet, careful regimen, and alkaline medicines. The gouty rheumatic constitution is often associated with congestion of the portal circulation, and this may become so important a factor in bringing on abortion that it deserves special mention. The late Dr. Edward Rigby constantly dwelt on the importance of keeping the bowels from being constipated in women liable to abortion, and he preferred saline aperients to aloes or other drastic purgatives, as easier in action and less likely to be injurious during pregnancy. The effect of carefully regulating the bowels is to lessen the tendency to congestion in the pelvic organs, and so aid in averting engorgement of the fœtal membranes and placenta. Care must be taken to choose such laxatives as are not likely to stimulate undue action of the bowels or straining, else the medicines may stir up the very mischief they are given to avoid. Compounds of sulphur, like the German compound liquorice powder, the confection of senna, and saline aperients seem best to fulfil the needful indications. Venesection has been recommended in cases of general plethora, and local depletion, where local congestion seemed to threaten abortion from the pain and sense of engorgement which it entailed. General bloodletting is now rarely employed in these instances. Its advantages are doubtful, and its employment may lead to harm instead of good. Where fainting is produced in the mother, the embryo may be destroyed and abortion follow. Local depletion by leeches is less objectionable, and leeches applied round the anus, as the best point for abstracting blood, will readily relieve tension in the hæmorrhoidal vessels. They may require repetition two or three times during the early months of gestation, if indications of congestion recur ; and as a rule they are of most use when applied just before the time which corresponds to the catamenial period.

The constitutional condition which, next to syphilis, seems to hold the most prominent place as predisposing to abortion, is anæmia, and for this it is plain a plan of treatment is called for the very opposite to a depleting one. Preparations of iron must be administered in some form least likely to disturb the digestive organs of the patient ; and these should be given not only antecedent to the occurrence of conception, but they should be continued with such modifications and in such combinations as may be suitable during the progress of pregnancy. It has been thought by some that iron is counter-indicated when gestation has once commenced, as it might favour the occurrence of abortion by inducing hæmorrhage. As a general rule there is no ground for this supposition, and iron, if cautiously given, may be taken by anæmic patients throughout pregnancy without harm. There is often the greatest tolerance of it where it is most urgently needed.

Cazeaux remarks that in ordinary pregnancy a state of chlorosis is produced—there is a relative anæmia, for there is a diminution of red globules, with increase of fibrin in the blood. A slight increase, therefore, of this anæmia may have the effect of deranging the progress of gestation by lessening the nutrition of the fœtus and by predisposing to fibrinous deposits in the placenta or membranes.

It is probable that some of the forms of degeneration found in the fœtal membranes and placenta are due to defects in the constitution of the blood in one or both parents. Whether the fault lies with the male or the female parent may not be easily determined. If there is obvious anæmia or deterioration of health in one or other, it may be enough to place the one apparently deranged under treatment ; but this indication not being forthcoming, it will be desirable to put both parents on iron, combined, perhaps, with quinine, arsenic, or other tonic remedies, as may seem suitable in each particular case.

Where local conditions have been ascertained or suspected to be the cause of repeated abortion, or of later fœtal death, the treatment must be directed in accordance with the special requirements of the case. Especial care should be taken to remove as far as possible all indications of endometritis prior to the commencement of pregnancy, as an unhealthy condition of the lining membrane of the uterus is regarded by most authorities as a potent cause of disease in the fœtal membranes and placenta.

In all instances where past experience has proved the proneness to miscarriage, it is an essential part of any plan of treatment that the patient should be habitually at rest in the recumbent position, so that the uterus may be affected as little as possible by the effects of gravitation. It is doubtful in most cases whether the patient should be entirely precluded from taking exercise and fresh air, lest the general health should so suffer as to undo some of the advantages of rest. This point deserves especial consideration, so far as anæmic and naturally bilious patients are concerned, both suffering if deprived of fresh air and exercise. A moderate amount of walking out of doors may, therefore, be permitted, with repose in the recumbent posture at other times. All carriage exercise and other forms of locomotion likely to jar the body should be sedulously avoided, and a carrying chair may be advantageously used to take the patient up and down stairs.

While this latitude of movement is permitted ordinarily, absolute rest on the sofa or in bed should be enjoined at the times which correspond to the days of the catamenial period. A greater tendency to abort has been noted at those times than at others, and, if abortion does not immediately take place then, damage is done, which culminates in miscarriage later, and is traced back to the menstrual epoch for its first symptoms. At those times, even during pregnancy, there is a nisus often distinctly observable in increased discomfort, or in some other way. It appears like a periodical tidal wave, which, in weakly women or those liable to go wrong, readily overflows its barriers, and ends in abortion. The influence of this menstrual wave is so fully acknowledged at all times in women, that, by common consent, operations are avoided during its continuance, in order to avoid the period of local hyperæmia with which it is accompanied. Charpentier remarks that, in certain women who abort frequently without known cause, there seems to be a peculiar irritability of the uterine fibre. The sphincter uteri seems weakened, and, when pregnancy occurs, the smallest effort promotes its dilatation. Irritability also determines premature contractions, and the sphincter being weak it easily yields, and so abortion occurs. It is obvious that in these cases, whatever else is prescribed, absolute rest in the recumbent posture is imperative so long as the irritability remains.

To Sir James Simpson we owe the suggestion that, in all cases where there is reason to believe the placenta is partially disabled by disease, chlorate of potash should be given, with the object of keeping the child alive during its further detention *in utero*. Simpson's theory was that, because chlorate of potash contained six atoms of oxygen to one of chlorine and one of potassium, it would sensibly increase the amount of oxygen in the mother's blood, and afford a larger proportion of this element for the placental respiration of the fœtus. The maternal blood-current being thus more abundantly charged with oxygen than under ordinary circumstances, a smaller portion of sound placenta could absorb more for the requirements of the fœtus, and so supplement the function of those parts of the organ damaged or destroyed. Whether this theory be true or not, it is certain that many practitioners have testified to its utility as well as to its harmlessness. Dr. Playfair suggests that it may act, in virtue of its tonic properties, on the constitution of the mother; and I think it may

act usefully as an alkaline salt in preventing the
formation of coagula and fibrinous deposits in the
placenta.   It is given in ten or fifteen grain doses
three times a day, and may be administered at any
period of pregnancy, but it is believed to be most
useful in the latter half.

The induction of premature labour, also recommended by Simpson as a means of averting the death
of the child *in utero*, is only available in those cases
where it dies in successive pregnancies after the
expiration of the seventh month.   At any period
antecedent to this the child would not be viable, or
would be so feeble that nothing would be gained by
the proceeding.   But in a limited number of instances
it has been observed that placental disease begins
apparently just before the seventh month, and
gradually and steadily advances until it kills the
child and its movements cease to be felt by the
mother.   With such experience of past times to
guide the practitioner, the induction of labour is
perfectly justifiable if the movements of the child
continue to be felt after the seventh month is completed ; and the operation is the more imperative if
the movements grow slower and feebler, and the
stethoscope indicates a declension of strength in the
beating of the fœtal heart.   In this way children's
lives have been saved which would probably have
been sacrificed by further delay.

In patients where intra-uterine death is threatened
or feared as the result of some form of poison, inorganic or organic, to which I have alluded, the
treatment must necessarily consist in removal of
the cause.   In those special instances where the pro-

gress of zymotic disease or of inflammation in some organ of the patient's body is attended with high temperature, it is possible some attempt may be made to avert the usual consequences so far as the pregnancy is concerned. As the experiments of Runge and others have shown that peril comes to the child *in utero* directly the temperature of the mother rises persistently up to 105°. while the infant's temperature rises still higher, it may be possible, in the progress of therapeutics, not only to keep down the general maternal hyperpyrexia, but I would throw out the suggestion that, where it is feasible, an attempt should be made to lower also the temperature of the uterus and of the fœtus, either by the application of ice-bags to the maternal abdomen, or of those tubular appliances so ingeniously invented for the application of cold, and which may be modified to fit any part of the body.

When all our most ingenious methods of diagnosis and treatment are exhausted in attempting to obviate intra-uterine death, there will still be a large number of cases in which no further clue can be found than an obvious constitutional feebleness, permanent or temporary, in one or both parents. In some of these the organic weakness or degeneration in health may be of such character that it is hopeless to expect a remedy, and perhaps it is well for the race in general that such constitutional faults or diseases should not be perpetuated in progeny. But where the constitutional weakness may be but temporary, attempts should be made to resuscitate the health. Everything that science and practice teaches to be useful for the restoration of strength in single organs and in the entire system should be called into requisition.

Boerhaave is said to have recommended horse-riding as a remedy for abortion. In any case where this proved useful it would probably be by improving the general health. Apropos of this I may mention a case within my own experience of a lady in India who, after aborting several times under the most careful system of rest—in some pregnancies amounting to absolute repose for many months in the recumbent posture—at length gave up the hope of bearing children, and took to riding on horseback, not only before a fresh gestation began, but after she had reason to believe that she was again pregnant. As the result she went for the first time to the full period, and was delivered of a living child.

Some of the baths and waters on the Continent have a high reputation for their tonic properties and their favourable influence on pregnancy. Aix-les-Bains is said to be useful in these cases. I have seen courses at Schwalbach and Kissingen followed by happy results. Schwalbach, perhaps, is more appropriate for patients who are more or less anæmic; Kissingen for those in whom the digestion and portal system are at fault. One successful case is fresh in my memory, where a mother who had previously borne healthy children was stricken with severe pleuro-pneumonia, and continued for some time after in comparatively feeble health, although she resumed her place in society again after an interval. Not long afterwards she conceived, and at the end of six months lost her child. A little later a fresh pregnancy occurred, and this terminated, apparently without cause, at the end of four months. After this she went to Kissingen, experienced a notable improvement in health, and subsequently bore two healthy children without misadventure.

My task is now ended, however imperfectly it may have been completed. I have had a sense, in giving these lectures, as of rushing rapidly through a harvest field,—rich in pathological facts and illustrations,—and plucking a few ears by the way, while I have left an abundant crop to be garnered by any who may be able and willing to undertake the work.

PLATE I.

FIG. I.—The larger half of a placenta, showing in section infiltration of low inflammatory deposit, and apoplexies, formed by the breaking down of tissue. The child was born alive.

FIG. II.—A portion of the same placenta, showing masses of dense deposit, in contrast with the normal spongy tissue in its neighbourhood.

FIG. III.—A portion of the same placenta in section, showing deposit of low organization crumbling in the centre.

Specimen in Middlesex Hospital.

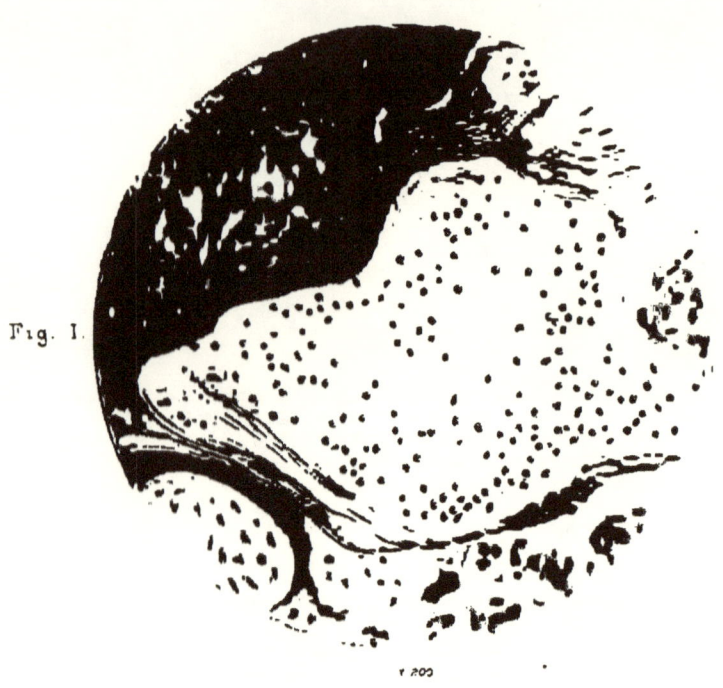

Fig. I.

r 200

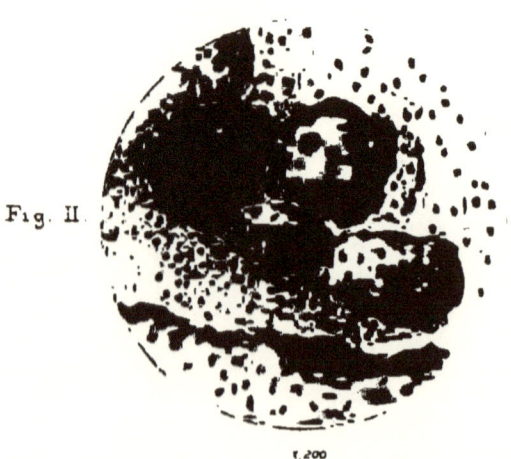

Fig. II.

r. 200

E. Thurston del   E. Burgess ch lith

PLATE II.

FIG. I.—Inflammatory deposit between the placental villi; pushing them aside and compressing them. The mass of deposit in the centre is almost structureless, and surrounded by a pseudo-capsule.

From Specimen in Middlesex Hospital.

FIG. II.—Microscopic section of a placenta, showing sections of atrophied and deformed villi, their vessels being obliterated. They are embedded in a fibroid stroma, which has contracted upon them.

Coll. of Surgeons Specimen.

Plate III

Fig. 1

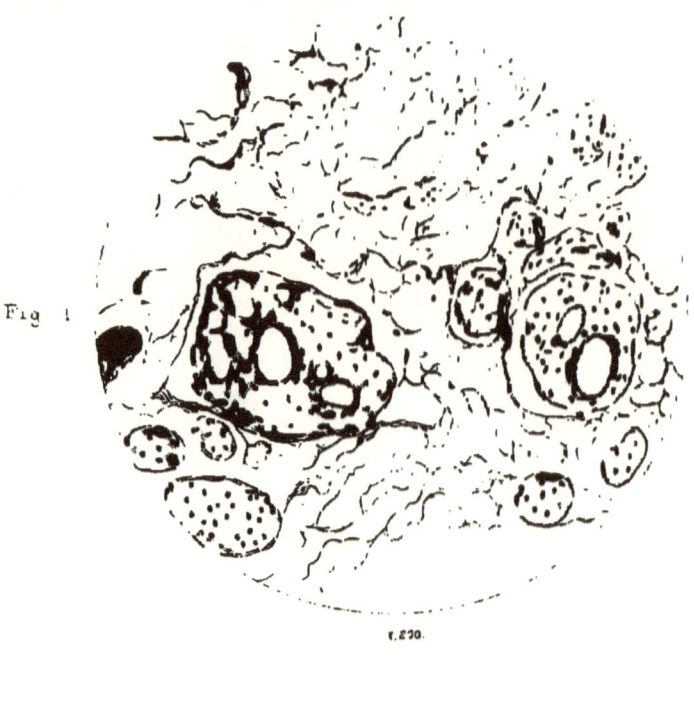

1.270.

Fig. II.

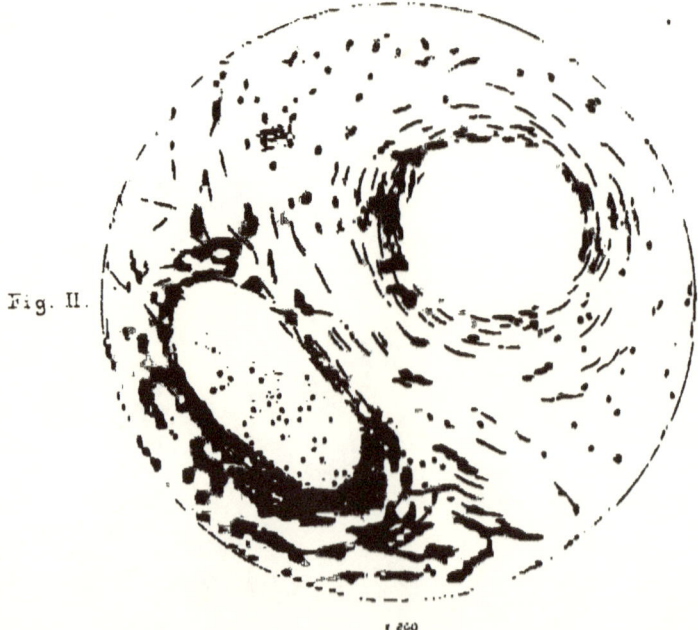

1.200.

PLATE III.

FIG. I.—Microscopic section of a placenta, showing the commencing conversion into fibroid tissue of inflammatory deposit between the villi.

King's Coll. Specimen.

FIG. II.—Microscopic section of the same placenta, showing great hypertrophy of vascular walls, and enlarged calibre of vessels.

King's Coll. Specimen.

INDEX.

ABORTION, frequent repetition of, 1–5
 chlorate of potash in, 182
 climate, predisposing to, 23
 deterioration of health, a cause of, 22
 difficulty of producing, in some cases, 5
 early, often overlooked, 12
 epidemics of, 29
 ergot as a cause of, 30
 frequency of, 6
 from syphilis in male, 17
  in female, 58
 impaired vitality a cause of, 14
 in animals, 14, 22, 27
 in connection with albuminuria, 49
  diabetes, 53
  phthisis, 51
 in trees and plants, 23, 27
 iodide of potassium in, 176
 iron in, 179
 mercury in treatment of, 175
 more frequent in later life, 28
 preventive treatment of, 174
 produced by losses of blood, 25
 ratio of, to pregnancies, 9
 sieges and famines producing, 30
 statistics of, 7, 8, 9
Acephalocysts in uterus, 95–112
" Adhesive endometritis," 88
Acute diseases, as a cause of intra-uterine death, 31
Age, as cause of intra-uterine death, 27
Altitude, as a cause of intra-uterine death, 27
Amnion, morbid changes in, 112
 adhesions of, 114

Amnion, blood extravasations into, 113
    development of, 112
    dropsy of, 115
    effects of rupture of, 113
    fragile structure of, 113
    inflammation of, 113
"Amniotic hydrorrhœa," 91
Anæmia, 25
    treatment of, 179
Antiseptic surgery as a preventive of intra-uterine death, 67
Apoplexy of ovum, 79–83

Carbonic acid poisoning a cause of abortion, 48
Catamenial period, uterus irritable during, 67
"Catarrhal endometritis," 90
"Cervical pregnancy," 75
Chlorate of potash in cases of intra-uterine death, 182
Cholera a cause of abortion, 55
Chorion, morbid changes in, 92
    partial disease of, 108
    cystic or vesicular, 92
        causes of, 110
        condition of embryo in, 105, 108
        different views concerning, 95
        essentially a product of pregnancy, 111
        forced into walls of uterus, 105
        its relation to death of embryo, 108
        minute structure of, 98
        period of its occurrence, 106
        relation of the decidua to, 103
        retention of, for long periods, 112
"Chronic diffuse endometritis," 85
Cod-liver oil in cases of intra-uterine death, 178

Decidua, structure of, 70
    apoplectic, 76
    arrested development of, 73
    atrophy of, 73
    congestion of, 84
    diseases of, 76
    fatty degeneration of, 81
    hypertrophy of, 74–87
    inflammation of, 85
    its liability to extravasations, 76
    reflexa, hæmorrhage into, 78
    weakness of, 75

Dysmenorrhœal membranes, 71

Eclampsia, causing fœtal death, 49
    temperature in, 50
Endometritis, causing inflammation of placenta, 132
    "interstitial," 132
Epidemics of abortion, 29
Ergot, as producing abortion, 30

Fertilising fluid, defects in, 15
Fœtal appendages, diseases of, 70
Fœtus, appearances of, after death from pyrexia, 46

Gastric irritation, producing abortion, 67

Habit of aborting, 5
Heart disease as cause of intra-uterine death, 55
Horse-riding during pregnancy, 185
Hydramnios, 114
    causes of, 116
    diabetes in connection with, 117
    effects and symptoms of, 115
    pathology of, 117
    period of its occurrence, 116
"Hydrorrhœa," 90
Hyperpyrexia a cause of intra-uterine death, 39
    treatment of, during pregnancy, 184

Induction of premature labour, 183
Inflammation of uterus as cause of intra-uterine death, 63
Injuries of uterus, &c., causing intra-uterine death, 65
Interbreeding as cause of intra-uterine death, 27
Intra-uterine death, causes referable to father, 15
    causes referable to mother, 22
    classification of causes, 14
    direct and specific causes of, 31
    in connection with diabetes, 53
        with albuminuria, 51
    over- and under-feeding causing, 23
    preventive treatment of, 174
Iodide of potassium in abortion, 176
Iron, influence of, on pregnancy, 179
Irritations, various, causing intra-uterine death, 65

Jaundice a cause of fœtal death, 54

LEAD-POISONING, 17, 57
Leucorrhœa, its relation to abortion, 63
Local conditions inducing abortion, 61
   treatment of, when causing intra-uterine death, 180

MALE parent may be cause of intra-uterine death, 15
   should be treated in some cases, 174
" Menstrual wave," importance of observing, 67, 181
Mental influences on pregnancy, 68
Mercurial treatment in syphilis, 175
Mineral waters and baths, 185
Moles, " cystic " and " carneous," 92, 104
Mortality, fœtal, in late periods of gestation, 11
Myxoma of chorion, 97
   partial, 106
" Myxoma fibrosum," 154

OPERATIONS during pregnancy, 67
Ovum, shape of, 70
   apoplexy of, 79
   insertion of, 74

PELVIC adhesions as cause of abortion, 64
Phthisis in relation to fœtal death, 51
Placenta, disease of, produced by general congestions, 57-61
   abscesses in, 132
   adhesions of, 132-136
   apoplexy of, 123
      its relation to other forms of apoplexy, 126
      generally preceded by degeneration, 126
   at third month, 120
   calcareous concretions in, 159
   " cellular hyperplasia," &c., of, 154
   congestion of, 123
   cysts and tumours of, 162-3
   diseases of, 119
   "disfiguring granulation-cell disease " of, 167
   early circulation in, 121
      structure of, 120
   extravasations in, 121
   exudations in, 133-137
   fatty degeneration of, 150
      a normal process, 153
   fibro-fatty degeneration in, 128
   hæmatosis of, 124
   hepatisation of, 131-139

Placenta, "hypertrophy of connective tissue " in, 133, 135, 145
    inflammation of, 130
    melanosis of, 158
    œdema of, 136
    organization of clots in, 130
    phthisis of, 136
    prævia, origin of, 74
    " sclerosis " of, 135
    syphilitic, 164
        a potent cause of abortion, 165
        opinions concerning, 165
        summary of conclusions, 172
    theories of disease in, 119
    thrombosis of, 125
Placental phthisis, 136
    syphilis, 164
        treatment of, 175
    villi, fibro-fatty degeneration of, 127
Placentitis, 130
    pathology of, 131
Pleurisy in pregnancy, 38
Plural births, 27
Pneumonia in pregnancy, 36
Poisoned blood a cause of abortion, 47, 57
Poisons, organic and inorganic, in pregnancy, 57
" Polypoid endometritis," 89
Prematurity as cause of intra-uterine death, 27
Procreating power different from development, 16
Purgatives in habitual abortion, 178
Pyrexia in relation to intra-uterine death, 39

" QUICKENING," abortion at time of, 13

REFLEX causes of abortion, 65
Rest, importance of, in preventing intra-uterine death, 181

SATURNINE intoxication, abortion from, 17, 57
Sieges and famine producing abortion, 29
Small-pox a cause of intra-uterine death, 31
Syphilis in the male, abortion from, 17
    in female, intra-uterine death from, 58
        causes disease in fœtal appendages, 61
        laws concerning its influence, 60
        prevention of, 59
Syphilitic placenta, 164

TEMPERATURE, high, a cause of fœtal death, 39
    fœtal, higher than maternal, 41
    Runge's experiments on, 40
Treatment, preventive, of intra-uterine death, 174
    anti-syphilitic, 175
    by baths and waters, 185
        chlorate of potash, 182
        iron, by cod-liver oil, &c., 178-9
    importance of rest in, 181
    of hyperpyrexia during pregnancy, 184

UTERINE congestion, &c., as cause of abortion, 62
    displacements, 64
    hæmorrhage, 129
        " concealed," 129
    inflammation and ulceration, 63
    other diseases, 64

VENESECTION generally to be avoided during pregnancy, 179
Vesicular chorion, 92
Villi, placental, fibro-fatty degeneration of, 123

PRINTED BY BALLANTYNE, HANSON AND CO.
LONDON AND EDINBURGH

SELECTION

FROM

J. & A. CHURCHILL'S GENERAL CATALOGUE

COMPRISING

ALL RECENT WORKS PUBLISHED BY THEM

ON THE

ART AND SCIENCE OF MEDICINE

N.B.—As far as possible, this List is arranged in the order in which medical study is usually pursued.

J. & A. CHURCHILL publish for the following Institutions and Public Bodies:—

ROYAL COLLEGE OF SURGEONS.
CATALOGUES OF THE MUSEUM.
Twenty-three separate Catalogues (List and Prices can be obtained of J. & A. CHURCHILL).

GUY'S HOSPITAL.
REPORTS BY THE MEDICAL AND SURGICAL STAFF.
Vol. XXVIII., Third Series. 7s. 6d.
FORMULÆ USED IN THE HOSPITAL IN ADDITION TO THOSE
IN THE B.P. 1s. 6d.

LONDON HOSPITAL.
PHARMACOPŒIA OF THE HOSPITAL. 3s.
CLINICAL LECTURES AND REPORTS BY THE MEDICAL AND
SURGICAL STAFF. Vols. I. to IV. 7s. 6d. each.

ST. BARTHOLOMEW'S HOSPITAL.
CATALOGUE OF THE ANATOMICAL AND PATHOLOGICAL
MUSEUM. Vol. I.—Pathology. 15s. Vol. II.—Teratology, Anatomy
and Physiology, Botany. 7s. 6d.

ST. GEORGE'S HOSPITAL.
REPORTS BY THE MEDICAL AND SURGICAL STAFF.
The last Volume (X.) was issued in 1880. Price 7s. 6d.
CATALOGUE OF THE PATHOLOGICAL MUSEUM. 15s.
SUPPLEMENTARY CATALOGUE (1882). 5s.

ST. THOMAS'S HOSPITAL.
REPORTS BY THE MEDICAL AND SURGICAL STAFF.
Annually. Vol. XV., New Series. 7s. 6d.

MIDDLESEX HOSPITAL.
CATALOGUE OF THE PATHOLOGICAL MUSEUM. 12s.

WESTMINSTER HOSPITAL.
REPORTS BY THE MEDICAL AND SURGICAL STAFF.
Annually. Vol. II. 6s.

ROYAL LONDON OPHTHALMIC HOSPITAL.
REPORTS BY THE MEDICAL AND SURGICAL STAFF.
Occasionally. Vol. XI., Part IV. 5s.

OPHTHALMOLOGICAL SOCIETY OF THE UNITED KINGDOM.
TRANSACTIONS.
Vol. VI. 12s. 6d.

MEDICO-PSYCHOLOGICAL ASSOCIATION.
JOURNAL OF MENTAL SCIENCE.
Quarterly. 3s. 6d. each, or 14s. per annum.

PHARMACEUTICAL SOCIETY OF GREAT BRITAIN.
PHARMACEUTICAL JOURNAL AND TRANSACTIONS.
Every Saturday. 4d. each, or 20s. per annum, post free.

BRITISH PHARMACEUTICAL CONFERENCE.
YEAR BOOK OF PHARMACY.
In December. 10s.

BRITISH DENTAL ASSOCIATION.
JOURNAL OF THE ASSOCIATION AND MONTHLY REVIEW
OF DENTAL SURGERY.
On the 15th of each Month. 6d. each, or 7s. per annum, post free.

A SELECTION

FROM

J. & A. CHURCHILL'S GENERAL CATALOGUE,

COMPRISING

ALL RECENT WORKS PUBLISHED BY THEM ON THE ART AND SCIENCE OF MEDICINE.

N.B.—*J. & A. Churchill's Descriptive List of Works on Chemistry, Materia Medica, Pharmacy, Botany, Photography, Zoology, the Microscope, and other Branches of Science, can be had on application.*

Practical Anatomy :
A Manual of Dissections. By CHRISTOPHER HEATH, Surgeon to University College Hospital. Sixth Edition. Revised by RICKMAN J. GODLEE, M.S. Lond., F.R.C.S., Demonstrator of Anatomy in University College, and Assistant Surgeon to the Hospital. Crown 8vo, with 24 Coloured Plates and 274 Engravings, 15s.

Wilson's Anatomist's Vade-Mecum. Tenth Edition. By GEORGE BUCHANAN, Professor of Clinical Surgery in the University of Glasgow ; and HENRY E. CLARK, M.R.C.S., Lecturer on Anatomy at the Glasgow Royal Infirmary School of Medicine. Crown 8vo, with 450 Engravings (including 26 Coloured Plates), 18s.

Braune's Atlas of Topographical Anatomy, after Plane Sections of Frozen Bodies. Translated by EDWARD BELLAMY, Surgeon to, and Lecturer on Anatomy, &c., at, Charing Cross Hospital. Large Imp. 8vo, with 34 Photolithographic Plates and 46 Woodcuts, 40s.

An Atlas of Human Anatomy. By RICKMAN J. GODLEE, M.S., F.R.C.S., Assistant Surgeon and Senior Demonstrator of Anatomy, University College Hospital. With 48 Imp. 4to Plates (112 figures), and a volume of Explanatory Text. 8vo, £4 14s. 6d.

Harvey's (Wm.) Manuscript Lectures. Prelections Anatomiæ Universalis. Edited, with an Autotype reproduction of the Original, by a Committee of the Royal College of Physicians of London. Crown 4to, half bound in Persian, 52s. 6d.

Anatomy of the Joints of Man. By HENRY MORRIS, Surgeon to, and Lecturer on Anatomy and Practical Surgery at, the Middlesex Hospital. 8vo, with 44 Lithographic Plates (several being coloured) and 13 Wood Engravings, 16s.

Manual of the Dissection of the Human Body. By LUTHER HOLDEN, Consulting Surgeon to St. Bartholomew's Hospital. Edited by JOHN LANGTON, F.R.C.S., Surgeon to, and Lecturer on Anatomy at, St. Bartholomew's Hospital. Fifth Edition. 8vo, with 208 Engravings. 20s.
By the same Author.

Human Osteology. Seventh Edition, edited by CHARLES STEWART, Conservator of the Museum R.C.S., and R. W. REID, M.D., F.R.C.S., Lecturer on Anatomy at St. Thomas's Hospital. 8vo, with 59 Lithographic Plates and 75 Engravings. 16s.
Also,

Landmarks, Medical and Surgical. Fourth Edition. 8vo. [*In the Press.*

The Student's Guide to Surgical Anatomy. By EDWARD BELLAMY, F.R.C.S. and Member of the Board of Examiners. Third Edition. Fcap. 8vo, with 81 Engravings. 7s. 6d.

The Anatomical Remembrancer ; or, Complete Pocket Anatomist. Eighth Edition. 32mo, 3s. 6d.

Diagrams of the Nerves of the Human Body, exhibiting their Origin, Divisions, and Connections, with their Distribution to the Various Regions of the Cutaneous Surface, and to all the Muscles. By W. H. FLOWER, C.B., F.R.S., F.R.C.S. Third Edition, with 6 Plates. Royal 4to, 12s.

General Pathology.

An Introduction to. By JOHN BLAND SUTTON, F.R.C.S., Sir E. Wilson Lecturer on Pathology, R.C.S.; Assistant Surgeon to, and Lecturer on Anatomy at, Middlesex Hospital. 8vo, with 149 Engravings, 14s.

Atlas of Pathological Anatomy.

By Dr. LANCEREAUX. Translated by W. S. GREENFIELD, M.D., Professor of Pathology in the University of Edinburgh. Imp. 8vo, with 70 Coloured Plates, £5 5s.

A Manual of Pathological Anatomy.

By C. HANDFIELD JONES, M.B., F.R.S., and E. H. SIEVEKING, M.D., F.R.C.P. Edited by J. F. PAYNE, M.D., F.R.C.P., Lecturer on General Pathology at St. Thomas's Hospital. Second Edition. Crown 8vo, with 195 Engravings, 16s.

Post-mortem Examinations:

A Description and Explanation of the Method of Performing them, with especial reference to Medico-Legal Practice. By Prof. VIRCHOW. Translated by Dr. T. P. SMITH. Second Edition. Fcap. 8vo, with 4 Plates, 3s. 6d.

The Human Brain:

Histological and Coarse Methods of Research. A Manual for Students and Asylum Medical Officers. By W. BEVAN LEWIS, L.R.C.P. Lond., Medical Superintendent, West Riding Lunatic Asylum. 8vo, with Wood Engravings and Photographs, 8s.

Manual of Physiology:

For the use of Junior Students of Medicine. By GERALD F. YEO, M.D., F.R.C.S., Professor of Physiology in King's College, London. Second Edition. Crown 8vo, with 318 Engravings, 14s.

Principles of Human Physiology.

By W. B. CARPENTER, C.B., M.D., F.R.S. Ninth Edition. By HENRY POWER, M.B., F.R.C.S. 8vo, with 3 Steel Plates and 377 Wood Engravings, 31s. 6d.

Elementary Practical Biology:

Vegetable. By THOMAS W. SHORE, M.D., B.Sc. Lond., Lecturer on Comparative Anatomy at St. Bartholomew's Hospital. 8vo, 6s.

Histology and Histo-Chemistry of Man.

By HEINRICH FREY, Professor of Medicine in Zurich. Translated by ARTHUR E. J. BARKER, Assistant Surgeon to University College Hospital. 8vo, with 608 Engravings, 21s.

A Text-Book of Medical Physics,

for Students and Practitioners. By J. C. DRAPER, M.D., LL.D., Professor of Physics in the University of New York. With 377 Engravings. 8vo, 18s.

Medical Jurisprudence:

Its Principles and Practice. By ALFRED S. TAYLOR, M.D., F.R.C.P., F.R.S. Third Edition, by THOMAS STEVENSON, M.D., F.R.C.P., Lecturer on Medical Jurisprudence at Guy's Hospital. 2 vols. 8vo, with 188 Engravings, 31s. 6d.

By the same Authors.

A Manual of Medical Jurisprudence.

Eleventh Edition. Crown 8vo, with 56 Engravings, 14s.

Also.

Poisons,

In Relation to Medical Jurisprudence and Medicine. Third Edition. Crown 8vo, with 104 Engravings, 16s.

Lectures on Medical Jurisprudence.

By FRANCIS OGSTON, M.D., late Professor in the University of Aberdeen. Edited by FRANCIS OGSTON, Jun., M.D. 8vo, with 12 Copper Plates, 18s.

The Student's Guide to Medical Jurisprudence.

By JOHN ABERCROMBIE, M.D., F.R.C.P., Lecturer on Forensic Medicine to Charing Cross Hospital. Fcap. 8vo, 7s. 6d.

Influence of Sex in Disease.

By W. ROGER WILLIAMS, F.R.C.S., Surgical Registrar to the Middlesex Hospital. 8vo, 3s. 6d.

Microscopical Examination of Drinking Water and of Air.

By J. D. MACDONALD, M.D., F.R.S., Ex-Professor of Naval Hygiene in the Army Medical School. Second Edition. 8vo, with 25 Plates, 7s. 6d.

Pay Hospitals and Paying Wards throughout the World.

By HENRY C. BURDETT. 8vo, 7s.

By the same Author.

Cottage Hospitals — General, Fever, and Convalescent:

Their Progress, Management, and Work. Second Edition, with many Plans and Illustrations. Crown 8vo, 14s.

Hospitals, Infirmaries, and Dispensaries:

Their Construction, Interior Arrangement, and Management; with Descriptions of existing Institutions, and 74 Illustrations. By F. OPPERT, M.D., M.R.C.P.L. Second Edition. Royal 8vo, 12s.

Hospital Construction and Management.

By F. J. MOUAT, M.D., Local Government Board Inspector, and H. SAXON SNELL, Fell. Roy. Inst. Brit. Architects. In 2 Parts, 4to, 15s. each; or, the whole work bound in half calf, with large Map, 54 Lithographic Plates, and 27 Woodcuts, 35s.

Public Health Reports.

By Sir JOHN SIMON, C.B., F.R.S. Edited by EDWARD SEATON, M.D., F.R.C.P. 2 vols. 8vo, with Portrait, 36s.

A Manual of Practical Hygiene.

By F. A. PARKES, M.D., F.R.S. Seventh Edition, by F. DE CHAUMONT, M.D., F.R.S., Professor of Military Hygiene in the Army Medical School. 8vo, with 9 Plates and 100 Engravings, 18s.

A Handbook of Hygiene and Sanitary Science.

By GEO. WILSON, M.A., M.D., F.R.S.E., Medical Officer of Health for Mid-Warwickshire. Sixth Edition. Crown 8vo, with Engravings. 10s. 6d.

By the same Author.

Healthy Life and Healthy Dwellings :

A Guide to Personal and Domestic Hygiene. Fcap. 8vo, 5s.

Sanitary Examinations

Of Water, Air, and Food. A Vade-Mecum for the Medical Officer of Health. By CORNELIUS B. FOX, M.D., F.R.C.P. Second Edition. Crown 8vo, with 110 Engravings, 12s. 6d.

Dangers to Health :

A Pictorial Guide to Domestic Sanitary Defects. By T. PRIDGIN TEALE, M.A., Surgeon to the Leeds General Infirmary. Fourth Edition. 8vo, with 70 Lithograph Plates (mostly coloured), 10s.

Manual of Anthropometry :

A Guide to the Measurement of the Human Body, containing an Anthropometrical Chart and Register, a Systematic Table of Measurements, &c. By CHARLES ROBERTS, F.R.C.S. 8vo, with numerous Illustrations and Tables, 8s. 6d.

By the same Author.

Detection of Colour-Blindness and Imperfect Eyesight.

8vo, with a Table of Coloured Wools, and Sheet of Test-types, 5s.

Illustrations of the Influence of the Mind upon the Body in Health and Disease :

Designed to elucidate the Action of the Imagination. By DANIEL HACK TUKE, M.D., F.R.C.P., LL.D. Second Edition. 2 vols. crown 8vo, 15s.

By the same Author.

Sleep-Walking and Hypnotism.

8vo, 5s.

A Manual of Psychological Medicine.

With an Appendix of Cases. By JOHN C. BUCKNILL, M.D., F.R.S., and D. HACK TUKE, M.D., F.R.C.P. Fourth Edition. 8vo, with 12 Plates (30 Figures) and Engravings, 25s.

Mental Affections of Childhood and Youth

(Lettsomian Lectures for 1887, &c.). By J. LANGDON DOWN, M.D., F.R.C.P., Senior Physician to the London Hospital. 8vo, 6s.

Private Treatment of the Insane as Single Patients.

By EDWARD EAST, M.R.C.S., L.S.A. Crown 8vo, 2s. 6d.

Mental Diseases.

Clinical Lectures. By T. S. CLOUSTON, M.D., F.R.C.P. Edin., Lecturer on Mental Diseases in the University of Edinburgh. Second Edition. Crown 8vo, with 8 Plates (6 Coloured), 12s. 6d.

Manual of Midwifery.

By ALFRED L. GALABIN, M.A., M.D., F.R.C.P., Obstetric Physician to, and Lecturer on Midwifery, &c. at, Guy's Hospital. Crown 8vo, with 227 Engravings, 15s.

The Student's Guide to the Practice of Midwifery.

By D. LLOYD ROBERTS, M.D., F.R.C.P., Lecturer on Clinical Midwifery and Diseases of Women at the Owens College ; Obstetric Physician to the Manchester Royal Infirmary. Third Edition. Fcap. 8vo, with 2 Coloured Plates and 127 Wood Engravings, 7s. 6d.

Lectures on Obstetric Operations :

Including the Treatment of Hæmorrhage, and forming a Guide to the Management of Difficult Labour. By ROBERT BARNES, M.D., F.R.C.P., Consulting Obstetric Physician to St. George's Hospital. Fourth Edition. 8vo, with 121 Engravings, 12s. 6d.

By the same Author.

A Clinical History of Medical and Surgical Diseases of Women.

Second Edition. 8vo, with 181 Engravings, 28s.

Clinical Lectures on Diseases of Women :

Delivered in St. Bartholomew's Hospital, by J. MATTHEWS DUNCAN, M.D., LL.D., F.R.S. Third Edition. 8vo, 16s.

By the same Author.

Sterility in Woman.

Being the Gulstonian Lectures, delivered in the Royal College of Physicians, in Feb., 1883. 8vo, 6s.

Notes on Diseases of Women :

Specially designed to assist the Student in preparing for Examination. By J. J. REYNOLDS, L.R.C.P., M.R.C.S. Third Edition. Fcap. 8vo, 2s. 6d.

By the same Author.

Notes on Midwifery :

Specially designed for Students preparing for Examination. Second Edition. Fcap. 8vo, with 15 Engravings, 4s.

Dysmenorrhœa, its Pathology and Treatment.

By HEYWOOD SMITH, M.D. Crown 8vo, with Engravings, 4s. 6d.

A Manual of Obstetrics.

By A. F. A. KING, A.M., M.D., Professor of Obstetrics, &c., in the Columbian University, Washington, and the University of Vermont. Third Edition. Crown 8vo, with 102 Engravings, 8s.

The Student's Guide to the

Diseases of Women. By ALFRED L. GALABIN, M.D., F.R.C.P., Obstetric Physician to Guy's Hospital. Fourth Edition. Fcap. 8vo, with 94 Engravings, 7s. 6d.

West on the Diseases of

Women. Fourth Edition, revised by the Author, with numerous Additions by J. MATTHEWS DUNCAN, M.D., F.R.C.P., F.R.S.E., Obstetric Physician to St. Bartholomew's Hospital. 8vo, 16s.

Obstetric Aphorisms:

For the Use of Students commencing Midwifery Practice. By JOSEPH G. SWAYNE, M.D. Eighth Edition. Fcap. 8vo, with Engravings, 3s. 6d.

Handbook of Midwifery for Mid-

wives: By J. E. BURTON, L.R.C.P. Lond., Surgeon to the Hospital for Women, Liverpool. Second Edition. With Engravings. Fcap. 8vo, 6s.

A Handbook of Uterine Thera-

peutics, and of Diseases of Women. By E. J. TILT, M.D., M.R.C.P. Fourth Edition. Post 8vo, 10s.

By the same Author.

The Change of Life

In Health and Disease: A Clinical Treatise on the Diseases of the Nervous System incidental to Women at the Decline of Life. Fourth Edition. 8vo, 10s. 6d.

Diseases of the Uterus, Ovaries,

and Fallopian Tubes: A Practical Treatise by A. COURTY, Professor of Clinical Surgery, Montpellier. Translated from Third Edition by his Pupil, AGNES McLAREN, M.D., M.K.Q.C.P.I., with Preface by J. MATTHEWS DUNCAN, M.D., F.R.C.P. 8vo, with 424 Engravings, 24s.

The Female Pelvic Organs:

Their Surgery, Surgical Pathology, and Surgical Anatomy. In a Series of Coloured Plates taken from Nature; with Commentaries, Notes, and Cases. By HENRY SAVAGE, M.D., F.R.C.S., Consulting Officer of the Samaritan Free Hospital. Fifth Edition. Roy. 4to, with 17 Lithographic Plates (15 coloured) and 52 Woodcuts, £1 15s.

A Practical Treatise on the

Diseases of Women. By T. GAILLARD THOMAS, M.D., Professor of Diseases of Women in the College of Physicians and Surgeons, New York. Fifth Edition. Roy. 8vo, with 266 Engravings, 25s.

Backward Displacements of the

Uterus and Prolapsus Uteri: Treatment by the New Method of Shortening the Round Ligaments. By WILLIAM ALEXANDER, M.D., M.Ch.Q.U.I., F.R.C.S., Surgeon to the Liverpool Infirmary. Crown 8vo, with Engravings, 3s. 6d.

Gynæcological Operations:

(Handbook of). By ALBAN H. G. DORAN, F.R.C.S., Surgeon to the Samaritan Hospital. 8vo, with 167 Engravings, 15s.

Abdominal Surgery.

By J. GREIG SMITH, M.A., F.R.S.E., Surgeon to the Bristol Royal Infirmary. 8vo, with 43 Engravings, 15s.

Ovarian and Uterine Tumours:

Their Pathology and Surgical Treatment. By Sir T. SPENCER WELLS, Bart., F.R.C.S., Consulting Surgeon to the Samaritan Hospital. 8vo, with Engravings, 21s.

By the same Author.

Abdominal Tumours:

Their Diagnosis and Surgical Treatment. 8vo, with Engravings, 3s. 6d.

The Student's Guide to Diseases

of Children. By JAS. F. GOODHART, M.D., F.R.C.P., Physician to Guy's Hospital, and to the Evelina Hospital for Sick Children. Second Edition. Fcap. 8vo, 10s. 6d.

Diseases of Children.

For Practitioners and Students. By W. H. DAY, M.D., Physician to the Samaritan Hospital. Second Edition. Crown 8vo, 12s. 6d.

A Practical Treatise on Disease

in Children. By EUSTACE SMITH, M.D., Physician to the King of the Belgians, Physician to the East London Hospital for Children. 8vo, 22s.

By the same Author.

Clinical Studies of Disease in

Children. Second Edition. Post 8vo, 7s. 6d.

Also.

The Wasting Diseases of Infants

and Children. Fourth Edition. Post 8vo, 8s. 6d.

A Practical Manual of the

Diseases of Children. With a Formulary. By EDWARD ELLIS, M.D. Fifth Edition. Crown 8vo, 10s.

A Manual for Hospital Nurses

and others engaged in Attending on the Sick. By EDWARD J. DOMVILLE, Surgeon to the Exeter Lying-in Charity. Fifth Edition. Crown 8vo, 2s. 6d.

A Manual of Nursing, Medical

and Surgical. By CHARLES J. CULLINGWORTH, M.D., Physician to St. Mary's Hospital, Manchester. Second Edition. Fcap. 8vo, with Engravings, 3s. 6d.

By the same Author.

A Short Manual for Monthly

Nurses. Second Edition. Fcap. 8vo, 1s. 6d.

Diseases and their Commence-

ment. Lectures to Trained Nurses. By DONALD W. C. HOOD, M.D., M.R.C.P., Physician to the West London Hospital. Crown 8vo, 2s. 6d.

Notes on Fever Nursing.

By J. W. ALLAN, M.B., Physician, Superintendent Glasgow Fever Hospital. Crown 8vo, with Engravings, 2s. 6d.

By the same Author.

Outlines of Infectious Diseases :

For the use of Clinical Students. Fcap. 8vo.

Hospital Sisters and their Duties.

By EVA C. E. LÜCKES, Matron to the London Hospital. Crown 8vo, 2s. 6d.

Infant Feeding and its Influence on Life ;

By C. H. F. ROUTH, M.D., Physician to the Samaritan Hospital. Fourth Edition. Fcap. 8vo. [*Preparing.*

Manual of Botany:

Including the Structure, Classification, Properties, Uses, and Functions of Plants. By ROBERT BENTLEY, Professor of Botany in King's College and to the Pharmaceutical Society. Fifth Edition. Crown 8vo, with 1,178 Engravings, 15s.

By the same Author.

The Student's Guide to Structural, Morphological, and Physiological Botany.

With 660 Engravings. Fcap. 8vo, 7s. 6d.

Also.

The Student's Guide to Systematic Botany,

including the Classification of Plants and Descriptive Botany. Fcap. 8vo, with 350 Engravings, 3s. 6d.

Medicinal Plants :

Being descriptions, with original figures, of the Principal Plants employed in Medicine, and an account of their Properties and Uses. By Prof. BENTLEY and Dr. H. TRIMEN. In 4 vols., large 8vo, with 306 Coloured Plates, bound in Half Morocco, Gilt Edges, £11 11s.

The National Dispensatory :

Containing the Natural History, Chemistry, Pharmacy, Actions and Uses of Medicines. By ALFRED STILLÉ, M.D., LL.D., and JOHN M. MAISCH, Ph.D. Fourth Edition. 8vo, with 311 Engravings, 36s.

Royle's Manual of Materia Medica and Therapeutics.

Sixth Edition, including additions and alterations in the B.P. 1885. By JOHN HARLEY, M.D., Physician to St. Thomas's Hospital. Crown 8vo, with 139 Engravings, 15s.

Materia Medica and Therapeutics :

Vegetable Kingdom — Organic Compounds — Animal Kingdom. By CHARLES D. F. PHILLIPS, M.D., F.R.S. Edin., late Lecturer on Materia Medica and Therapeutics at the Westminster Hospital Medical School. 8vo, 25s.

The Student's Guide to Materia Medica and Therapeutics.

By JOHN C. THOROWGOOD, M.D., F.R.C.P. Second Edition. Fcap. 8vo, 7s.

Materia Medica.

A Manual for the use of Students. By ISAMBARD OWEN, M.D., F.R.C.P., Lecturer on Materia Medica, &c., to St. George's Hospital. Second Edition. Crown 8vo, 6s. 6d.

The Pharmacopœia of the London Hospital.

Compiled under the direction of a Committee appointed by the Hospital Medical Council. Fcap. 8vo, 3s.

A Companion to the British Pharmacopœia.

By PETER SQUIRE, Revised by his Sons, P. W. and A. H. SQUIRE. 14th Edition. 8vo, 10s. 6d.

By the same Authors.

The Pharmacopœias of the London Hospitals,

arranged in Groups for Easy Reference and Comparison. Fifth Edition. 18mo, 6s.

The Prescriber's Pharmacopœia:

The Medicines arranged in Classes according to their Action, with their Composition and Doses. By NESTOR J. C. TIRARD, M.D., F.R.C.P., Professor of Materia Medica and Therapeutics in King's College, London. Sixth Edition. 32mo, bound in leather, 3s.

A Treatise on the Principles and Practice of Medicine.

Sixth Edition. By AUSTIN FLINT, M.D., W.H. WELCH, M.D., and AUSTIN FLINT, jun., M.D. 8vo, with Engravings, 26s.

Climate and Fevers of India,

with a series of Cases (Croonian Lectures, 1882). By Sir JOSEPH FAYRER, K.C.S.I., M.D. 8vo, with 17 Temperature Charts, 12s.

Family Medicine for India.

A Manual. By WILLIAM J. MOORE, M.D., C.I.E., Honorary Surgeon to the Viceroy of India. Published under the Authority of the Government of India. Fifth Edition. Post 8vo, with Engravings. [*In the Press.*

By the same Author.

A Manual of the Diseases of India :

With a Compendium of Diseases generally. Second Edition. Post 8vo, 10s.

Also.

Health-Resorts for Tropical Invalids,

in India, at Home, and Abroad. Post 8vo, 5s.

Practical Therapeutics :

A Manual. By EDWARD J. WARING, C.I.E., M.D., F.R.C.P., and DUDLEY W. BUXTON, M.D., B.S. Lond. Fourth Edition. Crown 8vo, 14s.

By the same Author.

Bazaar Medicines of India,

And Common Medical Plants : With Full Index of Diseases, indicating their Treatment by these and other Agents procurable throughout India, &c. Fourth Edition. Fcap. 8vo, 5s.

Diseases of the Heart and Aorta :

Clinical Lectures. By G. W. BALFOUR, M.D., F.R.C.P., F.R.S. Edin., late Senior Physician and Lecturer on Clinical Medicine, Royal Infirmary, Edinburgh. Second Edition. 8vo, with Chromo-lithograph and Wood Engravings, 12s. 6d.

Medical Ophthalmoscopy :

A Manual and Atlas. By WILLIAM R. GOWERS, M.D., F.R.C.P., Professor of Clinical Medicine in University College, and Physician to the Hospital. Second Edition, with Coloured Autotype and Lithographic Plates and Woodcuts. 8vo, 18s.

By the same Author.

Pseudo-Hypertrophic Muscular

Paralysis : A Clinical Lecture. 8vo, with Engravings and Plate, 3s. 6d.

Also.

Diagnosis of Diseases of the

Spinal Cord. Third Edition. 8vo, with Engravings, 4s. 6d.

Also.

Diagnosis of Diseases of the

Brain. Second Edition. 8vo, with Engravings, 7s. 6d.

Also.

A Manual of Diseases of the

Nervous System. Vol. I. Diseases of the Spinal Cord and Nerves. Roy. 8vo, with 171 Engravings (many figures), 12s. 6d.

Diseases of the Nervous System.

Lectures delivered at Guy's Hospital. By SAMUEL WILKS, M.D., F.R.S. Second Edition. 8vo, 18s.

Diseases of the Nervous System:

Especially in Women. By S. WEIR MITCHELL, M.D., Physician to the Philadelphia Infirmary for Diseases of the Nervous System. Second Edition. 8vo, with 5 Plates, 8s.

Nerve Vibration and Excitation,

as Agents in the Treatment of Functional Disorder and Organic Disease. By J. MORTIMER GRANVILLE, M.D. 8vo, 5s.

By the same Author.

Gout in its Clinical Aspects.

Crown 8vo, 6s.

Regimen to be adopted in Cases

of Gout. By WILHELM EBSTEIN, M.D., Professor of Clinical Medicine in Göttingen. Translated by JOHN SCOTT, M.A., M.B. 8vo, 2s. 6d.

Diseases of the Nervous System.

Clinical Lectures. By THOMAS BUZZARD, M.D., F.R.C.P., Physician to the National Hospital for the Paralysed and Epileptic. With Engravings, 8vo. 15s.

By the same Author.

Some Forms of Paralysis from

Peripheral Neuritis : of Gouty, Alcoholic, Diphtheritic, and other origin. Crown 8vo, 5s.

Diseases of the Liver :

With and without Jaundice. By GEORGE HARLEY, M.D., F.R.C.P., F.R.S. 8vo, with 2 Plates and 36 Engravings, 21s.

By the same Author.

Inflammations of the Liver, and

their Sequelæ. Crown 8vo, with Engravings, 5s.

Gout, Rheumatism,

And the Allied Affections ; with Chapters on Longevity and Sleep. By PETER HOOD, M.D. Third Edition. Crown 8vo, 7s. 6d.

Diseases of the Stomach :

The Varieties of Dyspepsia, their Diagnosis and Treatment. By S. O. HABERSHON, M.D., F.R.C.P. Third Edition. Crown 8vo, 5s.

By the same Author.

Pathology of the Pneumo-

gastric Nerve : Lumleian Lectures for 1876. Second Edition. Post 8vo, 4s.

Also.

Diseases of the Abdomen,

Comprising those of the Stomach and other parts of the Alimentary Canal, Œsophagus, Cæcum, Intestines, and Peritoneum. Third Edition. 8vo, with 5 Plates, 21s.

Also.

Diseases of the Liver,

Their Pathology and Treatment. Lettsomian Lectures. Second Edition. Post 8vo, 4s.

Acute Intestinal Strangulation,

And Chronic Intestinal Obstruction (Mode of Death from). By THOMAS BRYANT, F.R.C.S., Senior Surgeon to Guy's Hospital. 8vo, 3s.

A Treatise on the Diseases of

the Nervous System. By JAMES ROSS, M.D., F.R.C.P., Assistant Physician to the Manchester Royal Infirmary. Second Edition. 2 vols. 8vo, with Lithographs, Photographs, and 332 Woodcuts, 52s. 6d.

By the same Author.

Handbook of the Diseases of

the Nervous System. Roy. 8vo, with 184 Engravings, 18s.

Also.

Aphasia :

Being a Contribution to the Subject of the Dissolution of Speech from Cerebral Disease. 8vo, with Engravings, 4s. 6d.

Spasm in Chronic Nerve Disease.

(Gulstonian Lectures.) By SEYMOUR J. SHARKEY, M.A., M.B., F.R.C.P., Assistant Physician to, and Joint Lecturer on Pathology at, St. Thomas's Hospital. 8vo, with Engravings, 5s.

On Megrim, Sick Headache, and

some Allied Disorders : A Contribution to the Pathology of Nerve Storms. By E. LIVEING, M.D., F.R.C.P. 8vo, 15s.

Food and Dietetics,

Physiologically and Therapeutically Considered. By F. W. PAVY, M.D., F.R.S., Physician to Guy's Hospital. Second Edition. 8vo, 15s.

By the same Author.

Croonian Lectures on Certain Points connected with Diabetes.
8vo, 4s. 6d.

Headaches :

Their Nature, Causes, and Treatment. By W. H. DAY, M.D., Physician to the Samaritan Hospital. Fourth Edition. Crown 8vo, with Engravings. [*In the Press.*

Health Resorts at Home and Abroad.
By MATTHEW CHARTERIS, M.D., Physician to the Glasgow Royal Infirmary. Second Edition. Crown 8vo, with Map, 5s. 6d.

The Principal Southern and Swiss Health-Resorts : their Climate and Medical Aspect.
By WILLIAM MARCET, M.D., F.R.C.P., F.R.S. With Illustrations. Crown 8vo, 7s. 6d.

Winter and Spring

On the Shores of the Mediterranean. By HENRY BENNET, M.D. Fifth Edition. Post 8vo, with numerous Plates, Maps, and Engravings, 12s. 6d.

By the same Author.

Treatment of Pulmonary Consumption by Hygiene, Climate, and Medicine.
Third Edition. 8vo, 7s. 6d.

Medical Guide to the Mineral Waters of France and its Wintering Stations.
With a Special Map. By A. VINTRAS, M.D., Physician to the French Embassy, and to the French Hospital, London. Crown 8vo, 8s.

The Ocean as a Health-Resort :

A Practical Handbook of the Sea, for the use of Tourists and Health-Seekers. By WILLIAM S. WILSON, L.R.C.P. Second Edition, with Chart of Ocean Routes, &c. Crown 8vo, 7s. 6d.

Ambulance Handbook for Volunteers and Others.
By J. ARDAVON RAYE, L.K. & Q.C.P.I., L.R.C.S.I., late Surgeon to H.B.M. Transport No. 14, Zulu Campaign, and Surgeon E.I.R. Rifles. 8vo, with 16 Plates (50 figures), 3s. 6d.

Ambulance Lectures :

To which is added a NURSING LECTURE. By JOHN M. H. MARTIN, Honorary Surgeon to the Blackburn Infirmary. Crown 8vo, with 53 Engravings, 2s.

Commoner Diseases and Accidents to Life and Limb: their Prevention and Immediate Treatment.
By M. M. BASIL, M.A., M.B., C.M. Crown 8vo, 2s. 6d.

Handbook of Medical and Surgical Electricity.
By HERBERT TIBBITS, M.D., F.R.C.P.E., Senior Physician to the West London Hospital for Paralysis and Epilepsy. Second Edition. 8vo, with 95 Engravings, 9s.

By the same Author.

How to Use a Galvanic Battery in Medicine and Surgery.
Third Edition. 8vo, with Engravings, 4s.

Also.

A Map of Ziemssen's Motor Points of the Human Body :
A Guide to Localised Electrisation. Mounted on Rollers, 35 × 21. With 20 Illustrations, 5s.   *Also.*

Electrical and Anatomical Demonstrations.
A Handbook for Trained Nurses and Masseuses. Crown 8vo, with 44 Illustrations, 5s.

Spina Bifida :

Its Treatment by a New Method. By JAS. MORTON, M.D., L.R.C.S.E., Professor of Materia Medica in Anderson's College, Glasgow. 8vo, with Plates, 7s. 6d.

Surgical Emergencies :

Together with the Emergencies attendant on Parturition and the Treatment of Poisoning. By W. PAUL SWAIN, F.R.C.S., Surgeon to the South Devon and East Cornwall Hospital. Fourth Edition. Crown 8vo, with 120 Engravings, 5s.

Operative Surgery in the Calcutta Medical College Hospital.
Statistics, Cases, and Comments. By KENNETH MCLEOD, A.M., M.D., F.R.C.S.E., Surgeon-Major, Indian Medical Service, Professor of Surgery in Calcutta Medical College. 8vo, with Illustrations, 12s. 6d.

Surgical Pathology and Morbid Anatomy (Student's Guide).
By ANTHONY A. BOWLBY, F.R.C.S., Surgical Registrar and Demonstrator of Surgical Pathology to St. Bartholomew's Hospital. Fcap. 8vo, with 135 Engravings, 9s.

A Course of Operative Surgery.

By CHRISTOPHER HEATH, Surgeon to University College Hospital. Second Edition. With 20 coloured Plates (180 figures) from Nature, by M. LÉVEILLÉ, and several Woodcuts. Large 8vo, 30s.

By the same Author.

The Student's Guide to Surgical Diagnosis.
Second Edition. Fcap. 8vo, 6s. 6d.   *Also.*

Manual of Minor Surgery and Bandaging.
For the use of House-Surgeons, Dressers, and Junior Practitioners. Eighth Edition. Fcap. 8vo, with 142 Engravings, 6s.

Also.

Injuries and Diseases of the Jaws.
Third Edition. 8vo, with Plate and 206 Wood Engravings, 14s.

The Practice of Surgery:
A Manual. By THOMAS BRYANT, Surgeon to Guy's Hospital. Fourth Edition. 2 vols. crown 8vo, with 750 Engravings (many being coloured), and including 6 chromo plates, 32s.

Surgery: its Theory and Practice (Student's Guide). By WILLIAM J. WALSHAM, F.R.C.S., Assistant Surgeon to St. Bartholomew's Hospital. Fcap. 8vo, with 236 Engravings, 10s. 6d.

The Surgeon's Vade-Mecum:
A Manual of Modern Surgery. By R. DRUITT, F.R.C.S. Twelfth Edition. By STANLEY BOYD, M.B., F.R.C.S. Assistant Surgeon and Pathologist to Charing Cross Hospital. Crown 8vo, with 373 Engravings 16s.

Regional Surgery:
Including Surgical Diagnosis. A Manual for the use of Students. By F. A. SOUTHAM, M.A., M.B., F.R.C.S., Assistant Surgeon to the Manchester Royal Infirmary. Part I. The Head and Neck. Crown 8vo, 6s. 6d. — Part II. The Upper Extremity and Thorax. Crown 8vo, 7s. 6d. Part III. The Abdomen and Lower Extremity. Crown 8vo, 7s.

Illustrations of Clinical Surgery.
By JONATHAN HUTCHINSON, F.R.S., Senior Surgeon to the London Hospital. In occasional fasciculi. I. to XIX., 6s. 6d. each. Fasciculi I. to X. bound, with Appendix and Index, £3 10s.

By the same Author.

Pedigree of Disease:
Being Six Lectures on Temperament, Idiosyncrasy, and Diathesis. 8vo, 5s.

Treatment of Wounds and Fractures. Clinical Lectures. By SAMPSON GAMGEE, F.R.S.E., Surgeon to the Queen's Hospital, Birmingham. Second Edition. 8vo, with 40 Engravings, 10s.

Electricity and its Manner of Working in the Treatment of Disease. By WM. E. STEAVENSON, M.D., Physician and Electrician to St. Bartholomew's Hospital. 8vo, 4s. 6d.

Lectures on Orthopædic Surgery. By BERNARD E. BRODHURST, F.R.C.S., Surgeon to the Royal Orthopædic Hospital. Second Edition. 8vo, with Engravings, 12s. 6d.

By the same Author.

On Anchylosis, and the Treatment for the Removal of Deformity and the Restoration of Mobility in Various Joints. Fourth Edition. 8vo, with Engravings, 5s.

Also.

Curvatures and Diseases of the Spine. Third Edition. 8vo, with Engravings, 6s.

Diseases of Bones and Joints.
By CHARLES MACNAMARA, F.R.C.S., Surgeon to, and Lecturer on Surgery at, the Westminster Hospital. 8vo, with Plates and Engravings, 12s.

Injuries of the Spine and Spinal Cord, and NERVOUS SHOCK, in their Surgical and Medico-Legal Aspects. By HERBERT W. PAGE, M.C. Cantab., F.R.C.S., Surgeon to St. Mary's Hospital. Second Edition, post 8vo, 10s.

Face and Foot Deformities.
By FREDERICK CHURCHILL, C.M., Surgeon to the Victoria Hospital for Children. 8vo, with Plates and Illustrations, 10s. 6d.

Clubfoot:
Its Causes, Pathology, and Treatment. By WM. ADAMS, F.R.C.S., Surgeon to the Great Northern Hospital. Second Edition. 8vo, with 106 Engravings and 6 Lithographic Plates, 15s.

By the same Author.

On Contraction of the Fingers,
and its Treatment by Subcutaneous Operation; and on Obliteration of Depressed Cicatrices, by the same Method. 8vo, with 30 Engravings, 4s. 6d.

Also.

Lateral and other Forms of Curvature of the Spine: Their Pathology and Treatment. Second Edition. 8vo, with 5 Lithographic Plates and 72 Wood Engravings, 10s. 6d.

Spinal Curvatures:
Treatment by Extension and Jacket; with Remarks on some Affections of the Hip, Knee, and Ankle-joints. By H. MACNAUGHTON JONES, M.D., F.R.C.S. I. and Edin. Post 8vo, with 63 Engravings, 4s. 6d.

On Diseases and Injuries of the Eye: A Course of Systematic and Clinical Lectures to Students and Medical Practitioners. By J. R. WOLFE, M.D., F.R.C.S.E., Lecturer on Ophthalmic Medicine and Surgery in Anderson's College, Glasgow. With 10 Coloured Plates and 157 Wood Engravings. 8vo, £1 1s.

Hints on Ophthalmic Out-Patient Practice. By CHARLES HIGGENS, Ophthalmic Surgeon to Guy's Hospital. Third Edition. Fcap. 8vo, 3s.

Short Sight, Long Sight, and Astigmatism. By GEORGE F. HELM, M.A., M.D., F.R.C.S., formerly Demonstrator of Anatomy in the Cambridge Medical School. Crown 8vo, with 35 Engravings, 3s. 6d.

Manual of the Diseases of the Eye. By CHARLES MACNAMARA, F.R.C.S., Surgeon to Westminster Hospital. Fourth Edition. Crown 8vo, with 4 Coloured Plates and 66 Engravings, 10s. 6d.

The Student's Guide to Diseases
of the Eye. By EDWARD NETTLESHIP, F.R.C.S., Ophthalmic Surgeon to St. Thomas's Hospital. Fourth Edition. Fcap. 8vo, with 164 Engravings and a Set of Coloured Papers illustrating Colour-Blindness, 7s. 6d.

Normal and Pathological Histology of the Human Eye and Eyelids. By C. FRED. POLLOCK, M.D., F.R.C.S. and F.R.S.E., Surgeon for Diseases of the Eye to Anderson's College Dispensary, Glasgow. Crown 8vo, with 100 Plates (230 drawings), 15s.

Atlas of Ophthalmoscopy.
Composed of 12 Chromo-lithographic Plates (59 Figures drawn from nature) and Explanatory Text. By RICHARD LIEBREICH, M.R.C.S. Translated by H. ROSBOROUGH SWANZY, M.B. Third edition, 4to, 40s.

Glaucoma:
Its Causes, Symptoms, Pathology, and Treatment. By PRIESTLEY SMITH, M.R.C.S., Ophthalmic Surgeon to the Queen's Hospital, Birmingham. 8vo, with Lithographic Plates, 10s. 6d.

Refraction of the Eye:
A Manual for Students. By GUSTAVUS HARTRIDGE, F.R.C.S., Assistant Physician to the Royal Westminster Ophthalmic Hospital. Second Edition. Crown 8vo, with Lithographic Plate and 94 Woodcuts, 5s. 6d.

Squint:
(Clinical Investigations on). By C. SCHWEIGGER, M.D., Professor of Ophthalmology in the University of Berlin. Edited by GUSTAVUS HARTRIDGE, F.R.C.S. 8vo, 5s.

The Electro-Magnet,
And its Employment in Ophthalmic Surgery. By SIMEON SNELL, Ophthalmic Surgeon to the Sheffield General Infirmary, &c. Crown 8vo, 3s. 6d.

Practitioner's Handbook of Diseases of the Ear and Naso-Pharynx. By H. MACNAUGHTON JONES, M.D., late Professor of the Queen's University in Ireland, Surgeon to the Cork Ophthalmic and Aural Hospital. Third Edition of "Aural Surgery." Roy. 8vo, with 128 Engravings, 6s.

By the same Author.

Atlas of Diseases of the Membrana Tympani. In Coloured Plates, containing 62 Figures, with Text. Crown 4to, 21s.

Endemic Goitre or Thyreocele:
Its Etiology, Clinical Characters, Pathology, Distribution, Relations to Cretinism, Myxœdema, &c., and Treatment. By WILLIAM ROBINSON, M.D. 8vo, 5s.

Diseases and Injuries of the Ear. By Sir WILLIAM B. DALBY, Aural Surgeon to St. George's Hospital. Third Edition. Crown 8vo, with Engravings, 7s. 6d.

By the Same Author.

Short Contributions to Aural Surgery, between 1875 and 1886. 8vo, with Engravings, 3s. 6d.

Diseases of the Throat and Nose: A Manual. By Sir MORELL MACKENZIE, M.D., Senior Physician to the Hospital for Diseases of the Throat.
Vol. II. Diseases of the Nose and Naso-Pharynx; with a Section on Diseases of the Œsophagus. Post 8vo, with 93 Engravings, 12s. 6d.

By the same Author.

Diphtheria:
Its Nature and Treatment, Varieties, and Local Expressions. 8vo, 5s.

Sore Throat:
Its Nature, Varieties, and Treatment. By PROSSER JAMES, M.D., Physician to the Hospital for Diseases of the Throat. Fifth Edition. Post 8vo, with Coloured Plates and Engravings, 6s. 6d.

A Treatise on Vocal Physiology and Hygiene. By GORDON HOLMES, M.D., Physician to the Municipal Throat and Ear Infirmary. Second Edition, with Engravings. Crown 8vo, 6s. 6d.

A System of Dental Surgery.
By Sir JOHN TOMES, F.R.S., and C. S. TOMES, M.A., F.R.S. Third Edition. Crown 8vo, with 292 Engravings, 15s.

Dental Anatomy, Human and Comparative: A Manual. By CHARLES S. TOMES, M.A., F.R.S. Second Edition. Crown 8vo, with 191 Engravings, 12s. 6d.

The Student's Guide to Dental Anatomy and Surgery. By HENRY SEWILL, M.R.C.S., L.D.S. Second Edition. Fcap. 8vo, with 78 Engravings, 5s. 6d.

Notes on Dental Practice. By HENRY C. QUINBY, L.D.S.R.C.S.I. 8vo, with 87 Engravings, 9s.

Mechanical Dentistry in Gold and Vulcanite. By F. H. BALKWILL, L.D.S.R.C.S. 8vo, with 2 Lithographic Plates and 57 Engravings, 10s.

A Practical Treatise on Mechanical Dentistry. By JOSEPH RICHARDSON, M.D., D.D.S., late Emeritus Professor of Prosthetic Dentistry in the Indiana Medical College. Fourth Edition. Roy. 8vo, with 458 Engravings, 21s.

Principles and Practice of Dentistry : including Anatomy, Physiology, Pathology, Therapeutics, Dental Surgery, and Mechanism. By C. A. HARRIS, M.D., D.D.S. Edited by F. J. S. GORGAS, A.M., M.D., D.D.S., Professor in the Dental Department of Maryland University. Eleventh Edition. 8vo, with 750 Illustrations, 31s. 6d.

A Manual of Dental Mechanics.
By OAKLEY COLES, L.D.S.R.C.S. Second Edition. Crown 8vo, with 140 Engravings, 7s. 6d.

Elements of Dental Materia Medica and Therapeutics, with Pharmacopœia. By JAMES STOCKEN, L.D.S.R.C.S., Pereira Prizeman for Materia Medica, and THOMAS GADDES, L.D.S. Eng. and Edin. Third Edition. Fcap. 8vo, 7s. 6d.

Dental Medicine :
A Manual of Dental Materia Medica and Therapeutics. By F. J. S. GORGAS, A.M., M.D., D.D.S., Editor of "Harris's Principles and Practice of Dentistry," Professor in the Dental Department of Maryland University. 8vo, 14s.

Atlas of Skin Diseases.
By TILBURY FOX, M.D., F.R.C.P. With 72 Coloured Plates. Royal 4to, half morocco, £6 6s.

Diseases of the Skin :
With an Analysis of 8,000 Consecutive Cases and a Formulary. By L. D. BULKLEY, M.D., Physician for Skin Diseases at the New York Hospital. Crown 8vo, 6s. 6d.

By the same Author.

Acne : its Etiology, Pathology, and Treatment : Based upon a Study of 1,500 Cases. 8vo, with Engravings, 10s.

On Certain Rare Diseases of the Skin. BY JONATHAN HUTCHINSON, F.R.S., Senior Surgeon to the London Hospital, and to the Hospital for Diseases of the Skin. 8vo, 10s. 6d.

Diseases of the Skin :
A Practical Treatise for the Use of Students and Practitioners. By J. N. HYDE, A.M., M.D., Professor of Skin and Venereal Diseases, Rush Medical College, Chicago. 8vo, with 66 Engravings, 17s.

Parasites :
A Treatise on the Entozoa of Man and Animals, including some Account of the Ectozoa. By T. SPENCER COBBOLD, M.D., F.R.S. 8vo, with 85 Engravings, 15s.

Manual of Animal Vaccination, preceded by Considerations on Vaccination in general. By E. WARLOMONT, M.D., Founder of the State Vaccine Institute of Belgium. Translated and edited by ARTHUR J. HARRIES, M.D. Crown 8vo, 4s. 6d.

Leprosy in British Guiana.
By JOHN D. HILLIS, F.R.C.S., M.R.I.A., Medical Superintendent of the Leper Asylum, British Guiana. Imp. 8vo, with 22 Lithographic Coloured Plates and Wood Engravings, £1 11s. 6d.

Cancer of the Breast.
By THOMAS W. NUNN, F.R.C.S., Consulting Surgeon to the Middlesex Hospital. 4to, with 21 Coloured Plates, £2 2s.

On Cancer :
Its Allies, and other Tumours; their Medical and Surgical Treatment. By F. A. PURCELL, M.D., M.C., Surgeon to the Cancer Hospital, Brompton. 8vo, with 21 Engravings, 10s. 6d.

Sarcoma and Carcinoma :
Their Pathology, Diagnosis, and Treatment. By HENRY T. BUTLIN, F.R.C.S., Assistant Surgeon to St. Bartholomew's Hospital. 8vo, with 4 Plates, 8s.

By the same Author.

Malignant Disease of the Larynx (Sarcoma and Carcinoma). 8vo, with 5 Engravings, 5s.

Also.

Operative Surgery of Malignant Disease. 8vo, 14s.

Cancerous Affections of the Skin. (Epithelioma and Rodent Ulcer.) By GEORGE THIN, M.D. Post 8vo, with 8 Engravings, 5s.

By the same Author.

Pathology and Treatment of Ringworm. 8vo, with 21 Engravings, 5s.

Cancer of the Mouth, Tongue, and Alimentary Tract : their Pathology, Symptoms, Diagnosis, and Treatment. By FREDERIC B. JESSETT, F.R.C.S., Surgeon to the Cancer Hospital, Brompton. 8vo, 10s.

Clinical Notes on Cancer,
Its Etiology and Treatment ; with special reference to the Heredity-Fallacy, and to the Neurotic Origin of most Cases of Alveolar Carcinoma. By HERBERT L. SNOW, M.D. Lond., Surgeon to the Cancer Hospital, Brompton. Crown 8vo, 3s. 6d.

Lectures on the Surgical Disorders of the Urinary Organs. By REGINALD HARRISON, F.R.C.S., Surgeon to the Liverpool Royal Infirmary. Third Edition, with 117 Engravings. 8vo, 12s. 6d.

Hydrocele :
Its several Varieties and their Treatment. By SAMUEL OSBORN, late Surgical Registrar to St. Thomas's Hospital. Fcap. 8vo, with Engravings, 3s.

By the same Author.

Diseases of the Testis.
Fcap. 8vo, with Engravings, 3s. 6d.

Diseases of the Urinary Organs.
Clinical Lectures. By Sir HENRY THOMPSON, F.R.C.S., Emeritus Professor of Clinical Surgery in University College. Seventh (Students') Edition. 8vo, with 84 Engravings, 2s. 6d.

By the same Author.

Diseases of the Prostate :
Their Pathology and Treatment. Sixth Edition. 8vo, with 39 Engravings, 6s.

Also.

Surgery of the Urinary Organs.
Some Important Points connected therewith. Lectures delivered in the R.C.S. 8vo, with 44 Engravings. Students' Edition, 2s. 6d.

Also.

Practical Lithotomy and Lithotrity; or, An Inquiry into the Best Modes of Removing Stone from the Bladder. Third Edition. 8vo, with 87 Engravings, 10s.

Also.

The Preventive Treatment of Calculous Disease, and the Use of Solvent Remedies. Second Edition. Fcap. 8vo, 2s. 6d.

Also.

Tumours of the Bladder :
Their Nature, Symptoms, and Surgical Treatment. 8vo, with numerous Illustrations, 5s.

Also.

Stricture of the Urethra, and Urinary Fistulæ : their Pathology and Treatment. Fourth Edition. With 74 Engravings. 8vo, 6s.

Also.

The Suprapubic Operation of Opening the Bladder for the Stone and for Tumours. 8vo, with 14 Engravings, 3s. 6d.

The Surgery of the Rectum.
By HENRY SMITH, Professor of Surgery in King's College, Surgeon to the Hospital. Fifth Edition. 8vo, 6s.

Modern Treatment of Stone in the Bladder by Litholopaxy. By P. J. FREYER, M.A., M.D., M.Ch., Bengal Medical Service. 8vo, with Engravings, 5s.

Diseases of the Testis, Spermatic Cord, and Scrotum. By THOMAS B. CURLING, F.R.S., Consulting Surgeon to the London Hospital. Fourth Edition. 8vo, with Engravings, 16s.

Diseases of the Rectum and Anus. By W. HARRISON CRIPPS, F.R.C.S., Assistant Surgeon to St. Bartholomew's Hospital, &c. 8vo, with 13 Lithographic Plates and numerous Wood Engravings, 12s. 6d.

Urinary and Renal Derangements and Calculous Disorders.
By LIONEL S. BEALE, F.R.C.P., F.R.S., Physician to King's College Hospital. 8vo, 5s.

Fistula, Hæmorrhoids, Painful Ulcer, Stricture, Prolapsus, and other Diseases of the Rectum :
Their Diagnosis and Treatment. By WILLIAM ALLINGHAM, Surgeon to St. Mark's Hospital for Fistula. Fourth Edition. 8vo, with Engravings, 10s. 6d.

Pathology of the Urine.
Including a Complete Guide to its Analysis. By J. L. W. THUDICHUM, M.D., F.R.C.P. Second Edition, rewritten and enlarged. 8vo, with Engravings, 15s.

Student's Primer on the Urine.
By J. TRAVIS WHITTAKER, M.D., Clinical Demonstrator at the Royal Infirmary, Glasgow. With 16 Plates etched on Copper. Post 8vo, 4s. 6d.

Syphilis and Pseudo-Syphilis.
By ALFRED COOPER, F.R.C.S., Surgeon to the Lock Hospital, to St. Mark's and the West London Hospitals. 8vo, 10s. 6d.

Diagnosis and Treatment of Syphilis. By TOM ROBINSON, M.D., Physician to St. John's Hospital for Diseases of the Skin. Crown 8vo, 3s. 6d.

By the same Author.

Eczema : its Etiology, Pathology, and Treatment. Crown 8vo, 3s. 6d.

Coulson on Diseases of the Bladder and Prostate Gland.
Sixth Edition. By WALTER J. COULSON, Surgeon to the Lock Hospital and to St. Peter's Hospital for Stone. 8vo, 16s.

The Medical Adviser in Life Assurance. By Sir E. H. SIEVEKING, M.D., F.R.C.P. Second Edition. Crown 8vo, 6s.

A Medical Vocabulary :
An Explanation of all Terms and Phrases used in the various Departments of Medical Science and Practice, their Derivation, Meaning, Application, and Pronunciation. By R. G. MAYNE, M.D., LL.D. Fifth Edition. Fcap. 8vo, 10s. 6d.

A Dictionary of Medical Science :
Containing a concise Explanation of the various Subjects and Terms of Medicine, &c. By ROBLEY DUNGLISON, M.D., LL.D. Royal 8vo, 28s.

Medical Education
And Practice in all parts of the World. By H. J. HARDWICKE, M.D., M.R.C.P. 8vo, 10s.

INDEX.

Abercrombie's Medical Jurisprudence, 4
Adams (W.) on Clubfoot, 11
—————— on Contraction of the Fingers, 11
—————— on Curvature of the Spine, 11
Alexander's Displacements of the Uterus, 6
Allan on Fever Nursing, 7
—————— Outlines of Infectious Diseases, 7
Allingham on Diseases of the Rectum, 14
Anatomical Remembrancer, 3
Balfour's Diseases of the Heart and Aorta, 9
Balkwill's Mechanical Dentistry, 12
Barnes (R.) on Obstetric Operations, 5
—————— on Diseases of Women, 5
Basil's Commoner Diseases and Accidents, 10
Beale's Microscope in Medicine, 8
—————— Slight Ailments, 8
—————— Urinary and Renal Derangements, 14
Bellamy's Surgical Anatomy, 3
Bennet (J. H.) on the Mediterranean, 10
—————— on Pulmonary Consumption, 10
Bentley and Trimen's Medicinal Plants, 7
Bentley's Manual of Botany, 7
—————— Structural Botany, 7
—————— Systematic Botany, 7
Bowlby's Surgical Pathology and Morbid Anatomy, 10
Braune's Topographical Anatomy, 3
Brodhurst's Anchylosis, 11
—————— Curvatures, &c., of the Spine, 11
—————— Orthopœdic Surgery, 11
Bryant's Acute Intestinal Strangulation, 9
—————— Practice of Surgery, 11
Bucknill and Tuke's Psychological Medicine, 5
Buist's Vaccinia and Variola, 8
Bulkley's Acne, 13
—————— Diseases of the Skin, 13
Burdett's Cottage Hospitals, 4
—————— Pay Hospitals, 4
Burton's Midwifery for Midwives, 6
Butlin's Malignant Disease of the Larynx, 13
—————— Operative Surgery of Malignant Disease, 13
—————— Sarcoma and Carcinoma, 13
Buzzard's Diseases of the Nervous System 9
—————— Peripheral Neuritis, 9
Carpenter's Human Physiology, 4
Cayley's Typhoid Fever, 8
Charteris on Health Resorts, 10
—————— Practice of Medicine, 8
Chavers' Diseases of India, 8
Churchill's Face and Foot Deformities, 11
Clouston's Lectures on Mental Diseases, 5
Cobbold on Parasites, 13
Coles' Dental Mechanics, 12
Cooper's Syphilis and Pseudo-Syphilis, 14
Coulson on Diseases of the Bladder, 14
Courty's Diseases of the Uterus, Ovaries, &c., 6
Cripps' Diseases of the Rectum and Anus, 14
Cullingworth's Manual of Nursing, 6
—————— Short Manual for Monthly Nurses, 6
Curling's Diseases of the Testis, 14
Dalby's Diseases and Injuries of the Ear, 12
Day on Diseases of Children, 6
—————— on Headaches, 10
Dobell's Lectures on Winter Cough, 8
—————— Loss of Weight, &c., 8
—————— Mont Doré Cure, 8
Domville's Manual for Nurses, 6
Doran's Gynæcological Operations, 6
Down's Mental Affections of Childhood, 5
Draper's Text Book of Medical Physics, 4
Druitt's Surgeon's Vade-Mecum, 11
Duncan on Diseases of Women, 5
—————— on Sterility in Woman, 5
Dunglison's Medical Dictionary, 14
East's Private Treatment of the Insane, 5
Ebstein on Regimen in Gout, 9
Ellis's Diseases of Children, 6
Fagge's Principles and Practice of Medicine,
Fayrer's Climate and Fevers of India, 7
Fenwick's Chronic Atrophy of the Stomach, 8
—————— Medical Diagnosis, 8
—————— Outlines of Medical Treatment, 8
Flint's Principles and Practice of Medicine, 7
Flower's Diagrams of the Nerves, 3
Fox's (C. B.) Examinations of Water, Air, and Food, 5
Fox's (T.) Atlas of Skin Diseases, 13
Freyer's Litholopaxy, 14
Frey's Histology and Histo-Chemistry, 4
Galabin's Diseases of Women, 6
—————— Manual of Midwifery, 5
Gamgee's Treatment of Wounds and Fractures, 11

Godlee's Atlas of Human Anatomy, 3
Goodhart's Diseases of Children, 6
Gorgas' Dental Medicine, 13
Gowers' Diseases of the Brain, 9
—————— Diseases of the Spinal Cord, 9
—————— Manual of Diseases of Nervous System, 9
—————— Medical Ophthalmoscopy, 9
—————— Pseudo-Hypertrophic Muscular Paralysis, 9
Granville on Gout, 9
—————— on Nerve Vibration and Excitation, 9
Guy's Hospital Formulæ, 2
—————— Reports, 2
Habershon's Diseases of the Abdomen, 9
—————————————— Liver, 9
—————————————— Stomach, 9
—————— Pneumogastric Nerve, 9
Hambleton's What is Consumption? 8
Hardwicke's Medical Education, 14
Harley on Diseases of the Liver, 9
—————— Inflammations of the Liver, 9
Harris's Dentistry, 13
Harrison's Surgical Disorders of the Urinary Organs, 13
Hartridge's Refraction of the Eye, 12
Harvey's Manuscript Lectures, 3
Heath's Injuries and Diseases of the Jaws, 10
—————— Minor Surgery and Bandaging, 10
—————— Operative Surgery, 10
—————— Practical Anatomy, 3
—————— Surgical Diagnosis, 10
Helm on Short and Long Sight, &c., 11
Higgens' Ophthalmic Out-patient Practice, 11
Hillis' Leprosy in British Guiana, 13
Holden's Dissections, 3
—————— Human Osteology, 3
—————— Landmarks, 3
Holmes' (G.) Vocal Physiology and Hygiene, 12
Hood's (D. C.) Diseases and their Commencement, 6
Hood (P.) on Gout, Rheumatism, &c., 9
Hooper's Physician's Vade-Mecum, 8
Hutchinson's Clinical Surgery, 11
—————— Pedigree of Disease, 11
—————— Rare Diseases of the Skin, 13
Hyde's Diseases of the Skin, 13
James (P.) on Sore Throat, 12
Jessett's Cancer of the Mouth, &c., 13
Johnson's Medical Lectures and Essays, 8
Jones (C. H.) and Sieveking's Pathological Anatomy, 4
Jones' (H. McN.) Diseases of the Ear and Pharynx, 12
—————— Atlas of Diseases of Membrana Tympani, 12
—————— Spinal Curvatures, 11
Journal of British Dental Association, 2
—————— Mental Science, 2
King's Manual of Obstetrics, 5
Lanceraux's Atlas of Pathological Anatomy, 4
Lewis (Bevan) on the Human Brain, 4
Liebreich's Atlas of Ophthalmoscopy, 12
Liveing's Megrim, Sick Headache, &c., 9
London Hospital Reports, 2
Lückes' Hospital Sisters and their Duties, 7
Macdonald's (J. D.) Examination of Water and Air, 4
Mackenzie on Diphtheria, 12
—————— on Diseases of the Throat and Nose, 12
McLeod's Operative Surgery, 10
MacMunn's Spectroscope in Medicine, 8
Macnamara's Diseases of the Eye, 11
—————— Bones and Joints, 11
Marcet's Southern and Swiss Health-Resorts, 10
Martin's Ambulance Lectures, 10
Mayne's Medical Vocabulary, 14
Middlesex Hospital Reports, 2
Mitchell's Diseases of the Nervous System, 9
Moore's Family Medicine for India, 7
—————— Health-Resorts for Tropical Invalids, 7
—————— Manual of the Diseases of India, 7
Morris' (H.) Anatomy of the Joints, 3
Morton's Spina Bifida, 10
Mount and Snell on Hospitals, 4
Nettleship's Diseases of the Eye, 12
Nunn's Cancer of the Breast, 13
Ogston's Medical Jurisprudence, 4
Ophthalmic (Royal London) Hospital Reports, 2
Ophthalmological Society's Transactions, 2
Oppert's Hospitals, Infirmaries, Dispensaries, &c., 4
Osborn on Diseases of the Testis, 13
—————— on Hydrocele, 13
Owen's Materia Medica, 7
Page's Injuries of the Spine, 11
Parkes' Practical Hygiene, 5
Pavy on Diabetes, 10
Pavy on Food and Dietetics, 10

[Continued on the next page.

Pharmaceutical Journal, 2
Pharmacopœia of the London Hospital, 7
Phillips' Materia Medica and Therapeutics, 7
Pollock's Histology of the Eye and Eyelids, 12
Porritt's Intra-Thoracic Effusion, 8
Purcell on Cancer, 13
Quinby's Notes on Dental Practice, 12
Raye's Ambulance Handbook, 10
Reynolds' (J. J.) Diseases of Women, 5
————— Notes on Midwifery, 5
Richardson's Mechanical Dentistry, 12
Roberts' (C.) Manual of Anthropometry, 5
————— Detection of Colour-Blindness, 5
Roberts' (D. Lloyd) Practice of Midwifery, 5
Robinson (Tom) on Eczema, 14
————— on Syphilis, 14
Robinson (W.) on Endemic Goitre or Thyreocele, 12
Ross's Aphasia, 9
————— Diseases of the Nervous System, 9
————— Handbook of ditto, 9
Routh's Infant Feeding, 7
Royal College of Surgeons Museum Catalogues, 2
Royle and Harley's Materia Medica, 7
St. Bartholomew's Hospital Catalogue, 2
St. George's Hospital Reports, 2
St. Thomas's Hospital Reports, 2
Sansom's Valvular Disease of the Heart, 8
Savage on the Female Pelvic Organs, 6
Schweigger on Squint, 12
Sewill's Dental Anatomy, 12
Sharkey's Spasm in Chronic Nerve Disease, 9
Shore's Elementary Practical Biology, 4
Sieveking's Life Assurance, 14
Simon's Public Health Reports, 4
Smith's (E.) Clinical Studies, 6
————— Diseases in Children, 6
————— Wasting Diseases of Infants and Children, 6
Smith's (J. Greig) Abdominal Surgery, 6
Smith's (Henry) Surgery of the Rectum, 14
Smith's (Heywood) Dysmenorrhœa, 5
Smith (Priestley) on Glaucoma, 12
Snell's Electro-Magnet in Ophthalmic Surgery, 12
Snow's Clinical Notes on Cancer, 13
Southam's Regional Surgery, 11
Squire's Companion to the Pharmacopœia, 7
————— Pharmacopœias of London Hospitals, 7
Steavenson's Electricity, 11
Stillé and Maisch's National Dispensatory, 7
Stocken's Dental Materia Medica and Therapeutics, 13
Sutton's General Pathology, 4
Swain's Surgical Emergencies, 10
Swayne's Obstetric Aphorisms, 6
Taylor's Medical Jurisprudence, 4

Taylor's Poisons in relation to Medical Jurisprudence, 4
Teale's Dangers to Health, 5
Thin's Cancerous Affections of the Skin, 13
————— Pathology and Treatment of Ringworm,
Thomas's Diseases of Women, 6
Thompson's (Sir H.) Calculous Disease, 14
————— Diseases of the Prostate, 14
————— Diseases of the Urinary Organs, 14
————— Lithotomy and Lithotrity, 14
————— Stricture of the Urethra, 14
————— Suprapubic Operation, 14
————— Surgery of the Urinary Organs, 14
————— Tumours of the Bladder, 14
Thorowgood on Asthma, 8
————— on Materia Medica and Therapeutics, 7
Thudichum's Pathology of the Urine, 14
Tibbits' Medical and Surgical Electricity, 10
————— Map of Motor Points, 10
————— How to use a Galvanic Battery, 10
————— Electrical and Anatomical Demonstrations, 10
Tilt's Change of Life, 6
————— Uterine Therapeutics, 6
Tirard's Prescriber's Pharmacopœia, 7
Tomes' (C. S.) Dental Anatomy, 12
Tomes' (J. and C. S.) Dental Surgery, 12
Tuke's Influence of the Mind upon the Body, 5
————— Sleep-Walking and Hypnotism, 5
Vintras on the Mineral Waters, &c., of France, 10
Virchow's Post-mortem Examinations, 4
Walsham's Surgery: its Theory and Practice, 11
Waring's Indian Bazaar Medicines, 7
————— Practical Therapeutics, 7
Warlomont's Animal Vaccination, 13
Warner's Guide to Medical Case-Taking, 8
Waters' (A. T. H.) Diseases of the Chest, 8
Weaver's Pulmonary Consumption, 8
Wells' (Spencer) Abdominal Tumours, 6
————— Ovarian and Uterine Tumours, 6
West and Duncan's Diseases of Women, 6
West's (S.) How to Examine the Chest, 8
Whittaker's Primer on the Urine, 14
Wilks' Diseases of the Nervous System, 8
Williams' (Roger) Influence of Sex, 4
Wilson's (Sir E.) Anatomists' Vade-Mecum, 3
Wilson's (G.) Handbook of Hygiene, 5
————— Healthy Life and Dwellings, 5
Wilson's (W. S.) Ocean as a Health-Resort, 10
Wolfe's Diseases and Injuries of the Eye, 11
Year Book of Pharmacy, 2
Yeo's (G. F.) Manual of Physiology, 4
Yeo's (J. B.) Contagiousness of Pulmonary Consumption, 8

The following CATALOGUES issued by J. & A. CHURCHILL will be forwarded post free on application:—

A. *J. & A. Churchill's General List of about 650 works on Anatomy, Physiology, Hygiene, Midwifery, Materia Medica, Medicine, Surgery, Chemistry, Botany, &c., &c., with a complete Index to their Subjects, for easy reference.* N.B.—*This List includes B, C, & D.*

B. *Selection from J. & A. Churchill's General List, comprising all recent Works published by them on the Art and Science of Medicine.*

C. *J. & A. Churchill's Catalogue of Text Books specially arranged for Students.*

D. *A selected and descriptive List of J. & A. Churchill's Works on Chemistry, Materia Medica, Pharmacy, Botany, Photography, Zoology, the Microscope, and other branches of Science.*

E. *The Half-yearly List of New Works and New Editions published by J. & A. Churchill during the previous six months, together with particulars of the Periodicals issued from their House.*

[Sent in January and July of each year to every Medical Practitioner in the United Kingdom whose name and address can be ascertained. A large number are also sent to the United States of America, Continental Europe, India, and the Colonies.]

AMERICA.—*J. & A. Churchill being in constant communication with various publishing houses in Boston, New York, and Philadelphia, are able, notwithstanding the absence of international copyright, to conduct negotiations favourable to English Authors.*

LONDON: 11, NEW BURLINGTON STREET.

Pardon & Sons, Printers,]   [*Wine Office Court, Fleet Street, E.C.*